MADDIE'S IN THE MIDDLE

MARIAH CLARK SKEWES

Li'l Hedgehog Publishing

Dedicated to those children whose great misfortune
is to have been born into chaotic families
who cannot meet their needs.
Find your defenders and your helpers.
Your happiness will be what you create.
Continue to move forward.
Make good choices.
Forgive yourself for your mistakes.
Find the people who care.
Life does get better.

❤

With special thanks to my critique partners
without whom this book never would have been completed:
Terri, Allison, Tzeli, Libby, Rose & Dora.
Your patience in reading and re-reading the early versions
and your offerings of insights and revisions were priceless.
Thank you.
Additional thanks to the Gold Country Writers
of Auburn, CA.
An amazing group of dedicated authors!

MADDIE'S IN THE MIDDLE

SEVENTH GRADE

1.

"Your dad is dead."

Our stepmom's blunt words seemed to be suspended in midair, not completely entering my brain. I couldn't make sense of them. When she had said that we needed to sit down on the couch together, I knew something serious was happening. Something bad. We only had to sit on the couch together when we three kids were in deep trouble.

She seemed to rethink her words, as if clarification was needed.

"I learned that your dad died three days ago," she added.

This time her words permeated my brain. Our dad is dead? Really dead? Truly and completely dead? Totally and permanently never coming back dead? How could that be? My mind drifted back to the tidepools at the beach where we had sometimes gone with him, but this time the three of us kids seemed to be looking down from the high cliffs above the rocks, slowly sliding toward the edge. The abyss. And our dad wasn't there to save us.

My blood blocked out all other sounds as it rushed wildly past my ears. It roared like the wind. Beach wind.

Annie reached out and grabbed Max and me into a tight hug.

My mind took a short trip. It brought up Mrs. Klocki, my seventh grade English teacher. Mrs. Klocki would say, "Maddie, the concept is unclear. Was your stepmom told three days ago that your dad died? Or did your stepmom learn today that your dad actually died three days ago?"

Mrs. Klocki is a stickler for clarity. If I turned in a story with that kind of opening, she would give it back to me with a bunch of red marks and tell me to make some changes.

My mind stayed with Mrs. Klocki. She weighs about 500 pounds. I'm not exaggerating! She thinks we won't notice how big she is because she always wears this enormous leopard print coat that goes from just below her chin (and it's a really *big* chin!) down past her knees. Even when it's over 100 degrees outside and the air conditioning isn't working in her classroom. Really! I'm not kidding. And she has to walk up three flights of stairs to get to her classroom. I think it's the principal's way of putting her on a weight-loss program or something. But it doesn't help. She's been this big forever.

I don't know why Mrs. Klocki doesn't get a staff key to the elevator. Maybe she thinks it would just confirm how big she is if she started using it. But she never leaves her classroom anyway, so she only has to do the stairs twice a day: once in the morning before school starts (she always gets there super early so the kids won't see her come in) and then again at the end of the day after the final bell rings and everyone has gone home. No one has ever seen her walking anywhere. Ever.

And now that I think about it, maybe she *does* have an elevator key, and she just uses it when we're not there to see it. She never leaves her desk during the day, not even to eat or to go to the bathroom. She just sits there behind her enormous desk (she has the biggest desk in the whole school), wearing her enormous coat, and she tells us to make our writing more clear.

"It's all about clarity", Mrs. Klocki always says. "Meaning can be implied but it should never be confusing."

But then just as unexpectedly as she had appeared in my mind, Mrs. Klocki disappeared. I was back in our current mess. Back to our dad – or our lack of dad, that is. Our dead dad. Clarity. I wondered what I had missed.

"Your dad is dead," our stepmom said again. She tried to reframe it.

"Your dad was just found in his apartment, and he must have died a few days ago. Probably the day after Annie and I went to see him for some child support money. Which he didn't have, by the way. As usual."

The three of us started to cry. The three of us kids, that is. Not our stepmom. Clarity.

2.

I thought things would get better three years ago when we went to live with our dad. Like maybe leaving the whacky world we'd been living in with our mum would make life a little less crazy – a little more predictable. It's not like we didn't like the oddness of it all – it was sort of fun in its own weird way. But things were starting to spin out of control. Even for our family. So, I thought maybe living with our dad would make us more like other families. Peeing in toilets instead of in the backyard bushes when the plumbing backed up. Having friends over to the house to play. Wearing clean clothes to school. Going on family vacations. Normal. But that's not what happened. That's not the way it turned out at all.

I was only eight and in the fourth grade when our lives completely changed. I had been moved up a grade in school cuz I guess they thought I needed more of a challenge or something. I've always been about the youngest one in my class. Mr. Esperanza was dictating the bonus words for our weekly spelling test. I loved the bonus words. Getting them right made me feel like my world was in some sort of order. Like I was in control of it. I liked that feeling.

"Disequilibrium," I remember Mr. Esperanza saying. "The state of feeling unbalanced."

Our school counselor came into our classroom just as Mr. Esperanza was about to use 'disequilibrium' in a sentence, and she walked over to talk to him. They whispered back and forth for a while, and they kept glancing over in my direction. The class got super quiet. I looked around at the other kids nearby. Maybe it was someone else the adults were talking about. I sure hoped so. But the other kids were all looking back at me. Everyone seemed to know that something important was going on. And then my heart stopped. I mean it literally stopped beating. My chest was tight and I couldn't breathe. My teacher looked up, right at me.

"Maddie," Mr. Esperanza said. "You're needed in the office. Please go with Ms. Blitz. And you'll need to take your backpack with you."

'*Oh no!*' I remember thinking. '*Something bad is happening. Something really bad!*'

Mr. Esperanza was super tall and when he walked, he looked like a big stork. His legs just sort of stretched out in front of him and then folded back under him in a weird way. He sometimes wore pink shirts which reminded me of a flamingo. I like flamingos. He came up to my desk, leaned way over, and gave me a big hug. Totally unexpected. He usually wasn't much of a hugger.

"It will all be OK," he said quietly, as he handed me a book that he knew I loved. "You can keep this."

That made me even more nervous. My heart started beating again, but now it was beating too fast. I could feel it in my chest pounding and pounding like it was trying to get out. I could actually hear it. I wondered if anyone else could hear it, too. I looked down at my old scuffed up running shoes with my toes sticking out of the holes at the ends and at my dirty mismatched socks. A knot was forming in the pit of my stomach and it began to tighten, like someone was tying a huge rope around my belly. I felt like a pirate who was about to walk the plank, with her arms pinned down, facing the unknown.

"Thanks," I mumbled.

I stuffed the book into the bright purple backpack with the yellow sunshine flowers that the school people had given me. I dragged it behind me as I left my classroom with the counselor. Ms. Blitz was talking to me, but her words seemed to be caught in an underwater echo chamber and I couldn't understand what she was saying. Something was wrong with my ears. I tugged at them thinking maybe that would clear them. It didn't help.

When we got to the office, we found complete chaos.

My older sister, Annie, was already there. She was in fifth grade at the time and was supposed to be going on a field trip to a museum that day. Annie told me later that they had pulled her off the bus just before it took off. She was wearing an oversized white sweatshirt with the school logo and a smiling panda, the school's mascot, over torn blue shorts, not enough to keep her warm on the cold fall day. I guessed that the sweatshirt had come from the Clothes Closet in the office since I had never seen it before. At least it was clean. Annie was standing just inside the office door with one foot outside, looking like she was ready to make a run for it. She looked right at me blinking her eyes rapidly as if she were trying to give me a secret signal or something. Or maybe she was just trying not to cry. Her face was super red. That's when I realized she was angry.

There were police officers in the office. They were waving a bunch of official looking papers at the principal while she was holding onto our little brother, Max, who was only in first grade.

He was screaming and sobbing loudly as he tried to pull away from her. The principal looked like she was about to cry, too.

And our mum was there, right in the middle of everything. More police officers were holding onto her, telling her she needed to calm down or they'd have to handcuff and arrest her.

"Unhand me, you hooligans," Mummy was shouting as she tried to reach for us. "You have no authority here! You are trespassing and you will soon be answering to the highest of authorities! I am calling my cousin, the Queen. You'll be dragged to the dungeon under The Tower hence! You don't know with whom you are dealing! Unhand me, I say!"

And in the middle of all this clamor and noise I heard a jovial greeting.

"Hi, kiddos!"

I turned around. It was our dad.

I recognized him since we'd seen him a few times, but we really didn't know him all that well. He was standing in the office, looking handsome and full of himself in his cool jeans and T-shirt, and his brown leather flip flop sandals, and his super black hair brushed back and cut short on the sides, his sunglasses on top of his head, and his piercing blue eyes taking everything in. He was laughing as he talked it up with the secretaries who looked completely overwhelmed and confused, like they didn't know what to do. He was the only one in the room who seemed to be calm.

I didn't know what was happening. I thought about grabbing Max and making a run for Annie and the door. Or telling everyone to go away and just leave us alone. Or trying to explain that they had the wrong family, that whatever this was, it was a terrible mistake.

But then everything completely slowed down. All the voices merged with Ms. Blitz's in the underwater echo chamber and became an overwhelming dull pulsing drone. A voice somewhere burbled something about a Court decision, and we were now supposed to live with our dad. The slow-motion movie continued as the police officers surrounded our mum, pressing her back and away from us. My muscles refused to move. Our dad took hold of our hands as the principal slowly herded us out of the office, saying that everything was going to be OK. One by one, our dad loaded us into his super cool red convertible sportscar that didn't even have a booster seat for Max, and then the movie began to speed up, back to real time. Our dad put the top down so the sun was shining on us, and he began singing silly songs and whistling as we drove away, with our mum still screaming in the background.

"I'm calling the Queen! You can't take my children away from me! That man is a madman! And a jailbird! Where are my solicitors? You're going to have to answer to the Queen!"

That was three years ago. And things did get better for a while after that, but it didn't last long. It didn't last long at all.

3

Our dad's house turned out to be less than an hour away. When we got there, it was kind of awkward, but also pretty amazing. The house was built out over a steep hill overlooking the Pacific Ocean. When you went in the front door you were on the upper level. You could go straight through to sliding glass doors off the family room and onto a deck where you could stand outside and feel the ocean breeze and see Catalina Island in the distance. And then you could go downstairs to the kids' bedrooms and out to a huge backyard with a picnic table and swings. Everything looked pretty much brand new – the hardwood flooring and the rugs and the paint. And it was super clean, and everything worked! I guess it was built in the 1960's. But it had all been redone. And it had a turquoise blue front door and a small wall in the front yard made out of big square cement bricks with open geometric patterns in them. Our dad called them breeze bricks. Super cool.

"Hey, Kids," our dad said when we first arrived. "Come on over and sit down on the couch so we can talk about things." That was the first time we had to sit on the couch together. We sat down and looked at each other not knowing what to expect next. But he seemed pretty friendly.

"I want you to meet your new stepmom," he said. "She's going to explain how things run around here. I'll be off at my job teaching science during the day so she's going to be in charge of you."

'*So far so good,*' I thought. Then I looked over at Annie. She was rolling her eyes. Uh oh. Not a good sign.

"Welcome," our new stepmom said. She was wearing really clean new clothes and her hair was done in a pretty cool style, but I could see a big scar on her forehead under her bangs. It was thick and pink and kind of ropey looking – and I immediately wondered how she'd gotten it.

"This is a newly remodeled house, so we have to make sure to keep it nice and clean," she said. "We have plastic runners on the carpet where you can walk, and there are also runners under the barstools where you'll be eating your breakfast and dinner. And I have something special for each of you. I hope you like what I've chosen."

And then she smiled as she handed each of us a bib. I couldn't believe it!! Annie started coughing loudly but I could tell she was really laughing, and Max started to object.

"But I'm six!" said Max.

"Oh no, you're still five," our stepmom replied. "Your birthday isn't until tomorrow. We'll have to think of some sort of a party for you. You can think of this as an early birthday present."

"Oh, my God!" Annie said out loud, but luckily our new stepmom didn't hear her.

"Thanks, I guess," said Max.

I didn't know what to say. Having six and eight and ten-year-old kids wear bibs? That was crazy!

"Now you can keep your clothes clean when you eat. Not the clothes you're wearing, of course. Those are going straight into the trash! They're not worth saving. There are new clothes that I ordered for you downstairs on your beds. Off you go to put on your new things."

Our stepmom seemed like she was trying, but she didn't understand kids at all. Annie and I exchanged glances as we headed down the stairs.

"This is never going to work," Annie mumbled. I had a sinking feeling that she might be right.

4.

Before we went to live with our dad, we'd been living with our real mum forever. We called her "Mummy" since she's from England and that's what English children call their mums. But she had a lot of mental problems and couldn't take care of us anymore. She'd been arrested a few times for shoplifting since she didn't have much money, and we'd been put in a couple of children's receiving homes (that's where Social Services puts kids when their parents aren't around, and they don't know what else to do with them). And I guess everyone just decided we needed a new place to live.

So, the Court found our dad and sent us off to live with him.

And he actually turned out to be OK. At first anyway.

Our dad had our new school change our classes a few days after we enrolled there to give us more of a challenge. Even though he doesn't like our real mum (he says she's crazy), he knows she's super smart and that she was always teaching us stuff about biology and history and reading to us from the classics like Shakespeare and The Odyssey. So, he let our new school know that we needed advanced classes, and they were pretty surprised. I don't know what they were expecting – that we were going to be stupid or something? But we surprised them instead.

And our dad took us to the tidepools at the beach every weekend when we first went to live with him. He taught us about all the sea life that we found there, like sea urchins and barnacles and sea anemones and abalone. One time we even found an octopus! He knew a lot about marine life, being a science teacher and all. And he told us to never turn our backs on the ocean.

"Some things are stronger than you might realize," he said to us at the tidepools one day. "Life is all about choices and consequences. You need to be aware of where the power lies in life. Respect it and when it's yours, use it wisely." Whatever that meant. He liked to get philosophical sometimes.

Our dad even took us out in a boat to check on the lobster pots he had put in the ocean. We located them by looking for the red and white buoys with orange flags he had attached to them, that floated on the water's bobbing surface. The pots were actually cages made of strong rope and metal bars. Over time, they'd become covered with seaweed and barnacles, brown and dark green and slimy. We hauled up the pots and pulled the lobsters out, handling them carefully, so they didn't pinch us with their sharp red claws. When we brought them home, our dad dropped them into a huge pot of boiling water that our stepmom had prepared – while they were still alive! The lobsters let out a horrible scream when they hit the water. I screamed, too, the first time I heard it.

"I'm never eating any of that lobster meat!" I yelled in protest. "I don't care how sweet and wonderful you say it is!"

"Don't worry, Maddie," our dad replied. "That scream is actually just the air escaping out from under the lobsters' shells and whistling as it comes out. It's just the release of pressure, like a tea kettle on the stove. The lobsters aren't really feeling anything."

"But how do you know?" I sobbed. "Are you a lobster? Have you ever been dropped into a pot of boiling water?" And I stuck to my promise. I didn't eat any of the lobster meat that night.

Speaking of whistling, we learned that our dad was a great whistler. He could whistle any song you named. He could whistle super high and super low and super soft and super loud. He tried to teach all of us how to whistle, but we couldn't do it like he could. He was the champion whistler.

And it turned out he was a champion ice skater, too. He skated with a Cirque du Soleil ice show for a while when he was younger. Growing up in Wisconsin, he would skate on frozen lakes in the winter and that led to his job as a professional ice skater. He travelled all over the country skating with beautiful women in bright shiny costumes in front of big crowds. He showed us the pictures. And he said he loved it.

That was all before he went back to college to become a science teacher, and after he had joined the Army. He did a lot of things, but never stuck with anything for very long. At least that's what our stepmom said a couple of years later, after he left all of us. Again. Our stepmom said the only thing our dad stuck with at all was drinking and chasing women. I guess she might have been right about that cuz he sure didn't stick around to be a dad. All those trips to the ocean and the tidepools, and learning how to whistle, and listening to his stories just disappeared one day. Just like he did. Maybe he got bored easily. He said he was struck with wanderlust, meaning he was always searching for the next new thing that would excite him and make him happy. I don't think he ever found it.

5.

But back to the present. Seventh grade. Eleven years old. Our dead dad. Real life. I'm starting to think that life just sucks.

At first when our stepmom told us to sit down on the couch this time, I thought we were being kicked out of the house. Again. I wish now that it were that simple.

I remember shooting my sister Annie a pleading look. I could see the intensity in her green eyes. Her fireworks had already started, and her open mouth told me she was just about to let them loose. But when Annie caught my gaze, her eyes softened a bit. She knew I was right. This was not the time. We knew from our stepmom's tone that we were probably in enough trouble already. *Big* trouble. We could read the clues. The ropey pink scar on her forehead that she tries to hide with her bangs was already starting to darken and bulge. And her voice was super stern. And she was slurring her words cuz she'd already had too much to drink even though it was still morning. And it felt like the air was getting sucked out of the room. We were pretty good at reading the clues by now.

And I remember not being able to catch my breath. I felt like I was drowning. But before our stepmom had a chance to speak, my brain went somewhere else, like it sometimes does when things get too unpredictable. I thought about the orange juice incident.

'Oh no!' I thought. *'Did someone hide a glass of orange juice in the cupboard again?'*

Last time it was me. I hid my little brother's orange juice in the cupboard one Saturday morning as a joke but then I forgot all about it. Our stepmom found it when she was looking for a glass for her vodka later when she finally got up around noon. And she went nuts. I mean certifiably nuts!

"Who put this G.D. glass of orange juice in the cupboard? What the Hell?" (She actually says 'G.D.' like that won't count as cussing. She does say the "H" word, though.) "Do you know how expensive orange juice is? You G.D. kids don't care about anything, do you? All you care about is your own G.D. selves!"

I felt badly that time with the orange juice cuz we got kicked out of the house for the day and it was my fault. But all three of us got blamed. I knew I should have said something, but I was too scared. So, I just stood there, and I didn't say a thing. Our stepmom did eventually let us back in that day. When it started to get dark out. So far, she's always let us back in when she's kicked us out.

I was hoping that if she kicked us out today, she would let us back in again, too. Because there's another problem this time. It's my cat, Sailor. She's pregnant. If we get kicked out and she doesn't let us back in, we'll have to walk to our real mum's house. Our real mum lives about 20 miles away. At least we think she does. We haven't seen her much since we were taken away from her that day at school three years ago, and she's moved a couple of times since then. How am I gonna carry Sailor all that way? I'm thinking I could probably use a big brown paper shopping bag. Sailor would fit in that. But she might get sick. And what if she had her kittens along the way? Maybe I could put a towel in the bottom?

But then our stepmom started to speak. It turned out that we weren't getting kicked out of our house after all and I didn't need to worry about Sailor and her kittens. We weren't in any trouble. It was just our dad dying. That was all. I picked up Sailor and buried my nose in her soft fur. Clarity.

6.

The worst time we all had to sit down on the couch up until now was when my dad and stepmom were still married. Not even two years after we started living with them. They said they needed to talk to us. We knew it meant trouble. We knew the pattern by then.

"Hey, Kids," our dad had said one Saturday morning while we were watching a Disney movie on the big screen. "Come on over and sit down on the couch. We need to talk about something."

The three of us kids sat down on the couch wondering what was going on. Things had seemed kind of strained between our dad and our stepmom for a while. They were fighting a lot. But I was secretly hoping they were going to say we were going on a vacation. Maybe we'd be going to Disneyland! That might make things better.

"Your stepmother and I are getting a divorce," our dad said. "She's going to stay in the house and I'm going to move into a new apartment. We need to know where you would like to live – here with your stepmother or in an apartment with me?"

'*What?*' I thought. '*A divorce? Really? Where did that come from? We just got here!*'

I looked at Annie. She was seething. She had this really weird look on her face like she was one of the lobsters in the pot of boiling water, under pressure and about ready to let out a scream.

I looked at our dad. He was standing awkwardly, and shifting his weight back and forth and looked like he just wanted to get out of there as quickly as he could.

I looked at our stepmom. She looked really angry, and the giant scar on her forehead began to turn a dark purple and it looked like it was throbbing or something.

I looked at Max. He just looked really sad and lost.

And then I started to cry.

"Your stepmother is going to stay in the house," our dad repeated. "We need to know where you would like to live – here with your stepmother or in an apartment with me?"

I just stared at the drapes, not knowing what to say, and waiting for Annie to answer for us. There are actually drapes in the living room, the old-fashioned kind with the pleats and lining that hang on sharp metal hooks and everything. My stepmom calls them drapes but everyone else calls them curtains. They go with the décor, from the 1960's like she always says.

Annie usually takes charge at times like this. And finally, she answered.

"I want to stay here in the house," she said, and she stared straight at our dad. And she just kept staring at him and our dad was looking back at her, and she didn't stop staring until he finally looked away.

I thought about it for just a second after that. I wanted to go wherever Annie went and after all, this was where our friends were, the few friends that we had.

"I want to stay in the house, too," I said.

But our little brother, Max, started crying loudly.

"I want to go live in the apartment with Daddy," Max sobbed.

Annie looked at Max sadly.

"We don't split up, Max. Ever. Remember? It's one for all and all for one. Just like The Three Musketeers. It's you and me and Maddie. Together. Always and forever."

So, it was decided. We would all three stay in the house and live with our stepmom, and our dad would live alone in his new apartment. Poor Max. He was pretty disappointed. It sucks to be the youngest, I guess. No one ever listens to you.

7.

Looking back, I'm thinking we should have known something like this would happen. We already knew that life was never fair. Never calm. Never predictable. That homes shifted as quickly as the sands on the beach - the sandscape where you had walked looking totally different just a couple of hours later when you returned. I wondered if maybe we were like three little hermit crabs – leaving one shell home behind to find another in hopes the next one might fit better. Always searching and never secure.

Annie soon told me the rest of the story. The part that our dad and stepmom had left out.

Our dad was a science teacher at the same middle school where Annie and I go now. He had to leave his job last year cuz he was showing up drunk and he was carrying on with another science teacher there. There were rumors that they might have gotten caught kissing in the back room or something.

The other teacher's name is Mrs. Shambles. At least that's what Annie calls her. She left our family in shambles. Mrs. Shambles, that is, not Annie. (Mrs. Klocki would like that clarity.) But she didn't have to leave. She's still teaching there. Totally unfair, Annie says.

Our dad had to leave. The school people were all hoping he would get better with his drinking and then come back because he was actually a pretty decent science teacher. But he didn't.

I was still in elementary school at that time, in sixth grade, so I didn't really understand everything that was going on. But Annie did. Annie was in seventh grade at the middle school with our dad. Poor Annie. I took second place in the school Spelling Bee that year, and my dad was actually in the audience and saw me. That was pretty cool.

Anyway, we kids stayed in the house with our stepmom after the divorce. And it wasn't so bad. Our dad had only lived there for about a year and a half anyway. And after he left us, we got to see him every other weekend. He seemed more interested in Mrs. Shambles than in us, though. She was always there when we went to a park or the beach with him. And our stepmom started drinking more. She would call Mrs. Shambles' cell phone (I guess she got kicked out by her husband – Mrs. Shambles, not our stepmom – clarity again!) and she would have us all listen in to see if we could hear our dad's voice in the background. Kind of weird, I know, but life was pretty weird at that point.

I think our dad dying is harder on Annie than on Max and me because she remembers him more since she would see him at school all the time last year. She used to go into his classroom during morning break and sometimes at lunch to say hi until his drinking got completely out of control, and he started seeing Mrs. Shambles. It got to be pretty embarrassing for her. For Annie, that is, not Mrs. Shambles. But maybe for Mrs. Shambles, too. Who knows? Annie says the kids were all talking about it. So, after a while, Annie stopped going to his classroom.

But now our dad is dead. And it serves Mrs. Shambles right. She left her own husband to carry on with our dad and look where that got her. No husband and no boyfriend. I don't feel sorry for her, not at all, not even a little. She had it coming. Annie thinks so, too.

We got to skip school for two days after he died. We cried a little at first, and then we went over to Mr. and Mrs. Johnson's house and got to play a bunch of video games. Mr. Johnson taught with our dad, and he was our dad's best friend. He drinks a lot too, but never at school. Only at home, I guess.

There's going to be a small funeral – it's called a service – that the funeral home people planned. But our stepmom said not to expect a lot of people to show up. I'm not sure why. I guess he didn't have a lot of friends left with his drinking too much and carrying on and all. Quite a change from when we first came to live with him and our stepmom. They had parties all the time back then. And lots of friends. Oh well. It's like I said. Sometimes life just sucks.

8.

We had to go back to school today and it was a little awkward. Everyone was saying they were sorry, and I was thinking why should they be sorry? They didn't do anything. Our dad is the one who basically drank himself to death. At least that's what Annie says.

First period was pretty embarrassing. Mrs. Dick is my music teacher. Can you believe her name? I don't know why she doesn't change it to Mrs. Mick or Mrs. Flick or something.

At least once a week, Jesse yells out in the middle of class, "Hey, Mrs. Dick! Is your husband's first name Harry?"

And the whole class laughs and then she sends Jesse to the office. We don't see him for a few days after that cuz I guess he gets detention or suspension or something. And that works for a week or two until he does it again. He didn't do it today, though. I wish he would have cuz then maybe I wouldn't have been the center of attention. Because today, Mrs. Dick decided she would have me go to the cafeteria a couple of minutes before our morning break to get her the two hard boiled eggs she always has for a snack. I was SO embarrassed.

"Maddie", she said. "I need you to do a special errand for me. I know I can count on you because you're very responsible. I need you to fetch my two hard boiled eggs from the staff cafeteria. Just tell them they are for me."

Like I'm a dog or something! Going to fetch her eggs! Should I bring back a ball, too? Or a bone? The whole class was grinning at me. They were glad they weren't the ones being singled out for this special attention. Who wants to go to the cafeteria anyway and say, "Hi. I'm supposed to fetch two hard boiled eggs for Mrs. Dick!" I thought I was going to die!

By the time I got back with her eggs, class was over and morning break had started which meant I wouldn't be at the front of the line to buy the giant cinnamon rolls that they make at the Snack Shack, and Mrs. Dick wanted to talk to me about how sorry she was that my dad had died.

Really? I just wanted my cinnamon roll, not to have to listen to her sappy stories about how much she had enjoyed the parties at our house a few years ago. Like this is helping me or something.

But I listened politely, and said, "Thank you", and then I ran off to the Snack Shack but by the time I got there they were out of cinnamon rolls anyway.

The day didn't get any better after that either.

After morning break, I have Ancient History. And my teacher is Mr. Johnson. Yeah, the same Mr. Johnson who used to be my dad's best friend. So that's pretty awkward. And the guy really likes his mummies and his pyramids and his Sphinx and his other Egyptian stuff. It's all he ever really talks about.

And today he must have called on me at least ten times to answer questions. I always get them right cuz I have a good memory and I read everything in our textbook and all, but after a while it was pretty obvious to everyone that he was trying to be extra nice to me and it just got to be really embarrassing. And he's not the most popular teacher in the world. He's pretty strict and a hard grader so the kids don't really like him all that much. I don't know why he and my dad were best friends cuz the kids really liked my dad – at least that's what Annie says.

I couldn't wait for class to be over.

But at least Mr. Johnson's not as bad as Bulldog Burgess. I was in his class for a few days at the beginning of the school year (Bulldog's not Mr. Johnson's – clarity!) but I guess the school counselor decided I needed a different class, so she changed my schedule and I got transferred to Mr. Johnson's instead.

Bulldog Burgess also teaches Ancient History, and no one likes him. And I mean no one. Not the kids, not the other teachers, not even our custodian, Mr. Dyanchenko. And Mr. D. likes everybody! He's more than just a custodian and he's really nice. He helps you open your locker if you can't remember how to work the combination, and he's always cleaning up after everyone else's messes. Bulldog orders Mr. D. around and isn't respectful to him at all, but Mr. D. just has to put up with it. I can tell he doesn't like him, though. No one likes Bulldog Burgess. He's just really mean to everyone.

Bulldog Burgess looks just like a bulldog. That's where he got his nickname. He knows that's what the kids call him, but no one would ever dare to say it to his face. He's got really heavy jowls that hang down practically to his chest so his whole face looks like it's melting right off his head! He doesn't have much hair which makes his head look super big, and when he talks, his cheeks and his neck all wiggle at the same time. When Bulldog gets mad, which is practically all the time, he yells really loudly and his cheeks and neck jiggle even more and his face gets super red. It looks like he's having a heart attack or something! And he picks on kids – in a really mean way. If a kid doesn't know something, he tells them to think harder and to use their brain next time.

One time while I was in his class, a kid hesitated and then started to say, "I didn't think....." but before he could finish his sentence, Bulldog Burgess cut him off.

"You're right! You never think, do you?" And all the kids laughed. I didn't laugh though. I thought Bulldog was just being mean. It wasn't the kid's fault that he didn't know the answer. He was doing the best he could.

So being in Mr. Johnson's class hasn't been all that bad. Except for today when he kept calling on me. And except for me being nervous that he might say something about my dad dying. And except for me worrying that he might say something about my dad's service. Or about our hanging out at his house yesterday. But he didn't say anything. So, I guess I should count that as a good day. At least a better day.

9.

"Maddie, you have bird crap on your shoulder!" someone yelled.

I had made it to lunch today without any more embarrassing incidents and I thought the day might get better. But I guess I was wrong.

I was sitting outside at the picnic tables with my one friend Gracie. Gracie is in most of my classes this year and she's really smart. She went to a different elementary school than I did cuz she lives way on the other side of town, so I just met her this year in seventh grade. But I really like her and we're like practically best friends now. Actually, she's my only friend and we do everything together. Except for going up to the Snack Shack if only one of us wants to buy something or going to the bathroom together if only one of us has to pee. The other girls always seem to have to take a support person with them – like people who take dogs into grocery stores cuz they're too afraid to go in by themselves. I don't mean the service dogs like for blind people. I mean the ones that people carry in their arms or their purses or their backpacks. Or the worst – the ones that they push in a baby stroller. The ones that aren't really necessary. Gracie and I aren't scared, so we do stuff by ourselves when having a support person isn't necessary.

But sometimes having a support person is helpful. Like today, my first day back at school, Gracie just put her arm around me and hugged me and didn't ask any questions. She gets it – life I mean. And she gets me. She knows there are some things you just don't ask about. And I know that about her too. I've been a little worried about her lately though cuz she seems kind of sad all the time, not just for a day or two but all the time. I've hinted about it, but she doesn't want to talk about whatever it is. And so, I leave it alone and we sit together at lunch, and we just talk about other stuff.

I always bring my lunch. So does Gracie. We both bring our lunches in paper sacks, not the cool insulated lunch bags that the other kids who aren't buying the school lunch have.

This morning before school I asked my stepmom if I could get an insulated lunch bag.

"They're on sale," I said. "Two for one at Lucky Market. And all the other kids have them." I thought I could give one to Gracie.

"Paper bags were good enough for me and they're good enough for you," my stepmom replied. "You don't need an insulated lunch bag 'like all the other kids have'," she said imitating my voice in a really mean way. "Besides, they're too expensive."

"What's too expensive? The lunch bags or the kids?" I asked. Usually, I'm polite but I guess I was just in a bad mood and I didn't like how she had answered me.

"Don't get snippy with me, Missy," my stepmom said. "We have to watch our money now that your dad is dead. We're sticking with the brown paper bags."

'But don't a bunch of brown paper bags that you have to keep replacing cost more than just one insulated lunch bag in a super cool color that you can reuse?' I wanted to ask. *'And wouldn't it*

be better for the environment to have reusable lunch bags instead of throw-away paper bags that you have to cut down a bunch of trees for?' But I didn't dare say anything more, so I just grabbed the bag and stuffed it in my backpack as I headed out the door for school.

So there Gracie and I were today, sitting at the outdoor lunch tables eating our brown paper bag lunches and talking about small stuff when all of a sudden the kids behind us started laughing really loudly.

"Maddie, it really is bird crap!" someone else yelled. "All over your shoulder!" And everyone started laughing and pointing at me.

I looked back over my shoulder and sure enough, there was a small grey and white gooey pile of bird crap sitting right on the back of my shirt. A sea gull had taken a crap and it had landed right on MY shoulder.

What are you supposed to do when a sea gull craps on your shoulder right in front of the whole school? Do you wipe it off? Ignore it? Go to the bathroom and try to clean it with a paper towel?

That's what I decided to do. I ran to the bathroom to try to clean it off while all of the kids at the lunch tables just kept on laughing.

Gracie came with me cuz there was a reason to have a support person then and she tried to help. We grabbed a bunch of paper towels from the bathroom dispenser and wet them down with water and wiped and scrubbed, but the crap just seemed to spread into more of a mess.

And while we were scrubbing, two voices in loud whispers started coming from the last stall, the extra big one that's made for wheelchairs.

"Did you hear about Maddie's dad? He died and no one even knew for a couple of days!" It was Taylor's voice, and she used to be one of my best friends. We were in sixth grade together last year in elementary school.

"Yeah, how disgusting. Figures. You know how her family is!" The second voice was Olivia's. She used to be my other best friend from elementary school. And last year, the three of us were together all the time.

I pretended I didn't hear anything. So did Gracie. Like I said, she gets it. But I was actually pretty hurt. I missed being friends with Olivia and Taylor, and I didn't really know what happened that made them not like me anymore. Last year in sixth grade, everything seemed fine. And now this year in middle school, it's like they don't even know me, and they just hang out together. The two of them. All the time. Without me.

Gracie and I kept trying to clean up the bird crap, hurrying so Olivia and Taylor wouldn't come out of their stall where they were still whispering and find us there.

Suddenly, the bell rang. We didn't even get to finish our lunches. We just stuffed our lunch bags back into our backpacks and bolted for PE.

"We're probably going to die of starvation!" I said to Gracie as we ran toward the gym.

"Yeah," she replied. "And we have to run the mile today!"

But at least we were getting away from Olivia and Taylor. They're both pretty stupid to think that a bathroom stall is a place where they won't be overheard gossiping. I knew their schedules and they had already had their PE class so they would be going in the opposite direction. Anyway, Gracie and I both like running the mile, even when we're starving. We're the fastest runners in our class! Of all the girls, that is. A lot faster than Olivia and Taylor will ever be.

10.

"Hey, Maddie. Want to race?"

It was Jesse. He's in our class, and he always makes PE fun. He's a super good athlete and he and I usually race around the track when we're supposed to be jogging it as a warmup. He almost always beats me – he is a boy after all. We learned in Life Science that boys have larger muscles than girls and thinner fat layers, so I guess it makes sense that he usually beats me. But I've beaten him a couple of times – and he was pretty cool about it.

"Sure!" I answered. And we were off, tearing around the track together.

I guess it's a good thing Jesse's such a good athlete cuz he sure doesn't seem to be very smart. He never does his homework and he'd rather give a funny answer in class than the right answer and he never brings a backpack to school or any paper or books. He usually has a pen and a pencil tucked behind his ear and his cell phone in his back pocket, and that's it. So at least he's funny and good at PE.

Jesse beat me this time. But not by much. I was gaining on him at the end.

Class started and we had to do a bunch of warmup exercises and then a slow jog around the track. Jesse and I looked at each other and rolled our eyes. We were already warmed up. I caught Gracie's eye. She had a funny look on her face.

And then we ran the mile. Most kids complain about it, but I **love** running! It's like when I run my mind just leaves my body and travels around to other places. Sometimes it goes into a book I'm reading or into a movie I've watched online. Other times it goes backward in time to a birthday party with my real mum before her mental problems got so bad. And other times it goes back to the tide pools and I'm with my dad and he's laughing and saying, "Never turn your back on the ocean. It's more powerful than you may realize, and every choice has a consequence." Today, though, I'm flying over clouds in my mind in an airplane going to England to see my Grandpa when I was five.

Before I knew it the mile was over, and I had beaten my PR! (That's Personal Record.) I ran it in 6:15! Pretty good, huh?

"Hey, Maddie," I heard Jesse yell. "Great time! That's a PR, right?"

'How did he know that?' I wondered to myself. *'Maybe just a good guess,'* I thought. But I was grinning. And Gracie was watching.

"Yeah! My best time ever! How did you do?"

"I PR'd, too! I ran it in under 6 – a 5:47!"

"Wow! That's amazing. I think that's a school record."

"Nah – not yet. The school record is 5:32 but I'm gonna beat it. By the end of 8th grade next year, I'm hoping for a sub 5."

We headed to the locker room to change our clothes. Gracie came up beside me as we entered.

"You like Jesse!" Gracie whispered in a sing-song voice under her breath.

"No way!" I answered loudly. The other kids turned around to stare at me.

"I mean, he's OK and all. Just not my type," I whispered back. But I smiled to myself. Jesse was kind of cute. And he was in most of my classes, including French which was next. After French, my first day back would be over. I couldn't wait. Until PE, this had been my worst day of school ever! But maybe it was going to end on a good note after all.

11.

Jesse and I got to our French class at about the same time. He sits in the row next to me. I unloaded my backpack and put my French book and my notes and my pens and pencils on my desk. He leaned over and before he could ask, I gave him a couple of sheets of paper. He grinned. He might be cute and charming, but he's totally irresponsible and like I said, I don't think he's all that smart.

Mademoiselle Cesoir greeted our class.

"Bonjour, bonjour!" she called out in a singsong voice.

"Bonjour," we all responded together.

And then, Jesse started up.

"Hey, Mlle Cesoir! Do you have a date ce soir?" he called out.

The whole class laughed. Me included. It's like every teacher at our school has a weird name and hers is no different. "Ce soir" means "tonight" in French. Even the teacher in the room next to ours has a weird name – Mrs. Mann! Can you believe it? What's with these names anyway?

Mlle Cesoir didn't react at all. She's got great control! She just stared at Jesse and eventually the class quieted down. But she just kept staring. And it started getting really uncomfortable. Someone cleared their throat, and Mlle Cesoir just kept staring. Jesse started squirming in his seat, and we were all watching him, and he opened his mouth like he was going to say something, and we were all hoping it would be something really funny, but

Mlle Cesoir just kept staring him down. Eventually, he closed his mouth, and we realized we'd all been holding our breaths to see what was going to happen. But nothing happened.

"Stay after class, Jesse. I'd like to speak with you," is all Mlle Cesoir said. And she went on with the lesson.

Mlle Cesoir is as old as my real mum. She has some grey hair that she doesn't even bother to color, and she pulls it back off of her face in a low clip. She wears old fashioned pencil skirts and button-up blouses with a sweater over her shoulders. And she wears practically no makeup and ugly low shoes. I think she could be pretty if she worked at it, but obviously she doesn't. She speaks perfect English and perfect French.

Mlle Cesoir was sent to a boarding school in Switzerland when she was a teenager and she learned French there. We know she goes back every year to keep her French up cuz she shows us pictures from her trips. The pictures are pretty cool.

Everyone says that during one of her trips back to Switzerland when she was a lot younger, she fell in love and they planned to get married, but he wasn't sure if he wanted to come to America and she wasn't sure if she wanted to live in Switzerland. While they were trying to decide what to do, he went and got himself killed in a motorcycle crash and she never dated again. At least that's what the rumors are. She plays sad French music on low during our class all the time, so I guess maybe it's true.

Class continued on. We worked on conjugating the verb "etre" – to be. Je suis, tu es, il/elle est, nous sommes, vous etes, ils/elles sont.

Mlle Cesoir ended the lesson with, "And what will each of you be in your futures? It is your decision you know. The choices are up to you."

And the final bell rang.

Jesse stayed after class, and I was super curious. Mlle Cesoir didn't yell at him or send him to the office. She didn't embarrass him. So, what was she saying to him now? I couldn't help it. I knew I should leave, but I didn't. I hung around outside the door. I got a drink of water from the fountain. I pretended like I was looking over my notes. And I waited.

After like forever, Jesse came out. And he had a strange look on his face.

"What happened?" I asked Jesse.

He didn't say anything for a while, and we started walking toward our lockers. Finally, he answered.

"She told me I have great potential," he said. "She told me that I'm super smart and that she knows that because she looked up all my past test scores and grades. And she said she knows something must have happened last year because all my grades fell apart in sixth grade, and I started getting into trouble. And she told me I'm a lot better than that. She said I'm one of the best students in her classes, one of the best students she's ever had, and that I'm picking up French without hardly trying. And that she thinks I could be a translator for the United Nations one day, or I could write a travel blog and travel around the world, or I could open my own businesses in lots of different countries. And she told me to have a good evening and she would see me tomorrow."

"Wow!" I answered. "No detention? No suspension? What did you say?"

"I didn't say anything," Jesse answered. "I just left." And he didn't say anything more all the way to our lockers.

12.

When I got home that afternoon, I pulled out one of my favorite children's picture books – Madeline, by Ludwig Bemelmans.

> "In an old house in Paris
> That was covered in vines
> Lived twelve little girls
> In two straight lines
> The smallest one was Madeline!"

That's where I got my name – from the Madeline books, even though my name is spelled differently. At least that's what Mummy, my real mother, always said. And it seems to fit. Madeline tries to do the right thing, but she is always getting herself into scrapes because she is super curious. Just like me. And she doesn't always follow directions perfectly, even though she tries to. Sometimes she sort of interprets them for herself. Just like me. But she is fearless and courageous and adventurous and kind. I hope that's like me. I love the Madeline books. And I sometimes wonder what would have happened if Mummy had named my sister Madeline and I had been named Annie instead? Would we have turned out differently?

"Tenacious!"

That's how Mummy used to describe me when we lived with her. Because she was from England, she used a very specific vocabulary. Mrs. Klocki would have loved her if they had ever met. Which they didn't. Mrs. Klocki thinks it's important to read good books and I think she would like the Madeline books if she were to read them. I'll have to ask her if she knows about Madeline some time if I get my courage up to approach her. I'll just have to be more Madeline-like!

I got to thinking more about Mummy. I knew she was born in England, but she always claimed she was an American. Which was kind of funny because she would always say, "I'm an Americahn!" with this totally British accent.

I guess technically she was – she became an American citizen after being English first. But it was kind of confusing cuz she always talked about her ancestors coming over on the Mayflower. That was one of the big wooden sailing ships that first brought European people to the U.S. a long time ago. It wasn't the U.S. back then though; it was called the New World. And Mummy says her ancestors were on that boat. But then a bunch of generations later her great grandpa who was an American fell in love with a lady from England and he moved back there – to England. And eventually that's where Mummy was born. So, she was English first after all.

I don't know why I'm thinking about Mummy all of a sudden. We haven't seen her for a while. She came to visit a lot when we first came to live with our dad and our stepmom. It was pretty awkward though, and after a while she just stopped coming. And that sort of made things easier. I feel kind of guilty about that.

13.

"How is your mother, Madelleine?" Mademoiselle Cesoir asked me after class the next day. She's about the only one who calls me Madelleine. Everyone else just calls me Maddie.

It kind of surprised me. I knew that a lot of teachers at my school knew my dad cuz he had been a teacher here and all, but no one knows my real mum. At least that's what I thought. So when Mlle Cesoir asked about my mother, I thought she was talking about my stepmom. And when she asked me to stay after class, I was hoping she was going to tell me how smart I was and how much potential I had, like she did with Jesse. But that's not what happened.

"Are you alright, Madelleine?" Mlle Cesoir asked.

"I'm fine," I answered.

"You seem distracted. I was asking about your mother," she continued.

"She's fine," I answered. "She's just fine."

"Did you know we were sorority sisters?" she asked me.

"Um……no, I don't think so. She didn't go to college. She went to secretarial school," I answered.

"Oh, no. She went to college all right. She was brilliant! We were in the same sorority, and we had classes together at UCLA. She hardly had to study to get all A's. She was an amazing student. She majored in English Literature, and she loved

Shakespeare! I've often wondered how she got on after all of the difficulties started for her."

I suddenly realized that Mlle Cesoir was talking about my real mother. Mummy! I knew Mummy had gone to UCLA and she was super smart and stuff. And I knew she loved Shakespeare cuz she always used to quote him. But I didn't know Mlle Cesoir and Mummy knew each other, and I really didn't want to talk about it. Now there was one more teacher who knew more about my personal life than I wanted them to know.

"Do you see her?" Mlle Cesoir asked?

"Um.....sometimes," I answered.

"Well, do give her my best. It's such a shame that she's had such afflictions. (Mrs. Klocki would love that word.) She was truly a brilliant student!" Mlle Cesoir had tears in her eyes.

"Um.....OK," I said. And I hurried out the door. *So much for privacy,* I thought. *Why does everyone at this school have to know my own private business? I don't know any of theirs!*

14.

Well, it turns out that Mrs. Klocki knows about the Madeline books after all. Go figure! In class today, she was using Madeline to make a point about theme. I kind of liked that – Madeline being one of my favorite stories and all. After reading Madeline aloud to us, she told us we have to write our own poem about someone we know to show a theme. Like the theme of Madeline being about fearlessness and kindness. Whatever life throws at Madeline, she seems to get through it and sort of triumph, even though she's really little. We're supposed to pick a person to write about and then "show" through their actions what they are like.

"Show, don't tell," said Mrs. Klocki.

That's going to be kind of tough. And we have just a few days to get it done.

When I got home, I started working on my poem for Mrs. Klocki's class. Nothing seemed to be coming to me. I tried a lot of different starts, but nothing worked.

'*This is a stupid assignment!*' I thought and I bunched up my papers and threw them in the trash. I went outside completely frustrated and ran around the block as fast as I could to clear my mind.

And that's when it hit me. Without even trying, the ideas just started popping into my head, like they were talking to me in my mind. I was going to write a poem about my real mother,

Mummy. But I didn't want people to know it was about my mum, so I decided to pretend it was about a fake grandma instead. My Quirky Grandma Jean. I ran home quickly, and I wrote my poem:

My Quirky Grandma Jean
By Madelleine

I have a quirky Grandma Jean
She says she's a cousin of the Queen.
She came from Britain long ago
It could be true – how would we know?
Grandma's shoes don't often touch the rugs
She says if they do, they will fill with bugs.
Whenever her pens run out of ink
She throws them in the kitchen sink.
Grandma Jean doesn't really like to cook
She'd rather sing or read a book.
When we came to visit the other day
She offered us cookies made out of clay.
Grandma Jean bikes and walks everywhere
She likes the feel of the wind in her hair.
When I ask why she doesn't drive a car
She says, "Cars don't get you very far!"
When I ask Grandma Jean about her age
She answers, "Child, all the world's a stage.
And we are all players in it
I'll explain it if you have a minute."
And she tells me her age is forty-two

But that can't be. Mama's forty, too!
Grandma Jean says it's her professional age
"Remember, Child, all the world's a stage!"
Sometimes Grandma Jean does very strange things
Like when she pulled the elevator's emergency ring.
She said it was a test to make sure it would work
And meeting the kind firefighters was a very nice perk.
Once Grandma Jean asked a lady if she had ants in her pants
Because the lady was standing in a very odd stance.
The lady was shocked and looked at my mom
Who apologized and said, "I think it's best we move on."
Sometimes Grandma Jean talks to people who aren't really
there
She greets them and asks them to sit down in a chair.
She seems to be happy with all of her guests
Mama says in a very unique way she is blessed.
Since now Grandma Jean's not alone - she has friends
To give her some help with her odds and her ends.
She lives in her house and Mama visits every day
Grandma Jean reminds Mama to go out and play.
Grandma Jean doesn't realize that she acts in strange ways
As she fills up her time in what could be long days.
Mama says that as long as she's happy it's fine
Even though Grandma Jean's quirky, I'm glad that she's
mine!
P.S. - I've just found a letter buried deep in Grandma's trunk
Hidden way in the back beneath the very bottom bunk.
It starts with, 'My Dearest and Fondest and Most Loving
Cousin Jean'

And it ends with 'Kindest Regards, Your Fourth Cousin
Twice Removed the Queen'.
And I think I hear the voice of my sweet Grandma Jean
In my mind as I play on the slides and the swing.
Saying, "Things may not always be just what they seem
But remember, Child, to always follow your dream!"

I turned my poem in the very next day, and when I got it back from Mrs. Klocki later in the week, she had given me an "A+". I was surprised to see that she had written a note to me in the top corner of the first page.

"Well done, Maddie," it said. "I would suggest your poem has the theme of 'Perseverance' which is so important in life. Remember to persevere and to make good choices. And always follow your dreams! You're smart and you're resilient, Maddie. You're going to be OK. Fondly, Mrs. Klocki"

15.

"It looks like you two are going to Girl Scout Camp this summer," our stepmom said to Annie and me one evening right before the school year ended. It had been a long year and I couldn't believe we'd made it through. But we had. Even with our dad dying, even with all the social issues and being left out, Annie and I had kept our grades up in middle school, and Max had done well in elementary. No one seemed to notice, though. There were no "good job" or "proud of you" comments in our house. But we were still living in the same place, so we counted that as a win.

Our stepmom was holding up a letter from our school. I could see the name 'Mrs. Dulce, School Counselor' at the bottom of it.

Annie and I were pretty surprised.

"What?" our silent looks to each other said.

"I told your school counselor you were in Scouts when she called a while ago. I guess she found some donation money or something to cover the costs. She knows we could never afford it," our stepmom continued. "It's on Catalina Island," she added. "I don't know who's going to do your chores while you're gone. Max, I guess. It's for ten days. That ought to tire him out." She laughed at that as she picked at some lint on her bathrobe.

Camp? On Catalina Island? For ten whole days? That was actually pretty nice of Ms. Dulce, I thought. Especially since I would never say more than a couple of words to her whenever I talked with her. And I knew Annie wouldn't either. I started to feel a little guilty about that.

Mrs. Dulce had called me down to her office about every other week after my dad died - for the whole entire year.

"Is everything OK, Maddie? How are you doing this year?" she would always ask.

"I'm fine," I would answer. "Everything's good."

"Well, it seems like it's been a bit of a tough year for you," she would say as she fed the black and orange spotted goldfish that she kept in a glass bowl on her office desk. "Is there anything you'd like to talk about?" Ms. Dulce was young with long black curly hair and soft eyes that searched me in a gentle way. She really seemed to care.

"No. Everything's good. I'm fine." I would repeat politely, watching the goldfish flakes floating on the water. "There's nothing on my mind. Nothing I need to talk about."

The goldfish nibbled at the flakes. I could feel Ms. Dulce's kind eyes watching me. She kept trying but her questions never worked. No matter how many times she asked, I didn't say anything. It was always the same. I started thinking maybe she was a slow learner or something. But probably not. Probably she was just really persistent.

Ms. Dulce would try a few more times while the fish swam around his bowl, his bulging eyes watching us until she'd eventually give up and offer me a candy while she wrote me a pass back to class.

"Just know that people care, Maddie. And when you're ready, we're here to listen."

I appreciated her efforts, but honestly, I just wanted all of this stuff to end. I don't know how Annie got through last year all by herself at this school with our dad's stuff going on. I know the teachers and the counselors are trying to be nice, but their questions and their errands are really embarrassing. I'm not going to talk with anyone about it. I just want to be left alone. Well, not really alone. I guess I just want to stay in my classes and be like all the other kids for once.

Without any family issues that make me stand out.

Without other kids whispering and pointing at me as I walk by.

Without all the teachers knowing about my home life details and asking me if I'm OK.

Without the counselor calling me out of class all the time and trying to make me talk about it.

We're never going to tell anyone anything. Not Annie. Or me. Or Max. We've talked about it together a bunch of times. And we all agree. There's no point. Talking about it won't change anything. Besides, if we talk about what's going on we'll just get pulled out of our home again and sent away. And where else would we live anyway?

But now? Summer camp? Wow! That really was pretty cool of Ms. Dulce.

Annie and I won't know anyone at camp, just each other. And that's just fine with me. No one will know our family business. And we'll live in cabins, and we'll go on hikes, and go swimming and kayaking and stand-up paddleboarding. We'll be just like everyone else. Finally. I can't wait!

16.

We almost didn't make it to camp, though. I swear, nothing is ever easy.

First of all, we were worried about Max. He couldn't go because he wasn't in Girl Scouts. Obviously. I was a little worried about leaving him behind. I guess Annie was, too.

"Can we bring a cell phone so we can check on Max while we're gone?" Annie asked the day before we left.

"Who are you? The Little Mother?" our stepmom asked sarcastically. She calls Annie "The Little Mother" in a really mean way whenever Annie sticks up for us or worries about us.

"I just want to make sure he's OK," Annie said.

"Oh, he'll be just fine. I'll be taking good care of him," our stepmom laughed. Her words slurred just a little. I looked at Annie. Annie looked at Max. I could tell she was thinking it over.

Max looked scared.

"Max, you'll be OK," Annie said giving him a big hug. "It's only for ten days." Then she turned to our stepmom. "OK, we'll go."

"You're damned right you'll go," our stepmom replied. "It will be a good break for me."

But it turned out to be more complicated than that. There was going to be another custody hearing while we were at camp. That's where the Court decides who the kids should live with when their parents are all screwed up. I guess when our dad died, our stepmom just sort of kept us. But she didn't have any legal rights or anything since she and our dad were already divorced. And then our real mum showed up. Our real mum really wants us but can't take care of us. And our stepmom can take care of us (sort of) but doesn't really didn't want us. That's what Mrs. Klocki would call irony. What a mess. It will be up to a judge to sort it all out.

"Why is our stepmom asking to keep us when she doesn't seem to like us all that much?" I asked Annie the day before we left for camp.

"It's because of the money," Annie answered. "She gets our dad's Teacher's Retirement and his Social Security as long as she has us. And some Veteran's money. And the money from Grandpa's trust in England. Don't be so naïve, Maddie. Follow the money!"

Annie and Max and I had talked it over before leaving for camp and we eventually figured staying with our stepmom was probably the best option. She might be kind of mean and she definitely drinks too much, but we figured that was probably better than our mum's mental problems. Those just seemed to scare everybody and get her picked up by the police a lot. We thought someone from the Court might ask us where we wanted to live, so we wanted to be prepared. But they didn't. It turns out no one cares about that.

So off Annie and I went to camp. We had to take a boat across the 22 miles of ocean to get to Catalina Island and we both got really seasick. It was disgusting. Heaving over the sides of the boat and all. We couldn't even make it to the bathroom in time, so we just had to barf overboard. But once we landed, it turned out to be great! At least I thought so – Annie wasn't so sure. And we still didn't know where we'd be living when we got back.

17.

Camp started off with this big meeting in the Chow Hall (that's what they call the lunchroom) and all of us girls sat there at the tables while the camp counselors explained the rules. The camp counselors were so cool! They're totally different from our school counselors. They're like older teenagers and they all had fun made up names, like Mizzen (that's a type of mast on a big sailboat) and Gypsy and stuff like that. And they didn't pry into our personal lives. They just wanted us to be safe and to have fun and to be kind to each other.

Mizzen started off the meeting.

"Welcome, Campers!" she yelled. We all just sat there. And she laughed.

"Oh, come on!" she said. "When I yell 'Welcome Campers!' you yell back 'Welcome Back Atcha!' Let's try that again."

"Welcome, Campers!" Mizzen yelled again.

"WELCOME BACK ATCHA!" we all yelled back at her.

Mizzen seemed pretty happy with that.

"That's better! Now, whatever I say to you, you repeat it back to me – but louder! Ready? Here we go!"

"We're here to have fun!" yelled Mizzen.

"WE'RE HERE TO HAVE FUN!" we yelled back.

"We're here to make friends!" yelled Mizzen.

"WE'RE HERE TO MAKE FRIENDS!" we yelled back.

"We're here to be kind!" yelled Mizzen.

"WE'RE HERE TO BE KIND!" we yelled back.

"Awesome!" Mizzen said it more quietly, so we knew that the yelling was over. And then she said, "You can leave any problems you might have behind for the next ten days and just focus on having a good time and on making some new friends and on being kind to one another!"

That sounded good to me. Annie just rolled her eyes.

Next Mizzen led us in some fun chants and taught us some silly camp songs. She plays the guitar – it makes me want to learn, too! And then she went over a bunch of rules, but in a really funny way. I grinned at Annie. I think I'm going to like it here. But Annie still had a funny look on her face.

Gypsy was next.

"OK. Let's talk about safety," she said in a really little Minnie Mouse sort of squeaky voice. And we all laughed. We thought she was kidding around. But she wasn't. That was her real voice.

"This is my actual voice," she told us. She said her vocal cords didn't develop properly when she was little so she has this really tiny voice. And then we all felt badly for laughing at her.

But she told us it was OK.

"Everyone has something unique and different about them – something that maybe separates them from others a little bit. But really, we have more in common than we have differences," she said.

"We all want to be appreciated and we all want to be valued and we all want to be loved. And we all have something we're really good at and we all have something that we really struggle with and maybe need some help with. It might be different things, but those things make us who we are and bring us together. We need to appreciate our differences and be kind to one another."

And Gypsy told us that the thing that makes her unique and different is easy to see – or in her case to hear – but that some of us have things that make us unique and different that are on the inside and that aren't as easy to see or understand. And she challenged us to be kind to each other for the next ten days and to see if we could support each other, even if we didn't know what those differences were. I really like what Gypsy said. And I think Annie did too.

18.

"Good Morning, Campers. Welcome to the Swim Test!"

It was Mizzen using a bullhorn on our second day of camp. The waves were crashing loudly against the huge wooden pillars holding up the pier that we were standing on. All of us campers were there shivering in our bathing suits as we looked down at the cold, churning ocean water.

"You'll need to jump in and swim to the red buoy," she said pointing through the fog. "And then back here to the dock."

No one moved.

"It's only a hundred feet," she continued. "Two hundred there and back. If you don't think you can do it, let us know now."

I was scared. The camp counselors might be cool, but they were being pretty mean about the Swim Test. They said they wanted to make sure we were safe in the ocean, but I wasn't so sure.

"I think they're just trying to torture us," I whispered to Annie.

It was super early in the morning, foggy, and we were shaking from the freezing cold ocean breeze. I was pretty sure that the water would be freezing, too. They could have at least waited til the afternoon.

Mizzen and the other counselors were holding life preservers and they looked around the group waiting for anyone to speak up. No one said anything. That red buoy might as well have been a hundred miles away for me cuz I'm not a good swimmer. But I wasn't going to say I couldn't do it. That would have been really embarrassing.

I didn't even learn how to swim until just two summers ago when I was nine, and I'm still not very good at it. Our dad couldn't believe that none of us knew how to swim when we first came to live with him. But when you think about it, how would we have learned? It's not like he had been there to teach us. And our real mum sure couldn't afford to sign us up for expensive swim lessons!

Our dad used to work at a private swim club up the hill in the rich part of town during his summers off teaching. He was in charge of the swim program and the recreation area, so two summers ago he taught all of us to swim and also how to play chess. Chess is all about strategy and looking at the end game and being careful with your moves. You can't just move your pieces around the board and hope that everything will turn out OK. You have to have goals and be deliberate. I really like chess. And after our dad left, we kept playing chess. But we didn't have a pool so we couldn't keep practicing swimming.

"Maddie, your turn," Mizzen called out. "You need to jump in – unless you think you can't make it." I looked around and realized all the other girls were already in the water swimming for the buoy. I was the only one left standing on the dock. I guess my mind had drifted off. Again.

"You can do it, Maddie," Annie called to me from the water. "I'll swim right next to you."

So, I jumped in. I swear, I thought I was going to die! The water *was* freezing cold and I went all the way under and I wasn't sure which way was up. When I finally broke through the surface, I couldn't catch my breath. I was sputtering like crazy, and I was starting to panic.

"Come on, Maddie, I'll help you." It was Annie, right by my side and holding me up by my arm. I looked for the buoy. It was so far away.

"I can't do it!" I whispered to Annie, spitting salt water out of my mouth.

"Yes, you can," she whispered back. "You can do anything! You're strong! And I'll help you. Nothing can beat us!"

I looked at Annie. And I believed her. I started slapping my arms at the water and kicking my feet toward the buoy. Annie practically dragged me all the way there and back. And I made it.

But I didn't pass the test. No surprise there. At least I didn't drown. Thanks to Annie.

Because I didn't pass, I was going to have to wear a life jacket whenever I was in the water. Even if I just had my toes touching the water at the beach. That sucked. And there were only two other girls who didn't pass the Swim Test who were going to be living in life jackets like me. Annie passed though. She didn't have to wear a life jacket. But she offered to anyway just so I wouldn't feel so bad. That's Annie – the best sister ever.

19.

Except for the Swim Test, Annie and I had a blast at camp. But we seemed to like it in different ways.

We got to do some metal art and make necklaces during crafts time, and I was trying to decide whether to make my necklace in the shape of a daisy or a dolphin. That's what just about everyone else was choosing, too.

"What are you going to make?" I asked Annie.

"A peace sign," she replied. "I want to create a symbol for what's important in life."

When Annie noticed that a bunch of the girls at camp had pierced ears, she decided to pierce hers, too.

"No, Annie," I pleaded. "You're going to get in so much trouble when we get home! You know we've asked a million times to get our ears pierced and SHE always says no. And besides, Nurse Buttercup is never going to pierce them for you."

Annie laughed at that. "Don't worry about me, Little Sis," she replied. "SHE'll never even notice. I'll just wear my hair down all the time. And I'm not going to ask Nurse Buttercup. I still can't believe that stupid name! What do you think ice and safety pins are for?"

With that, Annie got one of the girls in our cabin to freeze her earlobes with ice cubes and pierce her ears with safety pins. She said her plan was to just leave the safety pins in until her ears healed!

It was like Annie really liked the freedom she found at camp, and I just liked being like everybody else.

There were things we both liked, though. We both loved the long hikes through the hills, sometimes learning about animal tracks and other times about edible plants. We had to pack our lunches in with us and pack our trash back out.

And we both loved collecting wild ginger root along the banks of the creek and bringing it back to camp to make ginger cookies.

And we both liked the service projects – making birdhouses and owl boxes for wildlife or Little Free Libraries to place in the community so that kids who couldn't get rides to the regular library on the mainland could borrow books.

On free choice days, we did different things. Annie usually went off by herself into the hills. And I usually chose kayaking. I loved paddling with strong fast strokes out over the water until camp was just a spec in the distance behind me, and then I would sit in my kayak and feel the stillness with the breeze in my hair and the sun on my face. It was so peaceful, and safe. I didn't even care that I was wearing a life jacket.

It was a great ten days but now it's almost over. We have to go home tomorrow. I can't believe it went by so fast. Annie and I still don't know where we'll be living when we get home. We thought we'd get that phone call by now. But we didn't. We're feeling kind of anxious about that. But we're going to be glad to see Max.

Tonight is our last campfire and we're supposed to write something down on a piece of paper and bring it to throw into the fire. It's to be something that's been bothering us that we want to let go of. I've thought a lot about that and I'm not sure what I'm going to write.

"What are you going to write, Annie?" I asked. We had just finished packing our bags to be ready to leave in the morning and we were sitting on the bunks in our cabin.

"I'm not sure," Annie answered. "But I think maybe I'm going to write something about our dad – to let go of him being such an irresponsible, narcissistic A-hole." Annie had some pretty strong feelings on that subject. And she sure has a great vocabulary!

"That's a good idea," I said. "Maybe I should write down that I forgive him for dying on us."

Annie laughed at that. I hadn't meant it to be funny, but I guess maybe it was in a weird sort of way.

The campfire was great. We sang a bunch of songs, and we all threw our papers into the fire. When we went back to our cabins, I felt kinda sad. I didn't really want camp to end. It was like we'd had ten days of not worrying about stuff all the time, except for sometimes worrying about where we were going to live when camp ended, of course. But the rest of the time it was just really calm and fun and nice. And predictable. With clear expectations. And no big surprises. And I felt like I was just like all the other kids here. Finally.

Our boat left the island at 8 a.m. sharp the next morning. Annie and I didn't get so seasick on the way back, so we were happy about that. Once the boat docked at the mainland marina an hour later, we walked down the ramp to the pier and then back up the second ramp to the parking lot. We saw our stepmom and little Max right away. They were standing next to our old beat-up car, waiting for us.

And Max had a giant smile on his face.

He ran over to Annie and me yelling.

"We get to stay! We get to stay! The Court says we don't have to go anywhere!"

Everyone looked over at us while Annie and I hugged little Max and we all started to cry. Even Annie.

Our stepmom didn't move. She just stayed leaning back on the car, watching us.

"Get in the G.D. car!" she yelled. "You're late! I've been waiting here for over an hour. I don't have all day. No one is very considerate around here. No consideration for anyone but themselves!"

We knew that wasn't true. We were right on time. And we knew that she'd already been drinking. That was pretty predictable. But most importantly, we knew we weren't going to have to live anywhere else. We were staying. Things were as good as they were going to get. We were home.

EIGHTH GRADE

20.

I was outside at the lunch picnic tables when the noon duty lady tapped me on the shoulder.

"What are those sandals you're wearing?" she asked. "Don't you know that flip flops are against the dress code?" She wrote me a referral and told me to go to the vice principal's office.

I swear, I HATE those lunch tables! First seagulls crapping on me and now the lunch ladies giving me more crap. It was super cold outside, and I didn't even have a sweatshirt on since I don't have one that fits me anymore, and everyone else was wearing a coat, and I was wearing old jeans and a cotton top with short sleeves, and I was freezing to death, and my teeth were chattering, and SHE says I'm breaking the dress code because I'm wearing the wrong shoes. She's a total piece of work!

"I'll go with you," Gracie offered as I was heading for the office.

"You will not!" the noon duty lady said. "Unless you want a referral, too."

Gracie started to say something, but I interrupted her. "It's OK, Gracie. I've got this," I said. I headed into the administration building.

I didn't want Gracie to get into trouble, too. But stupid noon duty lady. Doesn't she know when having a support person would be a good idea? Annie said later that I should have just skipped out and gone to my next class – she's pretty smart about that kind of stuff. But I usually try to follow the rules. Even when they don't make any sense.

It's been almost a year now since our dad died and we don't have any money. That sucks. It's hard to live without money. Our stepmom says our dad died without a will, so everything is in probate. I guess that means that whatever money you can scrounge up you spend on vodka.

We don't have any clothes that fit any more, so we go to school looking like we're homeless. (Mrs. Klocki might say that's a good character description.) My sandals have a strap around the back, so I thought they were OK and besides, I don't have any other shoes. I used to have some running shoes but they're too small now and my toes stick out of the holes in the ends. I guess I could have gone to my gym locker for the shoes I have there, but I didn't have time. So, I just wore my old flip flops to school instead. Even though it's winter.

The vice principal felt kind of sorry for me when I handed her the referral. She knew my dad and everything. She called my stepmom and told her that thongs weren't allowed at school. (I laughed at that.) She said she would find me some other shoes to wear.

"Here, Maddie. You can wear these and you don't even have to return them. They're yours to keep," she said smiling, trying to be helpful.

I looked at the shoes. They were hideous. They were bright yellow and had Pokemon characters on the sides. Oh my God! I'm in eighth grade!

"Thank you," I said politely.

I put the shoes on and went to class, hoping no one would notice. The vice principal didn't offer me a sweatshirt or anything even though I was obviously freezing. She just gave me the stupid shoes. Annie says I should have stuck them in my backpack or dropped them in a nearby trashcan and put my sandals back on. Like I said, she's pretty smart about that kind of stuff. But I wore the shoes back to class. The kids all stared at me when I came in late and started laughing behind their hands and pointing at my feet. So, I ended up freezing to death AND being late to class AND wearing ugly shoes. It was totally humiliating.

21.

Winter is coming and we still don't have any money. The weather is getting colder and the fog that rolls in from the ocean every night is coming in earlier than it used to. It stays around until late in the morning until it finally burns off. I could really use a jacket.

Annie, Max, our stepmom, and I were down at the docks one evening a few days ago wandering around before getting some cheap fish and chips take-out for dinner. Even though it's cold there, I love the docks. There are fishing boats everywhere, and seagulls that eat fries out of your hand, and a boardwalk with lots of people looking at stuff. You can smell the salty air and hear the old foghorns calling out from the lighthouse at the end of the breakwater. The small harbor waves lap against the dock making a soothing sound. It's pretty cool.

Max ran over to a long low salt-water tub that was sitting on the docks near the fishing boats.

"Look, Maddie," he yelled to me. "Big lobsters!"

I walked over to where he was standing, and Annie came up behind us. All of us bent over to look into the low stone tub. Sure enough, it was full of dozens of fresh lobsters that the fishermen had just brought in to sell to the restaurants and to the people on the docks. The large red claws were held closed with rubber bands so they couldn't pinch anyone who reached in. The lobsters made me think of going out on the boat with my dad to check on his lobster traps in the ocean. That seemed like a lifetime ago.

"What the hell are you looking at?" our stepmom slurred as she stumbled up behind us. She leaned over to look into the tub.

A slow-motion movie started in my mind as our stepmom leaned even further forward to see the lobsters and then started to fall into the tub! At the last moment, she overcorrected and fell over backward instead landing right on her back on the dock with her legs sticking up in the air. She was swearing up a storm. In front of a big crowd of people.

"GD it," she yelled. "Get me up. What the hell is wrong with all of you? What are you staring at? Get me up off this stinking dock!"

Annie refused to help, she was so angry. She just crossed her arms and walked away toward the fishing boats, getting lost in the crowd. But Max and I got our arms under her armpits and lifted her up, getting her away from all the people as quickly as we could. I could feel my cheeks burning. Everyone was watching us and whispering as we hurried away. We got our stepmom over to an outdoor table and Max watched her while I went to find her some coffee. We never did get our fish and chips for dinner. Annie ended up driving us all home that night. And she's only 13.

I'm learning that vodka is our stepmom's favorite drink. She goes through a whole bottle every day. And I'm noticing that it's a really BIG bottle! She buys it at different stores, one bottle at a time. I guess she thinks that way no one will notice. There's Lucky Liquor, The Quick Spot, Larry's Liquor and Spirits, and of course a bunch of grocery stores and quick stops. Annie says she drinks vodka because it's harder to smell on her breath. Like no one will see how weird she's acting, or how she's stumbling, or how she's slurring her words, or how she's falling down on the docks? She thinks no one is going to notice that she can't keep the car on the right side of the road when she drives? She thinks no one will notice any of that?

And more things just seem to be getting out of control lately. Like yesterday when our washing machine stopped working. Now we're going to have to do all our laundry at the laundromat. And our dishwasher broke a long time ago. And our car won't start, so we're having to beg for rides or walk the two miles to school. And even when our car does work, the cloth seats are so shredded that we have to cover them with old, faded beach towels so the stuffing doesn't get out and stick to all of our clothes. That's happened a couple of times already.

And Christmas is coming and we're not going to be able to buy a tree or get any gifts.

Life just gets suckier and suckier!

But then in the middle of all this craziness, something pretty amazing happened. One of the teachers that our dad used to work with, Mr. Whitley, came by our house unexpectedly. He wanted to look at our dad's tools in the garage to see if there was something he wanted to buy. No one is using the tools anymore so we may as well sell them. Our stepmom could probably advertise them on the internet and get a bunch of money for them but she's never going to get around to doing that, so it's a good thing Mr. Whitley is interested.

Our dad had a lot of woodworking stuff – he liked to make decorations out of wood. He made a really cool angel for

Christmas out of a big piece of plywood and painted her so she's wearing a long red dress with white ruffles at the bottom with her bare feet sticking out like she's walking. She has a really sweet face, with pink cheeks, and tiny white wings on her back. Her hair is up in a ponytail and she's carrying a candle on a flat brass colored holder with a ring at the end. Our dad hung her on the garage door the two Christmases that he lived with us. He even made her a little golden halo that hangs above and put a light on her so that the candle looks like it's burning. And he made a coffee table with a chess board embedded right in the middle of it. And he made seahorses out of walnut that he stained dark and decorated some of our inside walls with. (Uh oh, Mrs. Klocki would be upset. I just dangled a preposition!)

But all the tools just sit in boxes in the garage now, so when Mr. Whitley came by to take a look, we were pretty excited. I don't know what made him decide to do that.

"How much would you take for the table saw?" he asked our stepmom.

Annie, Max, and I were standing in a corner of the garage watching.

"It's not worth anything," she answered. "Just like the man who owned it."

Mr. Whitley looked over at the three of us kids.

"How about $300?" he asked.

Our stepmom looked surprised at that.

"OK," she answered. "But if it doesn't work, don't blame me."

Mr. Whitley paid her the $300 in cash and saved our Christmas. Our stepmom says now we can use some of the money to buy a tree and some presents! I'm pretty excited about that.

But Annie says the table saw was actually worth a lot more and Mr. Whitley was basically stealing from the poor.

I don't know about that. I think he was trying to help us out.

Annie also says that all of the money should go toward our Christmas, not just some of it.

I guess she's probably right about that but at least now we'll get to go shopping tomorrow.

And Max and I are going to hang up our dad's angel tonight.

It looks like we're going to have a Christmas after all!

22.

I got to thinking about the Christmas about a million years ago when we went off to England with our real mum to meet our grandpa. I guess he had sent her the plane tickets so we could come for the holidays, but I only remember a few things about the trip since I was only five at the time. When you think about it, I've lived more than half my life since then, so it makes sense that the memories are a little fuzzy. Kind of like the London fog that we found when we got there. Sometimes it's just hard to see things clearly.

Our mum must have lied about Max's age because he was two and a half and the four of us were sharing three seats on the plane. You're supposed to pay for a seat if a kid is two or older. At least that's what Annie says. I remember we were in the bulkhead – that's the space right behind first class where there's a wall in front of you instead of more seats and you get extra room on the floor to play. So, we weren't too squished.

When we got to London, we met our cousin Charlotte. She was pretty cool. She looked exactly like me, which is amazing since Annie and Max and I don't look anything alike. Annie has red hair with green eyes and millions of freckles and Max is blond with light blue eyes. I have brown hair with dark blue eyes, just like Charlotte. But my hair's not as dark as hers. And except for that and the fact that she's ten years older than me, Charlotte and I could be twins!

Charlotte told us a lot about our families. I remember she was rolling her own cigarettes in little white papers and smoking. She said everyone in England smoked when they were 15 so we shouldn't worry about it.

"I'm sorry about your mum's troubles," Charlotte said. "But I'm not terribly surprised. My mum says she was always a bit off. And besides, there are all of the family secrets."

She went on to tell us that we had an Auntie Bella who was living in an asylum at the time. I had never heard of Auntie Bella, and I wasn't sure what an asylum was cuz like I said, I was only five. Annie had to explain it all to me later.

"I don't really think there's anything terribly wrong with Auntie Bella," Charlotte went on. "Except that she wouldn't conform when she was younger. And you know that was simply unacceptable at the time, especially for a well-to-do British family!"

I guess conforming was a big deal when our mum and our aunties were younger. I remember I asked Charlotte what that meant.

"It means going along with the rules," Charlotte explained. "You see, our mums' family was pretty rich, and Bella was an independent sort. She ran a bit wild, you might say. Because she was the oldest of the three girls, she was expected to set an example for your mum and for mine. But when it was time for Auntie Bella to go off to boarding school, she simply refused to go."

Charlotte explained that all the rich families used to send their kids off to boarding school. And some still do. She said that her mum later went, and our mum who was the youngest eventually went, too. But Auntie Bella refused to go.

"That was just the beginning of her rebellion," Charlotte said. "Quite embarrassing for the family, you see. And she eventually ended up in an asylum."

I really didn't understand everything Charlotte was saying at the time. But now it makes me think of my favorite picture book, Madeline, and the movie they made from the book. In the movie, Madeline was made out to be an orphan, but she wasn't. Not really. She was just a rich kid from England whose parents sent her off to boarding school when she was really young. It makes me feel sorry for Auntie Bella, even though I've never even met her. And it makes me feel kind of sorry for Madeline. What kind of parents send you off to boarding school when you're little anyway? I knew Madeline had turned out all right. I hoped that maybe Auntie Bella might, too.

23.

We stayed in England for a couple of weeks then. I remember everyone had really cool accents. They sounded just like our mum! And they used super specific words. Mrs. Klocki should go to England; she would love it there. No one says "kinda" or "sorta" or "gonna" or "weird" or "cuz" or "cool". (I say cuz and cool a lot!) They say "a wee bit like" or "a small touch of" or "formulating a plan to" or "peculiar" or "due to the fact" or "indeed". Sometimes it sounded like a different language. It was awesome. Or as they say in London, "It was brilliant!" I guess I pick up accents pretty easily cuz we got back home, I answered the front door for a salesman and he asked me if I were from England. He said I had a British accent!

Our cousin Charlotte told us she hoped we were going to stay and live in England. She said our mum was asking our grandpa for money and he was going to set up some sort of fund to help her. Charlotte said he agreed to give her money, but he was concerned about "her mental state" and he thought she might do better in the States. (Annie told me later that he was just trying to make the problem go far away.) Charlotte said she didn't think he was going let us stay. I remember I started to cry.

"Don't fuss, Maddie," Charlotte said, and I remember she took a long drag on her cigarette. "The Queen delivered her annual Christmas message today. She reminded all of us to have fortitude and to be optimistic, that the difficulties in the world will pass and we shall all see better days ahead. So, you must be strong, Maddie. You must persevere. You're resilient! You'll be fine. Chin up, stiff upper lip and all that rot! We'll see you again soon."

Not long after, we got on another big jet and flew home. And we haven't been back since.

We're back in the rebel colonies now.

That's what my 8th grade U.S. History teacher, Mrs. Boardman, likes to call the U.S. She's from England, too. It's kind of fun having a U.S. History teacher who's from England, or the United Kingdom, the UK, as she calls it. I guess the UK includes England and Scotland and Wales and parts of Ireland. The parts of Ireland that weren't at war with England anyway, because of what our mum called "The Troubles".

Mrs. Boardman sometimes presents things from England's point of view. Instead of calling George Washington and his soldiers "patriots", she sometimes calls them "rebels". Instead of talking about the "Boston Tea Party" as an act of independence, she calls it "a treasonous theft". She says that in some ways England reacted to the colonists' wishes for more independence like some parents react to teenagers – by adding more rules when maybe relaxing them a bit and having a conversation about them would be better. (I wonder if that would have helped Auntie Bella.)

She also says it's important to look at how our decisions affect others and to consider whether we're getting the results we expect from the decisions we make. (And I wonder if that would have helped our dad.) Mrs. Boardman thinks it's important to discuss issues and to look at things from other people's points of view. She says that can be helpful in understanding others and the choices they make. Even if we don't agree with them. She's pretty smart about stuff like that.

I don't know – maybe she's right.

But I don't think I'll ever understand why a father would send his children away to live in an asylum or a foreign country just to get rid of them instead of trying to help them. And I don't think I'll ever understand why we couldn't stay in England back when I was five to be near our cousins and our grandpa. And I don't think I'll ever understand why our dad left us. I think those were all just selfish acts. With the people not thinking of anyone but themselves.

It does make me wonder about our stepmom, though. Sometimes she seems to be trying to be a decent parent – and at least she's stuck around. Maybe I should think about what life might look like from her point of view. I'm guessing it hasn't been all that easy for her either.

24.

Today we went Christmas shopping. It was so much fun! I bought some lipstick for Annie and a frisbee for Max. And I found a pretty cool ashtray for my stepmom. She smokes a lot. I wonder if she went to England when she was 15. When we got home, Annie and Max and I went into Annie and my bedroom to look at all of our purchases. We had to hide each other's gifts of course, but I couldn't believe how much extra stuff Annie and Max had bought! Annie had at least 10 lipsticks and lip glosses for herself, and some cool sunglasses, and a bunch of packs of gum. And Max had about 20 candy bars. I had only purchased 5 things – a gift for each of them, our stepmom, our dog, and something for myself.

"You're such a goody goody, Maddie!" Annie laughed. "You've gotta develop some sticky fingers!"

"What do you mean?" I asked.

"You gotta steal stuff!" Max blurted out. He's only 9 and he's stealing!

"What? You guys are stealing? You're gonna get in so much trouble! What if you get caught?"

Annie just laughed again. "We won't get caught. Who's gonna think a 13-year-old and a 9-year-old are thieves? It's fun. And look at all our cool stuff!"

All I could think of was the Boston Tea Party and the treasonous theft. But that was for a good cause, right? It wasn't just stealing stuff for the fun of it. There should be a good reason to break the law.

Annie eventually did get caught – but not for stealing.

25.

Annie is in high school now, in the ninth grade. She's a year older than me and she's really into boys. She's started sneaking out at night to hang with her friends. We share a bedroom and at least a couple of times a week, she stuffs her bed with pillows and sneaks out the back door. I'm not supposed to know about it, but I hear her go and I'm scared she's going to get caught. I've thought about talking to her about it, but she's older and she always seems to know better. Besides, I've never been able to win an argument with her. I'm just scared she's going to get into big trouble. I hope she's going to be OK.

One night after Annie had snuck out, our stepmom came downstairs for some reason. She never comes downstairs, and I mean *never*! So, I don't know what made her do it that night.

Our house is called a split level – which means that it's built on a hill and it looks like a one-story house when you enter the front door, but when you go downstairs there's a whole lower level. All the kids' bedrooms are downstairs and there's a den with a fireplace down there too, but our stepmom hasn't come downstairs for over a year. Really. I mean she literally *never* comes downstairs! Annie and I do all the cleaning on Saturdays and our stepmom doesn't use the den since there's a living room with a fireplace upstairs, and her bedroom and her bathroom and the kitchen and the dining room are all upstairs, too. So, there's really no reason for her to come down.

I don't know why she came down this time, but she did.

And she went right over to Annie's bed like she suspected something and pulled back the comforter and found it stuffed with pillows.

She went berserk! I mean *really* berserk! She was yelling and saying all kinds of nasty stuff about Annie and calling her awful names.

"Don't you let your skanky sister back in this house if you know what's good for you!" she shouted at me. "If she doesn't want to sleep here then she can just stay out all night and find somewhere else to sleep! She's nothing but a ho- just like just like your good-for-nothing father!"

There's a back door off of the bathroom down the hall on our lower level that leads to the backyard, and our stepmom went over to it and locked it. I guess Annie had left it unlocked so she could get back in. And then our stepmom came back into our bedroom.

"If you unlock that door, you'll be out on your ear just like your sister. You are not to unlock that door! Do you hear me? No matter what!"

She was yelling really loud and the scar on her forehead that we've noticed before was pulsating, like it had its own black heart. Like in *The Tell-Tale Heart* by Edgar Allen Poe that we're reading in English class.

I laid in my bed wide awake for hours after that until I finally heard a tapping on our window. I went over and looked outside and sure enough there was Annie.

"Let me in, Maddie! The door is locked," she said.

I went over to the bathroom back door carrying Annie's pillow and comforter and opened the door.

"She found out, Annie. She knows you snuck out. And if I let you back in, I'll get into big trouble!"

I handed her the pillow and comforter and she gave me a hug and laughed.

"Goody goody," Annie said and headed for the redwood picnic table that she used for a bed for the rest of the night.

Things got worse after that.

Our stepmom seemed to be drinking more and more and by ten o'clock in the morning she was usually thoroughly drunk and didn't even fuss with her bangs to hide her forehead scar. The three of us kids started getting kicked out of the house for the day pretty regularly, at least every other week. Annie started skipping school. I just kept studying and keeping my grades up and running track, anything to stay away from home. And I don't know what Max was doing. He seemed to follow Annie – breaking some of the rules and pushing the limits - but his grades were good, and he was going to school so I guessed he was OK. But I wasn't really sure. Except for the fact that I loved Annie and Max and I was worried about them, I wasn't really sure about anything anymore. Life was just one big mess.

26.

Not too many weeks later, things really bottomed out.

"Sit down on the couch. We need to talk." Our stepmom was drunk as usual, but she seemed pretty serious. And kind of angry. We knew the pattern. Max and I sat down, but Annie just stood there next to the couch. And our stepmom's forehead scar began to pulse. Like the tell-tale heart.

"I said, 'SIT DOWN!'" she yelled at Annie. But Annie didn't say a word and just continued to stand. Our stepmom and Annie stared at each other. Max and I didn't say a word. And then there was a knock at the front door. Our stepmom hesitated to answer it. There was something she needed to tell us first.

"Your mother is here. She's come to pick you up."

What? Our real mother? Our *mum*? We hadn't seen her in over two years! We thought she was crazy. Our dad said so lots of times before he died, and our stepmom told us stuff that made us kind of afraid of her. They both said she was too mentally ill to raise kids and that's why we were taken away from her. We had actually developed a secret call to let each other know if we ever spotted her in case she tried to kidnap us. None of this made any sense. I didn't know what to think.

And then we started to cry – Max and I that is – not Annie. I realized there must have been another Court case. There had been a bunch of custody battles over the years, and I guessed that a new judge must have decided we needed to go back to live with our real mum. Figures. Nothing ever seemed to be permanent or the least bit predictable.

Annie started shouting at our stepmom, "You're a cruel old witch!"

I was crying. "Annie, she can't help it," I said. "The Court must have decided it."

And Annie turned on me. "You're so naïve, Maddie," Annie shouted. "Don't be stupid! There hasn't been any Court case! There wasn't any custody battle. She just doesn't want us! I guess the money wasn't enough for her to keep us. We're an inconvenience to her and she's decided she's done with us. She's giving us back!"

So much for trying to understand our stepmom.

Max and I cried even harder then. And our stepmom's big scar continued to redden and throb as she headed toward the entry and opened the door.

27.

Our new life with our mum was crazy. Literally! Or as my British cousin would say, it was mad. Mum was super loving and kind and protective. With us anyway. She really wanted us to live with her and she had never wanted to give us up in the first place. She kept calling us 'her little prince and princesses' when she read us stories and tucked us into bed at night. And she said over and over how much she loved us and that she always knew we would finally come home to her.

Our mum was **super** smart. But she seemed to trip up over all the little stuff in life. Like she had kept all of our clothing from four years ago when we last lived with her and she gave it to us to wear, but of course none of it fit. And she didn't trust the neighbors, so we had to keep all the window shades down and we weren't supposed to talk to anyone, not even if they said, "Hi". And she also didn't trust our schools, so she didn't enroll us. She wasn't much of a cook either. But all of that just made life more interesting. And sometimes a little embarrassing.

We went to thrift shops for new clothes. Mum was really good at finding designer clothing at the thrift shops for super cheap prices. We all got a bunch of cool new-looking clothes that fit, and she only had to spend about $30!

And Mum homeschooled us. Like Mlle Cesoir said, she is brilliant. She had gotten a bunch of textbooks and she put us into advanced classes. We visited natural history museums and art galleries and libraries – like the Griffith Park Observatory and the Huntington Library which is really more like an art museum and a park with really cool peacocks wandering around everywhere.

Mummy said that learning opportunities are all around us and that we just needed to take advantage of them. She took us to UCLA to see the science displays and to hear famous people give talks on different topics in ginormous lecture halls. Mummy knew a lot about UCLA since she had attended there and the talks she found were really interesting. They were all free and open to the public so anyone could attend. My favorite was an anthropologist talking about ancient human skulls and what they could tell us about the development of the human brain. When he asked questions like, "What period do you suppose this skull represents?" Mummy always knew the right answers!

And we studied English and French. I was doing Algebra and I really liked it. We spent a lot of time in the house when we weren't out on field trips cuz Mummy said she didn't want people to take too much notice of us. We were reading Greek mythology and old classics like *Swiss Family Robinson* and *Little Women*. We learned all about Shakespeare and the Globe The-ater and about how because of his plays, even the masses (mean-ing the common people) got to go to the theatre. (That's how you spell "theater" in French!) I guess the UCLA lectures that we were attending were sort of the same thing - they were open to us masses!

We went on bike rides around the neighborhood and out on trails in ginormous parks. I wanted to be a veterinarian and Mum let me bring home bones from dead animals that I found on the road, and we boiled them in coffee cans on the stove to clean and sanitize them and then I put them back together on a shelf in the backyard shed to study. Annie thought that was disgusting.

Mum wasn't much of a cook though. Annie says it's because the British really can't cook and besides, what with boiling bones from road kills and all, it was probably best she didn't use the kitchen much anyway! So, we made a lot of things that were sort of like a mixture of meat and vegetables and Campbells soup – stuff you could bake in the oven or cook in a crock pot. And a lot of skim milk. Mum said whole milk wasn't good for us because it had too much fat and it wasn't good for our hearts. And we had a lot of whole grain bread. We went back to tuna sandwiches that were basically wet cuz she didn't know to drain the water from the can before she put it on the bread. We *never* had tuna packed in oil. And definitely no mayonnaise. She only used waxed paper for our sandwiches. She said plastic wrap wasn't good for the environment. We walked or rode our bikes instead of driving whenever possible. I thought it was to save money on gas, but Mummy said it was because it was good for our health and didn't contribute to global warming.

We found Mummy to be super encouraging. When Max used an entire roll of paper towels to make a scale drawing of a sperm whale with a sharpie pen, she called it "brilliant!" And when Annie needed help with a chemistry concept, Mummy brought out toothpicks and gumdrops to build molecular bonds with her. And when I had too many bones in my "bone box" and couldn't identify which ones had come from a snake and which ones had come from a cat or a bird, she pulled out the anatomy books to help me reconstruct them. And every night when we were going to bed, she would read to us from her favorite books until we fell asleep.

I guess you could say we weren't a very conventional family, but Mummy made life exciting even though it was pretty unpredictable in a good way. We'd wake up in the morning and never quite know what to expect for the day. It was sort of like the *Swiss Family Robinson* experience or being an explorer in the New World!

28.

But then after only a few weeks of living with Mummy, there was a knock on the door.

"Hide, children," Mummy said.

We could see through the window that there was a man standing on the doorstep who looked pretty official. He was wearing a button-down shirt and a tie and he had one of those official-looking lanyards with a name badge hanging around his neck.

We hid behind the couch and peeked out as our mum opened the door.

"Good morning," he said. "I'm Truancy Officer Stickler, from the local school district. I understand you have children living here who are not enrolled in school."

Our mum didn't even blink.

"Well of course my children are enrolled in school, Officer," she replied, in her totally British accent.

"That's not what the neighbors say," he said. "What is the name of the school?"

"Why Staysley School for the Gifted, of course!" our mum answered smiling. That's her last name. We started to giggle from behind the couch.

"I'll need some proof of that," Officer Stickler replied. "Do you have some enrollment papers that you can show me? Or Home School Certification?"

"My children don't need enrollment papers and my school doesn't require a certificate," Mum replied. "I am the Head Mistress, Head Mistress Staysley, appointed by the Queen. I can attest to the school's good standing and my children's enrollment."

Poor Officer Stickler didn't know what to say to that. He told our mum she could probably qualify for home schooling us and said that she could find the information online. He handed her a paper with a web address on it, but he didn't know that she couldn't even figure out how to work a toaster, much less the internet! Then he gave her a bunch of more papers to fill out.

"I'll be back to collect those forms in a week," he said. He handed her a card with his name and phone number on it. "If you need any help, you can call me," he added kindly.

"Thank you, no help is needed," Mum replied and she closed the door. Annie, Max and I scrambled out from behind the couch. All of us watched out the window together as Officer Stickler got into his blue truck and drove away. Mummy shook her head, turned to us, and smiled as she headed to the kitchen.

"That's the end of that rubbish!" she said as she dropped the papers and the little card right into the bin. (That's what she calls the trash can.) There were old tuna cans from breakfast that were still on the counter, and she knocked those in, too.

"Come along, children. Let's head out for an adventure."

And out the door we went.

Soon after that, stuff started happening that reminded me of what it is was like when we were little and lived with her before. The plumbing backed up and Mum didn't know what to do about it, so we had to go into the backyard and pee in the bushes again. And the glass top on the kitchen table broke, so we all sat around it for breakfast and dinner, just holding our cereal bowls and our plates on our laps. And when no one emptied the bin in the kitchen, we found maggots crawling all over the old spaghetti noodles and onto the floor. And when Mummy ran out of money and couldn't pay the bills, the electricity got shut off and we went out to diners to eat and then ran out without paying for the food.

And somehow, someone found out about all of our problems and the police showed up and took us away. Again. They located our stepmom and said they were bringing us to her house. Now we call that brief period with our real mum "The Six Weeks". The Six Weeks of loving encouragement, mad fun, and splendid adventures. But also of confusion and well-meant chaos. We were pretty worried and scared as we clung to each other in the back of the police cruiser and wondered whether our stepmom would take us back. We had no idea what the next six weeks would bring.

29.

When we got to our stepmom's house, the police told us to stay in the car with the social worker while they talked with our stepmom. They knocked on the door and when she answered, we could tell she was drunk as usual. We knew from the way she was leaning against the open doorframe and trying to flirt with the officers in a low sultry voice.

"Hello, Officers," she said. "What can I do for you today?" And she licked her lips and looked them up and down.

The police officers ignored that.

"These children are your charges," they said. "Unless you go to Court and the Judge decides something different, they are yours. Your responsibility."

"You have to keep them," the other officer added.

"Technically we're not even her stepkids anymore," Annie had said to Max and me just loud enough to be heard through the open window of the patrol car. Our stepmom turned and scowled at Annie.

The social worker tried to shush Annie from the front seat, but Annie continued.

"Since she and our dad divorced," Annie said loudly, "the Court said she's our legal guardian and we are her wards. That's what the Court decided while we were at Girl Scout Camp last summer." Our stepmom turned her attention back to the police officers.

"She could be in big trouble for kicking us out," Annie yelled, opening the car door and getting out, stretching her legs. "She basically abandoned us without the Court's permission," she shouted. Then before the social worker could intervene, Annie pulled Max and me out of the police cruiser and marched right past the police officers and our stepmom and into the house!

I guess you can't just kick your wards out into the wilderness when you get tired of them! I thought.

The police officers gave our stepmom their cards saying, "They look like pretty nice kids. Just give them a chance." The social worker handed her a card as well.

Our stepmom laughed at that.

"You have no idea, Officers," she slurred. And she shut the door as they remained standing on the porch.

"Sit down on the couch," our stepmom sputtered as the police cruiser left.

The three of us kids looked at each other. Max and I sat down on the couch while Annie remained standing and our stepmom called Mr. Johnson, our dead dad's best friend. I guess she didn't know what else to do. She obviously wasn't happy about getting us back. She kept yelling into the phone and glaring back in our direction.

Mr. Johnson arrived a short time later and he and our stepmom talked for a while in a separate room. Eventually they came back to where we were sitting on the couch. Max and I were sitting anyway. Annie was still standing.

"Your stepmom is willing to take you back if you promise to be good and not cause any trouble," Mr. Johnson said.

Annie snickered at that. Max and I looked at Annie and then back at Mr. Johnson and our stepmom.

"We promise," Max and I said almost immediately. But Annie just glared. Mr. Johnson stared at her for a while until he eventually realized she wasn't going to say anything.

"OK. I'm glad that's settled," he finally said. And then he left in a hurry.

We kept sitting on the couch for what seemed like forever (Annie standing) and when nothing else happened and we heard the clink of our stepmother's vodka glass hitting the kitchen counter, we headed down to our bedrooms and found them exactly as we had left them six weeks before. Nothing had changed. Our beds weren't made and our PJ's were lying on the floor where we'd left them. We were home.

30.

I'm in French II this year with Mlle Cesoir again and I'm loving it. I'm doing great in most of my classes and but I'm only doing barely OK in French, for my standards anyway. My "A" keeps dropping to a "B" and I have to work really hard to bring it back up to an "A".

I can read and write in French at a pretty basic level, but it's really hard to understand when someone is talking to you and it's impossible for me to speak it back. I'm trying, but it's hard. Jesse is in my French II class also, and this morning when I walked in before the bell rang he was having an actual conversation with Mlle Cesoir. In French! I couldn't believe it. I couldn't understand a word of it. I was super curious, so I hung around out in the hall after class, and then I caught him as he came out of the door.

"Hey, Jesse! You were actually speaking French with Mlle Cesoir before class today."

"Yeah – it is French class, right?" he responded. "I guess I should use French and not Chinese or something."

"Do you speak Chinese, too?" I asked dumbfounded.

"No, but I think I will take Chinese in high school." He grinned. "So far, I'm only just barely fluent in English."

I laughed.

"Just kidding," he said. "But I do speak Spanish. My grandma is from Mexico, and she only speaks to me in Spanish so I've learned a lot from her."

"No way. You can speak three languages?"

"Yeah – kind of. I'm working on being fluent in all three, anyway."

"I thought you didn't care about school and your grades," I said. He still didn't bring books or a backpack or anything other than a pen and a pencil to class, and sometimes a calculator to Algebra. And he still always borrowed paper, but I had noticed that he wasn't saying stupid stuff anymore to make the whole class laugh. I sort of missed that.

"Yeah, well, school isn't my highest priority, but I have gotten my grades up."

"Why?" I asked. "What changed?"

Now I was even more curious. We were almost halfway through our spring semester, and we'd be promoting to high school at the end of the year and heading to ninth grade in the fall. I always worked to keep my grades up, but Jesse never did.

"Well, I'm not supposed to say anything, but can you keep a secret, Maddie?"

I was intrigued.

"Of course. I won't tell anyone whatever it is. Unless it's like you're going to run away or hurt yourself or hurt someone else or something." I learned that during Ms. Dulce's failed attempts to offer me counseling last year. If someone's safety is involved, you have to share their secret.

Jesse laughed. "No, I'm not running away and I'm not going to hurt myself or someone else. But I really like French. And do you remember how Mlle Cesoir gave me a break last year when I was making fun of her in class?"

Of course, I remembered that. Everyone remembered that.

"Yeah," I replied.

"Well," Jesse said. "At the end of that semester, she asked me to stay after class again and she said I was doing a really good job in French. I was really picking it up. And she said she had checked my grades and she saw that I was getting an "A" in French and an "A" in P.E. But that I was pretty much failing all my other classes. And she said she was going to offer me a challenge - that if I would pick up all my grades and get straight A's that spring and again in eighth grade, she would sign a contract with me that if I got almost all A's for four years in high school, she would make sure I had my college paid for if I got in."

"What? That's crazy! Is that even legal?" I asked.

"Yeah, I know it's crazy. And I'm pretty sure it's legal. But even though I wasn't sure I completely believed her, I decided to give it a shot. I kinda like a challenge. And guess what? I'm getting all A's this semester."

Honestly, I didn't think Jesse was that smart. I knew he was funny, and I knew he was a good athlete. But then I remembered Annie telling me once that most comedians are really smart — that they know how to play with words or situations to tell a great story and how to make other people laugh. And that they have to time the punch lines just right. And that humor is a sign of intelligence. It suddenly dawned on me that maybe Jesse was actually really, really smart. He just didn't like to show it.

"Well, that's pretty cool," I said. "I hope it's true what she said."

"So do I," Jesse replied. "That would make me the first person in my family to go to college."

I went home that night thinking about how my parents had both gone to college, my real mum and my dad, that is, and how it was just an expectation that Annie and Max and I were going to go to college, too. Even our stepmom assumed we would go even though she hadn't. It never occurred to me that I wouldn't go to college. And now Jesse might be going, too.

31.

Gracie got transferred out of all of our advanced classes today.

The Counselor sent a call slip for her during second period Advanced English and Gracie seemed to know what it was. She didn't look surprised. She just looked sad. She glanced over at me and then grabbed her backpack and walked out of our classroom. And she didn't come back. She wasn't in any of my other classes for the rest of the day, either. I didn't know what was going on. She's been really distant and distracted lately and I'm worried about her.

"Hey, Mr. Garcia," I said to my last period teacher. "Where's Gracie? Why wasn't she in class today?"

"Gracie's schedule was changed," he answered me.

"What do you mean 'changed'?" I asked. "Why? She used to be in all my classes, and she wasn't in hardly any of them today."

"I'm sorry, Maddie, but it's nothing I can talk to you about," Mr. Garcia answered. "You would have to ask Gracie." He smiled at me kindly.

I left the classroom even more worried. I knew something was going on with Gracie, but I didn't know what. Cuz she won't talk about it – not to me, not to anyone. She just seems all alone.

I knew Gracie's grades had slipped. But it didn't make sense cuz she's super smart. She's probably the smartest person I know.

And I'd noticed her appearance had changed. Her long brown curly hair that used to kind of flow back and forth when she walked has been just hanging down limply lately.

And her clothes look all messed up – like they haven't been washed in a while. I can spot that one.

And she used to sort of bounce around with this great energy that made it hard to keep up with her and she was always smiling and joking around. But now she just looks beaten up. Not bruised or anything. Like she's carrying a really heavy weight on her shoulders.

Gracie doesn't pick up when I call her cell and she doesn't return my texts. We used to hang out before school and walk to classes together and sit at the same lunch table every day and talk on the phone all the time, but we don't anymore.

I miss her. I decided to make Gracie talk to me.

Today at the end of the day as I was leaving school, I spotted her.

"Hey, Gracie," I called as she was hurrying away. I ran to catch up to her. "Gracie, what's wrong? Are you OK? I'm worried about you."

Gracie didn't answer and kept walking, so I tried again.

"Hey, Gracie, it's me, Maddie. You know, your best friend?"

Gracie stopped then and she turned around and looked right at me just for a second. Then she looked down at the ground.

"What's wrong, Gracie?" I asked again. "You seem really sad, or maybe angry or something. What's happening? Did I do something to make you mad? And why did you get transferred out of all of our classes?"

Gracie looked up, past me. Then she turned and started to walk away.

"It's not you, Maddie. You're still my best friend. But I just think it's better if you don't hang around me anymore. And I couldn't keep up in our classes."

"That doesn't make any sense, Gracie," I said, catching up with her again. "How can we be best friends if we never hang around each other and you won't return my calls? And you're super smart. Of course, you can keep up in our classes."

"Trust me on this one, Maddie," she said over her shoulder. And she continued walking. Away from me.

None of this makes any sense. I don't know what's going on. I'm still worried about her. And I miss her. Gracie is supposed to be my best friend. In fact, she's really my only friend. And I'm also kind of embarrassed for myself cuz I don't have anyone else to hang out with. But lately it's just been me sitting by myself at lunch. Alone. And her sitting by herself at lunch. Alone, too. At the far end of the picnic tables. There's just this huge distance between us. And it looks like that's just how it's going to be.

I stood there feeling helpless as she moved further and further away from me. I was hoping that life would somehow get better for her. But I was afraid it wasn't going to.

32.

"Gracie, Sweetie! Where are you? Gracie, you forgot your homework!"

Gracie's mom showed up at school the next day and Gracie was *super* embarrassed. Her mom was wearing this really skimpy outfit with her fake boobs all sticking out of the clingy low-cut top, leopard print leggings hanging off of her skinny butt, and sparkly super red high heeled shoes. She was running around during lunch, her hair all piled high on top of her head, heavy make-up and bright red lipstick, waving a bunch of papers in front of her, and yelling at the top of her lungs.

"Gracie! I brought your homework!"

Poor Gracie! Everyone was at the outside lunch tables. Of course, that's where everything that's ever going to be super embarrassing starts. Gracie was sitting way off by herself like she's being doing lately, and she looked like she just wanted to crawl under the tables and hide.

Her mom headed for the lunch tables cuz I think she spotted Gracie and as she got closer, I noticed her teeth. They were disgusting. I mean really disgusting! They were grey and black and broken and missing. Here was this pretty lady in a weird too skinny and skanky sort of way with the ugliest teeth I'd ever seen.

Jesse was standing nearby so I went over to him, and whispered, "Hey, Jesse. What's with her teeth?"

Jesse answered, "They're meth teeth, Maddie. That's what happens with meth heads. They lose all their teeth. She's got a really bad case of meth mouth."

Jesse told me that he'd heard that Gracie's parents started using meth last year. He said that before they got so addicted to drugs, Gracie's parents didn't have much money, but they were really nice and hard-working people. He said now they're totally into meth and it's really hard on Gracie and her three sisters.

I asked Jesse if he thought Gracie's parents would stop using meth.

"No one ever stops on their own, Maddie. Not unless they get some serious help. And now I hear Gracie's older sister Charity might be using, too. She's in your sister's grade and she doesn't even come to school anymore. Gracie could be next."

At the lunch tables, all the kids just stared at Gracie and whispered behind their hands. I felt so sorry for her. I remembered how kind she had been to me last year on the first day I came back to school after my dad died. And I knew what it's like to have parents that embarrass you.

Dads that show up at work too drunk or high on prescription drugs to teach and who carry on with other teachers on campus and who abandon their kids.

Stepmoms who say mean things to you all the time and who can't keep their car on the right side of the road and who fall over backward in public because they're too drunk to hold their balance.

Mums who shout at people who aren't really there and who hear things that nobody else does and who don't know how to work a toaster.

But it's kind of like the caste system that we're learning about in history. Having parents who are alcoholics or prescription drug addicts or dead or crazy like mine is better than having parents that are meth heads like Gracie's. Meth head parents seem to be at the very bottom of the caste system.

I wanted to tell Gracie that everything was going to be OK. That she didn't have to be like her parents. That it wasn't her fault that her parents were using drugs. That things would get better. That we'd find someone who could help.

I headed toward Gracie just as Campus Security showed up and took her mom away while she was still yelling and waving the papers.

"Gracie, Honey, I'll be back. Don't worry, Gracie. I'm here for you!" Her words faded as she was carried away toward the office.

I continued toward Gracie, but it turned out she didn't want my help. She just pushed me away.

"Leave me alone!" Gracie yelled and ran toward the bathroom crying. She didn't want me to follow her, and I didn't know what to do or how to help her.

I stood there all by myself looking stupid.

33.

Speaking of teeth, I have braces. And I'm totally tired of them. No one calls me "brace face" or "tin grin" or "tinsel teeth" or "zipper lips" like I was afraid they might, but still. They're ugly and I was supposed to have them off by now since I'm in eighth grade.

I got braces at the beginning of sixth grade, so it's been like almost three years! And it was supposed to be for only two years. My dad said I needed them – back when he lived with us and before he and our stepmom divorced and before he died. Well, I guess that's kind of obvious. But anyway, he told our stepmom to research the local orthodontists, and she came up with two that were supposed to be pretty good – Dr. Goode and Dr. Goodrich. Like do all orthodontists have practically the same name?

"Who do you want to go to, Maddie?" she asked. "Dr. Goode or Dr. Goodrich? I hear they're both pretty good."

I was actually pretty surprised she had followed through on this and that she was asking my opinion. But how was I supposed to know who I wanted to go to? I was only in sixth grade and ten years old at the time. A bunch of the kids in my class were getting braces and I was trying to remember who they went to. I'm not very good with names and I was thinking that Dr. Goodrich was the younger and more popular one, so he was probably more up to date with stuff. (That's called deductive reasoning – using clues to decide.)

"Dr. Goodrich," I answered. "He's who all my friends go to, and I hear they really like him."

And guess what? We got to the office, and Dr. Goodrich turned out to be the old guy! Like practically 80 years old. Ready to retire. Figures!

So anyway, I think my dad worked out some sort of deal with him before he died (my dad, not Dr. Goodrich) cuz my stepmom told me that Dr. Goodrich was discounting the cost if we would be a part of his study. And I had to relearn how to swallow, and it was supposed to help straighten my teeth without having to pull any out. Really? That's ridiculous! My teeth were super crowded and even though I was only ten I could have told them it wouldn't work!

But anyway, the idea was that I had to roll my tongue up in the roof of my mouth when I swallowed, and it would make the roof of my mouth bigger. And that would somehow make it so he wouldn't have to pull any teeth. And then he would write up his study and he'd get published in some orthodontist journal and become famous right before he retired. He'd make a bunch of money on his research and we wouldn't have to pay so much money for my braces. Great plan.

There was only one problem. It didn't work. Three years later and I still had crooked teeth. No kidding! He says I didn't practice swallowing enough and now it's too late to pull any teeth and so I just have to keep the braces on for like forever, I guess. All the other kids in my classes who have braces are getting theirs off. Even though they didn't call me brace face or anything, they're now saying that if I kiss a boy who has braces, our braces will lock, and we'll be stuck together forever. And guess what? Jesse has braces, too. Life just sucks!

34.

Mrs. Boardman, my U.S. History teacher, has decided to team up with my English teacher, Mr. Litrate (like literate, I know – all my teachers have the stupidest names) to do a unit on the challenges of creating a new government. Kind of like what the colonists were facing a bunch of years ago when they came to the New World. Our teachers say it's all about choices and their consequences and thinking carefully about the long-term effects of decisions – good or bad.

We're reading *Lord of the Flies* in English and it's actually pretty cool. It's about all these boys that get dumped on this island when their plane goes down and how Ralph and Jack are both trying to be the leader of the boys, but they don't get along. They have really different personalities and super different ideas. And kids like Piggy and Sam'n'Eric (who are twins) just get caught in the middle, trying to decide which of the two philosophies they are going to follow and what kind of power is best. It's pretty ruthless! (I'm working on my vocabulary. Cool word, huh?) Ralph tries to be good and to keep everyone safe and to make rules that will protect everyone, but Jack seems to be a lot stronger and basically wants to explore and have fun and says that only the fittest are going to survive. The kids in my class are really getting into it.

And then people in the story start dying and the boys start wondering if they're making the right decisions. They begin to realize that their choices can have really dire (another cool word!) consequences. And they're British, so they know they are supposed to show "proper form" which basically means behave themselves. But they don't.

It makes me wonder. What do we do with parents like Gracie has or like I have? Can we help them show proper form and become better people or are they just doomed to always making bad choices that hurt the people around them, ignoring the consequences? And does anyone ever intervene to make it better? I think about Annie and me and Max. And I wonder who we would follow - Ralph or Jack? We always stick together. But then the more I thought about it, I wasn't so sure. And the possibilities began to make me feel sick to my stomach.

35.

Annie got in a lot of trouble a couple of days ago, and it was all my fault. Every Saturday we have chores at our house, and no one gets to do anything fun until all the chores are done. Annie and I dust and vacuum. One of us does the upstairs while the other one does the downstairs. And Max mows the grass and cleans up the yard and does the trash cans.

I'm glad I don't have Max's jobs cuz he has to pick up all the dog poop in the backyard. We have a dog named "Lucky' and we shop at 'Lucky Market' so I guess that makes us 'lucky'. Right? (That's called satire.)

When Max takes out the trash, all the vodka bottles rattle together. He has to sort them out from the other trash cuz our neighborhood does recycling, and you have to separate the glass and the aluminum cans from the rest of the trash. We don't have any aluminum cans though since we're not allowed to drink sodas. Our stepmom says they're bad for our health and they cost too much. (That's called irony.) So, there's just a bunch of empty glass vodka bottles for recycling. When Max rolls the trash can with the recyclables out to the curb for pickup every week, he always tries to push the top down on it so no one can look inside and see all the vodka bottles. It makes me wonder what the trash guys think.

So anyway, I had the upstairs to clean last weekend. There's a table in the living room, that we call the "three square table". It's basically a really long and low narrow heavy wooden rectangle, and it's made up of three big squares and the middle square has a cushion that's actually a seat. On top of one of the end squares we have this enormous lamp, and I mean really *enormous*. It's bigger than I am! And it's super heavy. We're supposed to carefully lift the lamp down (which is really hard to do by yourself) and dust the table under it, and then pull the table away from the wall and vacuum under it, and then move the table back to the wall, and then carefully pick the lamp back up and put it back on the table. I swear our stepmom has rules and procedures for the stupidest things. It takes *forever*. And then there's still a lot more dusting and vacuuming after that.

I wanted to get done early so I could go outside and hang. Not that I had anyone to hang with, but it was better than being inside and doing chores. I decided to move the table with the lamp still on it. I figured I would just drag the table carefully and then I could vacuum under it and then drag it back. That would save a lot of time. So, I started to drag the table with the heavy lamp still on it. All of a sudden, I heard this super loud and horrible CRACKKKKKKKK! It was so loud I was sure everyone else in the house heard it too. I quickly looked over my shoulder, but no one was around. And then I carefully looked under the table and my heart stopped. I mean it literally stopped! Or it at least skipped a few beats. There was a *huge* crack between the bottom of the table and the table leg which was just about ready to fall right off!

I was so scared! I didn't know what to do. I thought about finding my stepmom and confessing to breaking the table, but I knew I'd get into a lot of trouble. I looked around again. No one was nearby. No one would know if I just put everything back like it was in the first place. So that's what I decided to do. I had to lift the lamp off the table after all so I could carefully move the table back to where it belonged and then I pushed the leg in under it so that the table was sitting on it properly. I put the lamp back on top like it was before and I kept right on dusting and vacuuming. Like nothing had ever happened. My heart eventually calmed back down, and I thought I had gotten away with it.

But then a day later, Annie sat down on the middle cushion square of the table to watch TV and everything completely fell apart. And I mean literally fell apart. The table leg crumpled and the huge lamp fell to the floor with a deafening crash and broke into a thousand pieces. No one missed that one. And our stepmom went berserk! And she took it all out on Annie.

"You clumsy idiot! Look what you've done! You completely ruined my table and my lamp. And that lamp is one of a kind. Get out of my sight! Get down to your bedroom where you belong – I don't want to see your face. And leave your phone on the stereo. You don't deserve it. You're grounded for a week and you're cleaning the entire house by yourself next weekend!"

Poor Annie didn't know what had happened and I was too scared to tell. I let Annie take all the blame. I knew I was being a coward and that I was the one who broke the table, and I should say so. But I didn't. And Annie suffered the consequences.

36.

"Hey, Annie," I said one day. "How do you read books so fast? I know you're always reading but it's like you read faster than anyone I know."

Annie reads whenever she can. She's *always* reading. When Max and I are outside riding our bikes or rollerblading or skateboarding, Annie is inside reading. She reads really long books, like books that are 1,000 pages or longer. No kidding! I think that's why she's so smart. But she's not just book smart. She's really smart in other ways, too. She calls it 'life smart'. Jesse calls it 'street smart'.

Sometimes, though, she just seems to consume her books – like she just breathes them in. She goes through them in record time. I'm a good reader and everything but reading isn't my highest priority. I don't read books like Annie does.

"You gotta carve out time for reading, Maddie," she said. "When you and Max are outside hanging, I'm inside reading."

"Yeah, I know, but you seem to read more than just those times," I said.

"Well," Annie said. "I have a couple of tricks! But you can't tell. Promise?"

I promised.

"You know how we have to vacuum the backs of all the pleats of the drapes every weekend? And you know how long that takes?"

"Yeah," I said. I hated that job. It took forever.

"Whenever I have to do the downstairs drapes, I just plug in the vacuum and turn it on like I'm using it. I just leave it on, and then I lie down on my bed, and I read. Like for hours. The backs of the drapes don't really need vacuuming, and no one ever knows. And you know that *she* never comes downstairs so she just thinks I'm doing a great job of all the vacuuming. How is she going to check? She'd have to come downstairs. You know that'll never happen. Don't be so good all the time, Maddie. Be creative and find ways to do what you want!"

Annie laughed and I just stood there. I couldn't believe she wasn't vacuuming the backs of the drapes every weekend like we were supposed to. I always did. She could get in big trouble. Of course, I wasn't going to tell, but all I could think of was that it served her right that she got blamed for breaking that stupid table.

And then I wondered if maybe I was more like Jack, the ruthless leader in Lord of the Flies, than I had thought.

37.

Annie got blamed for other stuff, too, things that really weren't her fault. She always seemed to get into more trouble than Max and I did. We messed up, too, but we never got blamed like Annie did.

We'd only been living with our dad and stepmom for a few weeks when our stepmom gave Annie a bucket of soapy water and a mop and told her to clean the bathroom floor. It was the small bathroom on the main floor, right next to the carpeted master bedroom. Annie was only nine years old then and she'd never mopped a floor before, so I guess she did what she'd seen on TV in Cinderella or a pirate movie or something. She poured the entire bucket of water all over the floor and started swishing it around with the mop like she was swabbing a deck. Our stepmom went nuts! She must have heard the sloshing of water from way over in the kitchen where she was pouring herself some vodka and she came flying across the house yelling at Annie.

"What the hell are you doing?" she yelled, her words slurring. "That's a whole bucket of water! And it's bleeding into the carpeting! You're ruining the floor! And you're ruining the carpet! Don't you even know how to wash a floor properly? What's the matter with you damned kids? You think you're so GD smart but you really don't know anything, do you? You don't even know how to mop a floor!"

We really didn't know how to mop a floor. Our real mum was super creative and super smart and everything, but she didn't seem to do much cleaning, at least not like our stepmom. It just wasn't her priority, I guess. And I don't think she was ever taught how to clean since she had lived most of her life at boarding school. Our stepmom was totally different. She had cleaning procedures and rules for everything.

Our stepmom started throwing towels all over the floor and the carpeting to sop up all the water. I tried to help by stomping on the towels, thinking maybe that would help them soak up the water faster. It didn't work. The water just shot out and splashed all over the walls. And our stepmom just screamed louder.

I don't know where our dad was, probably out on a boat or something.

And poor Annie. She was crying. How would she know she wasn't supposed to pour a bucket of water on the floor to wash it?

Looking back now, it makes me wonder who our stepmom thought Annie was anyway? The servant? A deckhand? Cinderella? I remember that was the last time Annie ever cried because of something our stepmom said or did. Annie sure didn't cry when she got yelled at for breaking the three-square table. Or when our stepmom and our dad said they were getting a divorce. Or when our stepmom sent us back to live with our real mum. Annie never cried at those times. She just got angry.

38.

"Maddie," our stepmom said to me at the beginning of eighth grade this year. "You need to develop your self-esteem. I think being the middle child has made you not have a lot of confidence in yourself. That's called 'Middle Child Syndrome.' I heard about it on one of my talk shows. Taking Drama as an elective should help you with that."

Sometimes our stepmom actually tries to be kind and caring. I know she meant well this time. But really? Drama? Middle Child Syndrome?!? What was she thinking?

What about all the family chaos and never being sure of where we were going to be living? What about her being drunk by 10 o'clock every morning and saying horrible things to us? What about our dad dying and us having no idea where our real mum is? What about not being able to have friends over because I have no idea what condition she will be in and whether she'll say something insulting about my friends' families in front of them? (Which she's done before, by the way.) No. My lack of self-confidence is Middle Child Syndrome! Give me a break!

I don't know why my stepmom had the idea that acting in front of a bunch of people would somehow help me. Like I said, I think she meant well. But there was no way I was going to take Drama.

"Please don't make me take Drama," I pleaded. "I can hardly stand in front of the class to read one of my essays. There's no way I'll be able to act in a play!"

"That's exactly why Drama is the perfect class for you," she answered.

I know I don't argue like Annie does, but I begged and pleaded with her until she finally relented. Mrs. French is the Drama teacher. Another stupid name. She should be teaching French. But Mrs. French also teaches Public Speaking and when my stepmom realized that she said I could take Public Speaking instead.

I figured making a couple of speeches in front of my class would be better than acting in a play in front of the whole school, so I acquiesced. (Another cool word, right? It means "agreed".)

So now I'm in Public Speaking. Mrs. French knew my dad and she actually lives just a couple of blocks away from us so I'm starting to think the whole thing was a set-up. Between my stepmom and Mrs. French. Or maybe it was just Mrs. French's idea. Who knows? None of the grownups in my life is ever transparent about anything. Absolutely no clarity there. Ever.

OK – so the class is Public Speaking, but guess what? There's only one speech we have to do. That's the good news. The bad news is that there are three parts to the class: Speech, Debate, and The Dreaded Drama. Go figure.

We started with Speech. That went OK even though I was really nervous. We had to do a speech about someone who we admired, and I did my speech about Annie – about how smart she is and how brave she is. My stepmom wasn't real happy about that. I didn't put a lot of details in it and I didn't look at the class when I gave my speech or anything, so I only got a "B", but I wasn't going to spill all the family secrets. Like I said, it's an unwritten rule in our family that no one tells anyone what's really going on. But everyone probably knows about it anyway. And I was really nervous.

Mrs. French has all the students in class give the speaker feedback on their speech and their presentation afterward on little pieces of paper. She reads them all to make sure they are appropriate before she gives them to the person who made the speech so they can consider the comments to make their future speeches better. She calls it "critiquing". And she says it helps you to grow. The feedback I got was stuff like, "Good speech", and "Interesting", and "You need to put in more details", and "Your voice shakes too much", and "You should look at the class more." I guess it was all pretty true.

Gracie started off the year in my Public Speaking class before she got transferred out of all our advanced classes. Gracie was a natural when it came to Public Speaking. I was really glad she was having success in that class anyway. When she gave her speech, it was awesome! She talked about not judging other people based on preconceived ideas and presumptions. Like I said, she's super smart. But someone wrote on their feedback paper that they liked her speech, but they didn't like her mom or her dad or her older sister cuz they were all a bunch of druggies and meth heads and they were all probably going to OD (that means overdose) soon. And they wondered if Gracie was a druggie, too. The papers are anonymous so I guess the person thought they could get away with it.

But Mrs. French pulled it out of the feedback papers when she was reviewing them before she gave them to Gracie. She sent Gracie off to the office on a fake errand and while Gracie was gone, she went off on our class. Mrs. French was *super* mad.

"These comments are an act of COWARDICE!" she yelled at the class. And I mean really yelled! "This is NOT a critique. It is common cruelty. Whoever made these comments obviously missed the entire point of Gracie's speech and should be extremely ASHAMED of themselves. THIS PERSON shows no character whatsoever!"

No one said a word.

When Mrs. French gets all worked up like that, she pushes her heavy black bangs back off of her forehead with the back of her hand in a really dramatic way. She doesn't have a scar, so I guess she doesn't have anything to hide. Her face does get all red and contorted though. We knew she was serious. Whoever wrote that will never do it again. I'm glad Mrs. French went off on them.

Poor Gracie! I'm glad she didn't see those comments. But not long after, her mom showed up at school in her weird skanky outfit, and Gracie's grades all slipped, and she was transferred out of our class anyway.

39.

Next in my Public Speaking class came the Debate unit. I don't like arguing and I guess you could say I really don't like confrontation. Everyone always calls me a peacemaker. Maybe that is part of Middle Child Syndrome after all. Or maybe it's because when people get all heated up about something, I never know what's going to happen next. It just scares me and even if I open my mouth, no words come out.

Mrs. French had us rate a bunch of controversial topics like War, and Capital Punishment, and Gun Control, and Charter Schools, and Socialism to say which ones we would most like to debate. And we had to say if we were for or against them. And then she assigned us a partner to work with and she assigned us a topic and the position we were to argue when we went up against another team.

I was teamed with Venus and we got Capital Punishment. I was pretty happy about that cuz Venus is a great debater and we're both totally against Capital Punishment. What if the wrong person gets blamed for something they didn't do? If they really didn't do the crime and you kill them, you can't fix it! And if they did do it, wouldn't it be better if they had to live the whole rest of their life in a really crummy prison eating really awful food and doing super hard work? And who knows? Maybe over time they could become a decent human being and do something good for the world. Even from prison.

But then I looked at our paper more closely.

"Venus," I said. "We have to argue FOR Capital Punishment! I'm against it and I thought you were, too."

"I'm totally against it," Venus replied. "But it looks like Mrs. French tricked us!"

Mrs. French had assigned all the groups the opposite point of view of whatever they said they wanted to argue.

"This isn't fair," a bunch of the students in our class called out.

Mrs. French smiled.

"It's important to understand both sides of an argument," she replied calmly. "By digging deeply into the opposite point of view, you can better understand your own opinions and those of others who disagree with you. When you understand both sides of an issue, you can make better and more compassionate choices," she added. "You can begin to come together respectfully in situations, even if you continue to disagree."

All I could think of was that she was beginning to sound like Mrs. Boardman.

Venus and I prepped for the debate together. I tried to be helpful, but I was scared to death. I hate arguing. I get terrified when people don't like what I'm saying or when they disagree with me. I don't like having a strong opinion about anything – at least not out loud. It's like I'm scared that everyone is going to not like what I say, so they're not going to like me, and then they'll go away and abandon me, and I'll never have any friends or anyone who understands me. Or loves me. Or stays with me. Ever.

I know it's just a stupid debate, but I'm terrified.

And I feel sorry for Venus. She's super confident and super smart and a super good debater and she ended up being paired with me!

Even though Venus and I both ended up doing a ton of research and were really well prepared, when it came to the actual debate, I just folded. It's like my voice just wobbled, and my vocal cords shut down, and eventually I couldn't say anything at all. Not a word. No self-confidence whatsoever. Just like my stepmom said. Venus had to carry the whole thing.

Venus did great, though – no one can stand up to an argument with her! She was really kind to me after and said she knew I had given it my best. We got an "A" but it was only because our research was so good. It was totally Venus' effort when it came to debating the other team, and the feedback papers from our class said so.

After Debate, it was time for the final unit that I was dreading. Drama. Mrs. French loves drama; it's her favorite part of the class.

"Everyone wears a mask to some extent in life," Mrs. French told our class. "Through drama you can take off your own mask for a while and try on another one. You can actually see what it's like to be someone else."

I wondered about that.

"And you can also dig more deeply behind your own mask and express things that you normally might not feel comfortable saying or doing," she said, smiling right at me. Uh oh.

Mrs. French handed out the scripts.

She handed me a one-act play that had only one person in it! It was just going to be me doing all the acting. There wasn't going to be anyone I could hide behind or lean on!

"Mrs. French, can I change this for a different play? Maybe one with lots of characters in it?" I asked her once she had given out all the assignments.

"Maddie," she replied. "This is a very special play. I chose it specifically for you. It's one of my favorites. You'll do just fine."

Mrs. French was firm. She wouldn't change it.

The play was about a girl who was about my age, and she was walking down these empty railroad tracks and her family was having lots of problems. The girl was really lonely, and she was talking about her life and wondering if things would ever get any better. I guess the railroad tracks were sort of a metaphor for life, and they just looked really long and really endless and really empty.

I worked hard on my lines and Annie helped me. Annie likes Mrs. French. She's one of her favorite teachers. Annie calls her "bright and insightful."

When it was time to do the performances, Mrs. French took volunteers and of course I didn't raise my hand. I was the very last person in the whole class to perform. When it was my turn to go up to the front of the class, I was really nervous. I walked up slowly, looking down at my shoes and not at the audience. Not at all. I started saying my lines slowly and kind of quietly. My voice was shaking, just like during the debate.

But then the strangest thing happened. As I "walked down the tracks", I started getting into the character. My voice stopped trembling and pretty soon I was saying my lines more confidently.

And then it got easier and easier and I was shouting my lines, really feeling them from my heart. I began feeling and expressing the things that this girl was feeling and shaking my fist at the sky, and crying about the injustices in life, and the loneliness, and the emptiness, and the defeat. And then before I knew it, it was over. And I had done it!

At first the whole class was just super quiet, but then they all just started clapping, and I mean really clapping. They had clapped politely after all the other performances; that was what Mrs. French requires, calling it 'theater etiquette'. But they clapped really hard for me. And I looked out at them, and they were all crying. The girls were anyway. I wish that Gracie had been there. But the boys just looked really sad and uncomfortable. And Mrs. French was beaming at me, and calling, "Bravo! Bravo!" She was clapping too. And she wasn't even pushing the hair out of her eyes or anything!

40

This morning I got out of bed and stretched – a big smile on my face. I'm super excited because I'm promoting from eighth grade today. Finally. The end of middle school where all the teachers knew my dad. The end of counselors calling me out of my classes to talk. The end of everyone knowing my family business. I can't wait. After summer, I'll be in high school. And I'll have some privacy. Finally.

I love school. It's something I'm good at, and it's pretty predictable. Except for the social stuff and the lack-of-friends stuff and the being left out stuff. And the everyone knowing your business stuff. But in classes, you know what you're supposed to do and if you do it, life is good. I'm involved in a bunch of school clubs and activities. I take notes in all my classes, and I stay after school for track, and I study when I get home. And then I can't wait to go back to school again. I guess school is my safe place. I don't really want summer to come at all, but I am pretty stoked about high school next year.

But then I noticed a note taped to the mirror over the dresser Annie and I share. It was from Annie. I recognized her handwriting. And suddenly I wasn't so excited any more.

I pulled the note off of the mirror. I had a sinking feeling in the pit of my stomach. I looked over at Annie's bed. It looked like it hadn't been slept in. Uh oh.

Annie and Max are supposed to come to my promotion this afternoon. They're being excused from school early. I'm doing a speech at the ceremony because I'm one of the Eighth Grade Class Officers. Go figure! Me doing a speech. Maybe Mrs. French and my Public Speaking class really did help. But I'm still really nervous. Annie helped me with it since she's so good at English and I practiced it with her a lot of times last night, so I think it will go OK.

I opened up the note.

"Hey, Sister," it said. "Sorry, but I took all of your babysitting money. You had $165 in your drawer. Just tell our stepmom that she owes it to you. She never paid me back for all the money she borrowed from me, and it was a lot more than $165, so she can pay my money back to you. And just for the record, she took a bunch of money from the Parent Teacher Club when she was treasurer. I know cuz I found a bunch of IOU's in the money tray that she kept in her drawer right before they kicked her out as Treasurer. (Yeah – I snooped!) So anyway, tell her to pay you back. And tell her to pay the PTC back, too! I'm not coming home again - ever. I can't handle this place anymore. I love you. I know you'll do fine. Good luck at your promotion. You'll ace your speech. See ya – I love you. Annie"

My stomach felt like it turned completely over.

Annie was just finishing ninth grade, entering tenth grade in the fall. We were supposed to be in high school together next year. She was my big sister, my defender, my protector. I loved her. She was the one who held Max and me together. She was the one who explained life to us. She couldn't leave! What about the Three Musketeers? One for all and all for one! I started to cry.

But I guess Annie had just had enough. I had a feeling that something was coming the other day when we got home from school and our stepmom started in on Annie. It was like the storm that had been brewing finally burst. And the fallout was bad.

41.

"The school called today. You weren't there! You were truant again!" Our stepmom glared at Annie. "If you're going to live in my house you're going to have to go to school." She stumbled from the car and headed toward the house, still yelling at Annie. "You live in MY house, you live by MY rules!"

"Oh, the rules of a drunk?" Annie shouted back. "And you mean the house that our dad's teachers' retirement and our grandpa's trust fund pay for? I can't believe you haven't been arrested for a DUI yet. You're just a depressing deadbeat old drunk." Annie was glaring back at her.

"Don't use that tone of voice with me," our stepmom screamed, slurring her words. "You don't know what you're talking about. You always think you're so GD smart!"

And she reached out to slap Annie's face. Everything seemed to freeze and play out in slow motion after that. Annie caught her wrist in midair. I swear, the world tilted on its axis, and I could hear my dad saying, "Be careful with power. You have to treat it with respect." Max and I held our breaths and watched and didn't say a word.

"You'll never hit me again," Annie said slowly and quietly, still holding our stepmom's wrist. She waited a few more moments as if to let the words sink in, and then she slowly and deliberately released the wrist and stared our stepmom down until we all finally headed into the house. Not another word was spoken.

And now Annie is gone.

42.

I thought back again on what it was like when we first came to our dad and stepmom's house to live. I seem to be doing a lot of that lately. Maybe it was because I'd been noticing the signs that something was brewing with Annie. Or maybe it was because I was trying to understand our stepmom and our now-dead-dad. I don't know.

I remember that when we first came to live here, it was really hard to fall asleep at night. Max used to drag his comforter and pillow from his room down the hall into Annie's and my room.

"Can I sleep in here with you guys tonight?" Max would ask.

"Of course you can, Maxmax," Annie would reply.

And little Max would make a bed for himself on the floor between Annie's and my twin beds. Annie and I would hold hands in the dark over little Max, and Annie would tell us stories until we fell asleep.

"There was once a beautiful Snow Queen," Annie would always begin the stories, "Who lived in the land of cold. And although her world was very cold, it was also very beautiful, and the Snow Queen was very kind." At first I thought of the evil white queen, Jadis, from The Chronicles of Narnia, who made her collar out of Aslan's mane. The first time Annie told us the story I was afraid that her Snow Queen was evil too, and that she would make us live in an endless winter. But I was wrong.

"The Snow Queen would cocoon all the little animals and children in magical snowflakes," Annie would continue. "And the snowflakes protected the children and the animals and kept them warm. They knew they were cared for and loved." And then Annie would continue with wonderful tales of the adventures that the animals and the children had together, in a land where no one was ever lonely or lost, and everyone was always warm and loved. And Max and I would fall asleep to Annie's stories, knowing that Annie was there to protect us and that we would be OK.

43.

I went to my Eighth Grade Promotion Ceremony. The band played as we entered, and we all stood for the Pledge of Allegiance. The principal read all of our names and handed each of us a Certificate of Promotion as we crossed the stage.

The speeches were at the very end. Right before it was my turn to speak, I looked over at Mrs. French. She was standing to the side of the stage, behind the heavy red velvet curtain. She's our Class Advisor and she's the one who encouraged me to run for an office and helped me write my speech. I guess it was a good thing I took her class after all. She gave me an encouraging smile and pushed up at her bangs. I looked out at the audience, and I saw my stepmom and Max in the third row near the center aisle. My stepmom looked like she was at least partially sober, only leaning a bit to one side. And Max was smiling up at me proudly. There was an empty seat next to Max and I wished Annie were sitting there, too. But I knew I would try to make her proud anyway.

When it was my turn, I took a deep breath as I walked up to the microphone and cleared my throat. I started my speech, just like I had practiced with Annie. It was about doing your best, and not letting circumstances get you down. I didn't share any personal stuff – we still never talk about family stuff outside the family – but I did talk about getting back up after you've been knocked down, and overcoming your circumstances, and about finding your defenders and your support people that will help you along the way, and about setting goals and achieving them. And just when I was finishing my last line, I looked way out over the heads of the audience and standing just inside the double doors at the back of the auditorium was Annie. She was smiling at me and giving me a "two thumbs up" and she was even crying. Annie never cries. And then I was done, and everyone was clapping, and Mrs. French was beaming, and I looked back at the double doors to the auditorium, but Annie was already gone.

I do think I had made her proud though.

That night, Max came down to my room, which used to be Annie's and my room, with his pillow and his comforter and asked, "Can I sleep in here tonight, Maddie?" And I said, "Of course you can, Maxmax." And he made a bed for himself on the floor between Annie and my beds. But I didn't try to tell him any stories. I can't tell them like Annie does. And eventually we both fell asleep.

EIGHTH GRADE SUMMER

44.

It's already becoming a really long summer! I can't wait for school to start in the fall. Usually in the summer, Annie and I hang out. But not this year. Max is almost three years younger than I am and we do still go bike riding in the hills together, and skateboarding, and looking for snakes under the tumbleweeds, and stuff like that. One Saturday a couple of weeks ago we even rode way north along the coast on the highway! There's not much of a bike lane there, but Max and I are pretty good riders and we're careful, and besides, we wanted to be gone from the house, so it was a good day. And we wore our helmets. We must have ridden a total of 20 miles or more.

Most kids in our neighborhood are enrolled in Science Camp or Basketball Camp or Gymnastics Camp or some other camp that we can't afford. There's no Girl Scout Camp this summer either since I dropped out of Scouts toward the end of the school year. Max has friends his own age that he hangs with a lot. I don't really have any friends since Gracie just kind of slipped away and Taylor and Olivia haven't wanted anything to do with me for a really long time. My stepmom says I just need to develop some new friends – like that's so easy. Right.

I tried reaching out to Gracie again, but she still won't answer my phone calls. I don't know for sure what's going on with her. I guess it's all of her family drug stuff, but I still miss her. My stepmom says it's best to stay away from her anyway. Like she's such a good influence? My stepmom, I mean. Not Gracie.

Olivia and Taylor are the only other friends I've ever had here at my used-to-be-dad's house – and that was way back in elementary school. Things changed a lot between us after my dad died, when I heard them talking about him in the school bathroom in seventh grade. Maybe it had to do with us not having any money and me not having the right clothes and everything. I guess I became pretty uncool to hang around with. And I couldn't have them come over to my house anyway cuz I never knew what to expect with my stepmom. That meant we had to always hang out at their houses which I think they got kind of tired of. And then Olivia and Taylor had a falling out – I think it was over a boy or something but I'm not sure. So now I hear they don't even hang around with each other much anymore.

Olivia and Taylor's parents were pretty cool though. We had all been in Scouts together so their families had a ringside seat to all our family issues. But I think their parents sometimes thought my stepmom was pretty heroic or something. Like the time we were having a fundraiser one Saturday and we all had to show up at nine in the morning at Lucky Market to sell cookies. My stepmom was supposed to drive me to the fundraiser since it was over a mile away, but of course she didn't get up in time so I decided I would just run there instead. I didn't want to be late.

It was really cold and I didn't have any real running warmups or anything so I just wore shorts and a T- shirt. By the time I got there I was freezing.

Olivia and Taylor and their moms drove up in their cool SUV's just as I arrived, and we got the tables all set up and the cookies set out and then guess who came driving up an hour later? My stepmom. In our dumpy old car. She must have stopped at the ATM or something on the way cuz she handed Taylor and Olivia's moms $60 for a bunch of boxes of cookies! They thought she was just amazing.

Then my stepmom looked at me and said, "Maddie, you look so cold. I know you wanted to walk here this morning, but I told you I'd drive you. You should have at least worn a sweater. I'll go back home and get you one."

Off she went and Taylor and Olivia's moms both looked at me and told me how lucky I was that she came into our lives, and I just got all angry inside thinking, *"If you only knew!"* But I wasn't saying anything like that out loud of course.

"Yeah, we're pretty lucky all right," I said.

And my stepmom came back a couple of hours later right as we were breaking down the tables, totally drunk, and handed me an old torn sweater.

45.

So, dropping out of Scouts. Near the end of eighth grade this school year, it was almost time for the Bridge Ceremony where we would become First Class Scouts. It wasn't very cool to be in Scouts anymore cuz we were in middle school and there were only five of us left in the troop – Olivia, Taylor, a girl named Jackie, Mrs. McKay's daughter, and me. Even though Olivia and Taylor wouldn't acknowledge me at school, they had to be nice at Scouts. That was part of Scouting. None of us liked our Scout Leader Mrs. McKay very much though. She was really strict and not very much fun, and Jackie came up with this big plan to embarrass her at the final Bridge Ceremony.

"Here's what we're going to do," said Jackie to all of us girls except for Mrs. McKay's daughter. Jackie always came up with ideas that we were supposed to follow.

"We're all going to quit the troop right before the Bridge Ceremony. It'll serve Mrs. McKay right cuz she's so mean and she never lets us do what we want to do."

"I don't know," I said. "Is that really a good idea?"

"Goody goody," said Jackie in a really mean way. Taylor and Olivia laughed.

"I think that's a great idea!" Olivia and Taylor said at almost the same time. And they looked at each other and laughed again.

"But we're going to do it slowly, so she doesn't see it coming," Jackie went on. "We'll drop out one by one for the four weeks leading up to the Bridge Ceremony so the only person left in the troop will be Mrs. McKay's daughter!"

I didn't say anything. But Olivia and Taylor laughed again. Besties.

Our troop had been doing a bunch of fundraising and we'd been saving all our money so that after the Bridge Ceremony we could take the Amtrak train up north to the State Capitol in Sacramento. It was going to be a special week-long trip and since there were only five of us girls left in the Troop, including Mrs. McKay's daughter, the trip would be fully paid for. The train, the hotel, the meals and even the souvenirs. Jackie sure didn't like Mrs. McKay.

I knew the plan wasn't a good idea and it was really cruel, but I was secretly just mad all the time at everything in general and somehow hurting someone I didn't care about felt good. We all four agreed on it – Jackie, Olivia, Taylor and me. I remember telling my stepmom that I wanted to quit the Troop and she asked if I were sure since she knew I'd been working hard at fundraising and was looking forward to the trip.

"You know, Maddie. Some things can't be undone once you do them. But the choice is yours. Are you sure about this?" She sounded so reasonable that I hesitated for a minute. Every so often she's like a regular person. I don't get it. But then I told her that I was sure.

I called up Mrs. McKay and told her I was quitting. And over the next two weeks, so did Taylor and Olivia.

But Jackie never did.

It was Jackie's idea and she was supposed to be the last one to quit, but she backed out. She just put us up to it. I couldn't believe it! So, it was just Jackie and Mrs. McKay's daughter left in the Troop for the Bridge Ceremony and for the big train trip and overnight stay in a hotel in Sacramento. I heard they had a great time since there was so much money left and only two girls and their parent chaperones to spend it on. And I heard that Mrs. McKay was really hurt by what we did. Jackie made us look like jerks when it was all her idea to quit in the first place!

I tried to blame the whole thing on Jackie for a long time. But after a while I had to admit that I had gone along with the plan just to fit in even though I knew it was wrong. The whole thing had backfired on me. I didn't get to go on the trip, I hurt my Scout Leader, and Olivia and Taylor somehow blamed me for everything and there was no way they would ever be my friends again.

I felt awful. I got to thinking about choices and taking responsibility for them. And then I felt even worse.

Up until the Scouting debacle (great word!) Olivia's parents and Taylor's parents still really liked me even if Olivia and Taylor didn't. Both their families occasionally invited me on their family trips. They both had cabins in the mountains where I had done some vacationing with them, and I loved those trips. The families were all really nice and no one yelled at each other, and no one got drunk, and no one ran off with someone else's husband or wife. But still as families went, they were pretty different.

Olivia's little brother was deaf, and Olivia's mom was teaching him to read lips and to develop his speech so he could talk with other people who weren't deaf. The whole family had learned sign language, but his mom said she wanted him to "live in both the hearing world and the deaf world". I guess there's a big debate in the deaf world as to whether being deaf is a disability or just a difference and whether as a deaf person you should have to learn to talk like other people. But Olivia's mom was determined, and her little brother learned to talk pretty well after working at it for a lot of years. Because he couldn't hear, his mom would have him touch her nose and put his hand in front of her lips to "feel" the sounds. It was pretty cool actually. We did a lot of sledding in the winter at their cabin and canoeing in the lake in the summer and traipsing around in the woods on hikes. And sometimes we went fishing, but I didn't like that much.

Taylor's family was wilder than Olivia's. They rode snow-mobiles in the winter, and they taught me to ride a dirt bike and to waterski in the summer. And Taylor's mom taught us how to use tampons. I was a little bit embarrassed, but we were at the lake one weekend and Taylor was having her period and wanted to go swimming, so her mom said she was old enough to start using tampons. She asked me if my stepmom had taught me about tampons (hilarious!) and I said no, and so she explained to both Taylor and me how to use them.

We had campfires outside at night and one morning I stumbled and stepped right into the hot coals and burned my foot pretty badly. I didn't tell anyone about my burnt foot though cuz I wanted to be invited again. I didn't tell my stepmom when I got home either cuz I didn't want to get into trouble. But eventually my stepmom did find out and she was really concerned because my foot really was burned pretty badly. She took me to the doctor, and he got it all cleaned up. I wasn't in trouble after all. That surprised me. Like I said, sometimes my stepmom acts like a regular person. But that was a long time ago, now.

46.

"Hey, girl! Nice bike. Why don't you come over here and show it to us? Maybe we can share the seat with you and take you for a ride!"

Two creepy looking guys were calling out nasty stuff to me and laughing as they hung out on a corner near Gracie's house. It wasn't a very good neighborhood. I ignored them and kept pedaling but I did start to wonder if I should turn my bike around and head for home. Just then I saw Gracie's street sign up ahead.

I had decided to go and find Gracie and make her talk to me. I had her address, but I'd never been to her house. Whenever we would meet up on weekends it was always at a park or something. I guess she didn't want anybody coming to her house just like I didn't want anybody coming to mine.

Gracie lived way on the other side of town. It was about four miles away from my house, but I figured I could ride my bike there. I had bought a new bike with some of my babysitting money a few months ago, before Annie took the rest of it. I babysit a lot, and the kids really like me. I love hanging out with them and making up games and playing outside with them. We do art projects, and we bake stuff and I read them stories, and their parents always want me to come back. It's really nice to be wanted. And it fills up my time since I don't have anything else to do this summer. I'm making a bunch of money that I usually put in my savings account for college. I used some of it to buy my bike though, and Annie took the rest that I hadn't deposited yet. I think she probably needed it more than I did.

It was a Saturday morning. I had looked up Gracie's address on my cell phone map app. It looked like it should take me less than an hour to get there. I figured I could be there and back before my stepmom even woke up. Max left early on a hike with some friends today so no one will even know that I'm gone.

I'd never been to this side of town before. And I as I rode, I started noticing that the big houses like the one I live in were disappearing, and the houses were getting smaller. But they were really nice and they had lawns that were mowed and rose bushes and stuff. But then the cute little houses started disappearing and I was going through an area with a bunch of old stores and some of them were all boarded up. And there were a bunch of liquor stores on the corners. I wondered if my stepmom ever came here to buy her vodka. I kept riding and then after a while there were a bunch of empty lots and a couple of homeless camps. People living under tarps and in tents and with shopping carts just lying around and bikes with baby carriers attached to them but there weren't any babies. Just a lot of junk. It looked really sad and not very safe.

I kept going and following my phone app, and after I passed the creepy guys on the corner, I turned onto Gracie's street. Eventually I came to a vacant lot about halfway down the block.

It was a huge lot with a bunch of trash lying around and the grass was all dry and dead. Actually, it wasn't even grass, just weeds and a lot of dirt. Lots and lots of dirt. And there was this garage looking building at the very back of the lot. It was painted white, or at least it used to be white. It was almost grey now and the paint was peeling off and you could see the bare wood through the peeling paint. Some of the wood was crumbling. Dry rot. There was this apartment at the top of an old flight of wooden stairs on the outside of the building. I checked the address. I was at the right place. I headed up the stairs carrying my bike. I wasn't going to leave it at the bottom for those creepy guys to steal.

When I got to the top of the stairs, I knocked on the door which was really awkward cuz I was still holding my bike and there was only a tiny landing to stand on. No one answered. So, I knocked again, louder this time. I could hear a baby crying and some little kids yelling inside. Maybe I was at the wrong place. I knocked again. And then Gracie looked out the window. She looked really shocked to see me. She looked back over her shoulder and then looked at me again. She motioned for me to go away. I shook my head.

We looked at each other for a really long time. Eventually, she must have realized that I wasn't going anywhere, and she came to the door and opened it just a crack. She peeked out at me.

"Maddie! What are you doing here?" she asked in a low whisper.

"I'm worried about you, Gracie," I said. "I just want to talk with you. What's going on?"

"Close that damned door!" someone yelled at Gracie from inside.

I could see there was a haze of smoke in the apartment. And a lot of people inside, not just Gracie and her sisters. Other people and a baby and a bunch of other kids, too.

"Go home, Maddie," Gracie said. "You don't belong here." And she shut the door and didn't open it again, even though I kept knocking. I knocked and I knocked for a really long time, but the yelling in the apartment started getting louder and louder and I was afraid I might get Gracie into trouble.

I didn't know what to do. I stood there holding my bike and staring at the door. I thought about Gracie and what I knew about her family. I knew her real name was Grace and that her parents had given her and her three sisters really hopeful names. Maybe they thought the names would lead to happy futures. I knew Charity was the oldest, and her name meant love. Destiny and Nevaeh were a lot younger – like only 2 and 3 years old, and their names meant hopeful future and heaven, spelled backward. And I knew Grace meant forgiveness.

I wondered if Gracie's grandparents had named her parents something hopeful, maybe it would have helped them. But maybe not. And if I'm honest with myself, I'm not sure if it's going to work for Gracie and her sisters either.

I stood there for the longest time, and after a while, I gave up and carried my bike back down the stairs. As I pedaled past the creepy guys on the corner, past the homeless camps and the boarded-up buildings, past the houses that needed repair, and rode the long four miles home all I could think of was, '*You don't belong here either, Gracie. You deserve better than this.*'

47.

There was a knock on the door.

Max and I looked at each other. Noone ever came to our house. Ever. Unless it was a neighbor saying that our dog had pooped in their yard. Or that the yelling in our house was too loud. Or that we needed to move our junk car. Whenever someone knocked on our door we knew there was trouble brewing. It was a hot summer afternoon, Max and I were bored and were just thinking about heading out on our bikes, and we knew our stepmom had already been drinking. Whatever this was, we knew it wasn't good. We'd better stick around.

Our stepmom opened the door. She was still in her seethrough nightgown but at least she had a robe over it. Max and I peeked around the corner from the living room and saw a man with a nametag on a lanyard around his neck standing on the doorstep and looking inside. He introduced himself to our stepmom. Turns out he was a Probation Officer. Our stepmom didn't ask him in, so he just stood on the doorstep and talked to our stepmom while Max and I listened.

"We found Annie," he said. Our stepmom had reported her missing to the police after she ran away. "We can bring her back home for you. She's at the juvenile detention center now but we don't have to book her or anything. We just need your OK to bring her back home. She won't even have to spend the night there."

"She's not coming back here," our stepmom answered. Max and I looked at each other. We couldn't believe what we were hearing. "She can sit in that detention center and rot for all I care." Definitely drunk.

"If you won't let her come home, she may have to spend the night at the center and then go to a children's receiving home until a foster family is found," he replied.

"Good riddance to her," our stepmom answered. "She didn't like it here so she can just live somewhere else. After all I've done for her!"

The Probation Officer looked over at Max and me. He seemed to have kind eyes.

"OK," he answered. "But here's my card in case you change your mind."

"Don't hold your breath!" our stepmom answered. "That girl is nothing but trouble. You'll see." And she slammed the door and headed to the kitchen to pour herself some vodka.

A few weeks later, a Summons came. That's an invitation – actually it's an order – to go to Court for something. It was a hearing to send Annie into foster care.

"You're going to Court with me, Maddie," our stepmom said. "It will be good for you."

Good for me? In what way would that be good for me?

"I don't think I'd really like to go," I answered timidly. But she was firm.

"You'll get to see your precious sister," she laughed. "You're coming with me all right."

I was really nervous. I didn't want to be my stepmom's support person. But I did want to see Annie. And I really didn't have a choice.

A week later, we went to Court. Annie was there. So was the Probation Officer who had come to our house. I looked over at Annie trying to tell her with my eyes that I was really sorry that she couldn't come home. Annie knew what I was thinking – she always does – and her eyes were kind and telling me that it was all OK. There was another family there too that knew Annie from when we were younger. After the Judge heard all the details, the other family said they would take Annie and have her live with them. The parents were both social workers or psychologists or something and they knew Annie was super smart and that she had been through a lot. So, the Judge decided that Annie could live with them instead and she didn't have to go to a foster home after all. I guess that was good. But I still wished she was coming home.

After the Judge ordered the other family to become Annie's guardians, he spoke directly to our stepmom.

"You have lost one child," he said. "You have two others depending on you. I understand you have a drinking problem."

I looked at the Probation Officer. He smiled gently at me.

"You need to clean up your act and start behaving like a responsible parent," the Judge went on, speaking directly to our stepmom. "You need to stop drinking and take your two remaining children on a family vacation and make a new start of it. They deserve that." And he banged his gavel and closed his books for the day.

I liked what the Judge said. And I got to see Annie. It turned out I was glad I went to Court after all.

48.

"Welcome to San Diego!" "Sea World Ahead!" "Balboa Park next exit." "San Diego Zoo Two Miles." There were billboards and signs all along the freeway as we came into town. Max and I were looking out the rental car windows and we were super excited. We saw pictures of beaches with palm trees and dolphins jumping out of the water. And lots of buildings with red tile roofs. All we had to do now was get off the freeway and check into our hotel. We were going on vacation!

Our stepmom had done just what the Judge had ordered. She had stopped drinking the very afternoon that we went to Court. Max and I were shocked. How could someone go from drinking a quart of vodka a day to stone cold sober? In just one day! But our stepmom did. She even planned a family vacation for her and Max and me. She decided we should rent a car and go to San Diego for a few days and stay in a hotel, and swim in a pool, and go to Sea World and watch the dolphin shows. Like a real family vacation! Together. We couldn't believe it. Maybe things were going to get better after all.

"WHERE THE HELL IS THE OFFRAMP?" our stepmom was shouting. "I don't see how to get off this G.D. freeway!"

Max and I looked at each other. We knew our stepmom was sober, but she sounded just like she did when she was drunk. We'd been in the car for about three hours and now that it was time to exit the freeway, our stepmom couldn't figure out how to get off. Max and I looked out our windows frantically, trying to be helpful. We were stuck on a freeway cloverleaf! That's where you just keep going around in a figure eight loop over and over again and you never get off. If you're in the wrong lane, you can be stuck on the freeway. Forever. Really forever. And we were in the wrong lane.

Our stepmom kept yelling and cussing.

"This whole thing was a STUPID IDEA! If we can't get off the G.D. freeway, we're just going to turn around and drive right back home!" she yelled.

Max and I were trying to figure out which lane she should be in, and we were begging her not to go back home. But when you think about it, we couldn't have gone back home anyway cuz she couldn't even figure out how to get off the freeway! I figured we'd eventually either starve to death or maybe just run out of gas.

Finally, a miracle happened. Our stepmom got in the right lane and we found our exit and we got off the freeway. We checked into our hotel and we went swimming in the pool and we went to Sea World and we saw the dolphin shows. But the whole thing was so stressful for our stepmom that when we got back home a few days later, she started drinking again. And she drank even more than she did before.

49.

I ran into Jesse at the beach later this summer. Things were looking up. I get sunburned really easily, so I have to smear on a lot of sunblock and wear a hat and sit under an umbrella, so I definitely didn't look very cool. But Jesse didn't seem to mind.

"How's your summer going?" I asked him.

"It's OK," he replied. "I'm doing a lot of studying."

"Studying?" I was shocked. When did that change?

"Yeah," he said. "You remember our Eighth Grade Promotion Ceremony?"

Did I ever! Annie leaving, our stepmom half drunk, me giving a speech, little Max smiling.

"Well, right after the ceremony, Mlle Cesoir caught up with me and asked if I would follow her to the principal's office. I thought I was in a bunch of trouble or something even though I knew I hadn't done anything wrong. But she said she had something to give me. I followed her and the principal came too. That made me really nervous. And then she handed me a contract. And she asked if I were willing to sign it."

"A contract?" I asked. "What did it say?"

"Remember how Mlle Cesoir had told me that if I agreed to do my best to get all A's in my classes in high school she would make sure that my college was paid for? Well, she had the contract there for me to sign! It said that I had to sign up for advanced classes, and that I had to keep a 3.8 Grade Point Average or higher, and that I had to get admitted to a state university. And if I did all that, she would make sure it was paid for!"

"I remember. But that's almost all A's in super hard classes in high school. Did you get all A's this last semester in eighth grade?"

Max was kind of embarrassed.

"Remember this is our secret, right?" he asked.

"Sure!" I said.

"OK – yes, I got all A's. But I don't want anyone to know."

"Why not? It's cool to be smart," I said.

"Not really in my group of friends. It's more cool to be cool," Jesse answered.

And I got it. He was kind of caught between his rowdy group of friends and creating a different future for himself. I thought back on Mlle Cesoir's lesson about conjugating the verb "to be" and her question, "And what are all of you going to be in your futures?" And I realized that for some of us that's a harder question than for others, and that she was trying to help Jesse make the best choice.

50.

I saw a lot of Jesse this summer. He started coming over to my house and we would hang outside and sit on the breeze brick wall out front to talk. We never went inside for obvious reasons. And we texted all the time, too. Eventually, he told me the story about what had happened in sixth grade that caused him to start getting into trouble and letting his grades slip so badly.

Jesse told me he had an older brother, Zach, and Jesse really looked up to him. They did everything together, even though Jesse was about five years younger.

"It wasn't like he just tolerated me hanging around him. He was really great," Jesse began so softly I could hardly hear him. He picked at a spot on his T-shirt. "We were buds. He taught me to play basketball. And he helped me with my homework. And he was teaching me to play the guitar."

Jesse said he has really nice parents and a grandmother who lives with them, too. His abuela (that's his grandma) came from Mexico many years ago as an exchange student and married an American man. They had just one child, Jesse's mom, and Jesse's mom and dad had two children, Zach and then Jesse. The whole family speaks both Spanish and English and they own a Mexican restaurant in town that's really popular. That's where Gracie's mom used to work. Our family had actually gone there a couple of times. I wonder if she ever waited on us and we didn't even know it?

Jesse told me that Zach started hanging out with a pretty rough crowd when he was in tenth grade.

"My parents tried to convince him to stay away from that group," Jesse told me, looking down at his flip flops as he gently swung his legs over the side of the low wall. "My dad knew they were drinking a lot and doing drugs. He knew they were trouble. But Zach wouldn't listen. And he seemed to change. He started drinking and eventually got into a really bad drug habit. He couldn't seem to stop. He started skipping school and his grades dropped. Zach didn't even want to hang around with me anymore," he added softly.

That really made me sad.

Jesse went on.

"A year later in the middle of his junior year in high school, things got worse. He started stealing stuff to sell or trade for drugs. My parents tried to talk with him but he just ignored them. The last time I saw him, he took my dad's car and left the house in the middle of the night. My dad tried to stop him but Zach just pushed past him saying, 'Get out of my way old man!' and he left. My parents didn't know what to do. They were frantic. I didn't find out the rest until the next day."

Jesse said that Zach robbed a late-night liquor store for the money he needed for drugs that night. The police were called and chased after him. Zach sped off, lost control of his car and crashed into a light pole. He was killed instantly.

"I was in sixth grade at the time and my world just fell apart," Jesse said. "I loved Zach. He was my hero, my best friend. He called me 'Little Man'. We just always used to hang out together. I took it pretty hard."

I thought about Annie and Max and how awful it would be if I lost one of them. Even though Annie isn't living with us right now, I know she's OK and that we'll see each other again. I can't imagine knowing for my entire life that I was never going to see her or Max again.

I looked at Jesse. He seemed so lost and so sad. I wanted to put my arm around him. But I didn't.

"That's when I started acting out at school and not doing my classwork or my homework," he said. "My parents tried to get me to talk to a counselor, but I wouldn't. I mean – what was the point? It wouldn't bring Zach back."

I understood that.

And now it all began to make sense. Jesse the class clown and troublemaker.

Jesse said things just seemed to get worse for him. The more he acted out at school, the more trouble he got into and the less his teachers expected of him. It was like he was on a hamster wheel and he didn't know how to get off.

By the time I met Jesse last year in seventh grade, he said he loved making fun of authority and a lot of the teachers got really irritated with him. He sort of thrived on that. But he said that Mlle Cesoir was different. When she looked into his background, she saw how smart he was and how he fell apart after his brother died. He said that the day she kept him after class after he made fun of her, she told him that she had lost someone that she loved as well, and that at first she also fell apart. But she told him that she eventually realized that the person she loved would want her to go on living and to make a good life for herself. And she thought that's what Jesse's brother would want for him, too.

Jesse said he wasn't sure why, but for some reason that got through to him.

"Maybe it was just the timing," Jesse said to me. "Maybe I was just ready to hear that someone cared. But for whatever reason, I got to thinking about what Zach would want for me and I realized he'd be super ticked off that I was throwing my life away. He would want me to do better. And when Mlle Cesoir gave me the challenge of raising my grades, I guess it was a little bit of a wake-up call. I decided to try."

I thought about how kind Mlle Cesoir had been to ask about my mum a couple of years ago. I guess the timing wasn't right for me at that moment. I didn't realize then that she was just trying to be kind. I had only felt embarrassed.

I thought about Mrs. Klocki's note on my poem telling me I'd be OK and that I was resilient.

I thought about Mrs. French and the one-act play that she had assigned me. And the fact that she had encouraged me to run for a class office and to give a speech at our Promotion Ceremony.

I thought about Taylor and Olivia's parents and how they had included me in their family vacations.

And I realized that there truly were people who were looking out for me and who cared.

"Wow. That's pretty amazing," I said softly, looking at Jesse's sad face. "Sometimes I guess you just have to be ready to receive someone's kindness."

Jesse smiled shyly at me at that. Then he leaned over and gave me a hug. I didn't want it to end.

NINTH GRADE

51.

It's kind of cool being in high school finally. None of the teachers here knew my dad, except for Mr. Whitley who I guess transferred from the middle school this year. But even though the others might have heard the rumors, they didn't actually know him. My real mum has been out of the picture for a while. So, no embarrassing moments there. And my stepmom never shows up for parent conferences or anything – so it's like I can be anonymous at school. Finally. And I like it.

Annie goes to the continuation high school now. She says she likes it there, that she can be herself and not put up with a bunch of BS at the regular high school or at home. She says that the teachers at the continuation school really care about the kids, and they take a personal interest in them without prying. I guess that sounds pretty cool. I miss her though, but I'm glad she's OK. And Max is at the middle school and he's doing really well. At least I think he is. He's in all advanced classes and he's even got French with Mlle Cesoir and Journalism. He says he wants to be an investigative reporter when he grows up. I don't know where Gracie is. I never see her anymore. I'm wondering if maybe she moved.

I'm taking French III and Geometry and Advanced English and a bunch of other hard classes. Jesse is in most of my classes, and I like that. He's acing everything. I guess he's taking Mlle Cesoir's challenge seriously. But it's still our secret.

Jesse just told me he heard that Gracie didn't move and that she's skipping school and she's started doing drugs. That just makes me really sad. It would be terrible if she becomes a meth head like her parents. I tried calling her again, but she still doesn't pick up. And she still won't answer my texts either.

I ask Jesse how he knows what's going on with Gracie.

"Her mom worked at my family's restaurant for a long time," he told me.

I already knew that since he had mentioned it before. But I didn't know the rest.

"She was a waitress there and the customers really liked her," Jesse went on. "They always requested her tables. She was smart and funny and she would joke with everyone. She always got the best tips cuz she never messed up anyone's orders and she made everyone feel really good."

"She doesn't work there anymore?" I asked. "What happened?"

"She started coming to work stoned a while ago. Remember when she came to school that day last year and embarrassed Gracie? I'm sure she was loaded. She had changed so much by then. It got so bad that my dad had to send her home from work a few times. He felt badly about it cuz he knew that her husband didn't work – just Gracie's mom. And he knew they needed the money from her job and from her tips. But then she just started missing her shifts and eventually she stopped coming in at all. My dad was worried about her, and he went over to her house to see if he could help. You should see where they live, Maddie. I went over one day when my dad brought their family some food. It's really sad."

I didn't tell Jesse I had been there. I knew how sad it was.

"So eventually it's like Gracie's mom just fell off the map. My dad kept bringing food over until Gracie's dad threatened to call the police on him for trespassing. He knows Gracie's dad wouldn't follow through cuz the last thing Gracie's dad would want is the police showing up. But still, my dad didn't want to cause Gracie's mom any trouble, so he stopped going over. My dad says they're all using drugs now. Even Gracie and Charity."

And all I could think of was, 'Poor Gracie and Charity. Who was helping them?'

52.

I'm trying out for Dance Squad next week and I'm super excited about it. I'm running track and doing pretty well there, and so is Jesse. (And he *did* break the middle school record in the mile – he ran a 4:58!) I'm just trying to stay focused on school and keep all the crazy family stuff away. So far high school is going pretty well. And even home life seems a little easier.

Our stepmom doesn't get on Max and me as much as she used to. Maybe it's because Annie ran away. Or maybe it's because we're just staying out of the house as much as we can. But it really does seem like the whole world shifted on its axis the day that Annie stopped our stepmom's slap in midair. I'm taking Physics now and I'm wondering if that's actually possible. I mean can you dynamically change an emotional situation in a physical way? (I sound pretty smart, huh?) We're all basically just a bunch of electrons that respond electrically anyway, right? It's like Annie taking control in that moment literally took all the wind out of our stepmom's sails, and like Newton's Third Law of Physics states: 'For every action there is an opposite and equivalent reaction.'

Max and I have learned to pretty much stay out of our stepmom's way. We have a secret signal, 'Wow is red!' It means our stepmom is really mad and probably drunk. 'WOW' is MOM upside down (we couldn't figure out 'stepmom' upside down so we just went with 'mom') and red represents anger. We came up with it as a signal to watch out if one of us is just getting home and the other one knows things are already coming apart.

Our stepmom sends us to bed early a lot, even though I'm in high school and Max is in middle school and we really don't do much of anything wrong. I think she just can't handle the challenge of raising kids. She makes us leave our cell phones upstairs when we go down to our bedrooms at night so we can't play any games or watch anything on the internet.

Max and I have figured out that when we're sent to bed early, we can sneak back up from the lower level of the house where our bedrooms are to the middle landing of the stairs, and just stand there on the landing and watch TV. We're hidden by the mid-60's style stereo console that stands right next to the stair railing and we can look out under it and see the TV across the room. And we can also see our stepmom's legs hanging over the couch in the other direction. If she moves, we can just scoot back downstairs really fast so she doesn't catch us. It's sort of a fun game – but I wish we could choose our own TV shows. The stuff she watches is pretty much sappy old romance movies on Hallmark or Netflix – and they're really boring. So mostly we just stay in our rooms and talk or read or do homework.

Max and I are both pretty good students. We spend a lot of our evenings studying. That and snooping. We're determined to learn the backstory on our stepmom and where she got that scar. Every so often when she's not making our lives totally miserable, I feel sorry for her. I think I could have more empathy toward her if I knew more about her history.

I signed up for Psychology as my elective this year. I'm thinking I might want to become a psychologist and study mental illness or human behavior. I guess the reasons for that are kind of obvious. There's this big debate in psychology about whether mental illness and drug and alcohol addiction are due to nature (meaning they're inherited) or nurture (meaning due to the environment you're raised in). They're both considered to be diseases - mental illness and addictions - and they're both "dynamic", meaning that your choices and experiences might also influence how much a genetic predisposition, if there is one, might affect you. But I'm learning that there are ways to deal with mental illness and addictions if people are willing to get some help. Whatever the cause, nature or nurture, Annie and Max and I are pretty much doomed if we're not careful. We've got both nature and nurture working against us.

53.

I got a text. It was from Jamie.

"Hey, Maddie. No room in the car. Sorry. You'll need to find another ride to the dance tonight."

I don't know what happened. I tried calling Jamie, but she won't pick up. I've been hanging with her and her friends for a while since ninth grade started this year. They're a little bit older than me and they sort of tolerated me for a bit, but I guess that's over now.

It seems like all the social life stuff from middle school just moved right on up to high school. All the drama and the leaving other people out. Olivia and Taylor are still ignoring me, so I guess that's just over – like forever. Their parents don't even invite me on vacations with them anymore. The last time one of them did, it was Olivia's family last year. They invited me to their cabin for the weekend.

"Don't tell Taylor," Olivia had said. "It was my parents' idea to invite you, not mine. And if Taylor finds out, she'll be pissed. We're besties you know!"

It was awkward at the lake with Olivia and her family. When I got back to school on Monday morning, I had to lie to Taylor about the sunglasses' tan line on my face and the sunburn on my shoulders. I think she knew anyway, and then she and Olivia just started to hang out all the time. That sucked for me.

So, this year I tried hanging out with Jamie and her friends. That worked for a while but now I guess it's not going to work anymore either.

I tried to fit in with Angelika (that's our middle school custodian, Mr. D's daughter) and her friends at one point. They're all born again Christians and they believe in the Holy Spirit and stuff. I went to church with them a few times and it was actually pretty cool, and they were really nice. They have a Youth Group there and they do a bunch of fun activities. One night there was this team competition and someone on our team had to eat a peanut butter sandwich really fast, but it was so sticky that the person had trouble swallowing.

"Here, let me have it!" I said. I grabbed the sandwich when the judges weren't looking and took a big bite. I wanted to help the person out. I didn't want them choking to death on peanut butter. Plus, I wanted our team to win the competition.

But Angelika saw me do it.

"I'm really disappointed in you, Maddie," she said. "And Jesus would be, too."

I kind of stopped going to church with her after that. And then we stopped hanging out altogether. I figured I'd never be forgiven for taking a bite out of that peanut butter sandwich.

Before I latched onto Jamie and her friends, I pretty much just went to the library and studied during breaks and lunches. And I started playing more chess. There's a group of kids that aren't popular at all but they're really smart and they sometimes play chess in the library. I guess they're social losers, like me. And it's been kind of fun to work on strategy and on what moves will benefit you and what moves might spell ultimate disaster.

When to give up a pawn or sacrifice your rook or your knight for the greater good. And always protecting your queen, usually no matter what the cost.

With all the studying and being around the asocial geniuses I've actually been acing my classes. I'm a pretty good student. And I still like school. I'm just dedicating myself to getting through high school with the best grades I can so that I'll qualify for some scholarships and be able to go off to college somewhere. I can't wait to go away to college. No one will know that I'm not cool to be around there.

But none of that helps with the dance tonight. Since Jamie won't let me go with them and I can't drive yet, my stepmom is going to have to drive me. She's drunk, as usual, but I have to ask her for a ride. It's my only alternative.

"What happened? Did your new so-called friends dump you already?" My stepmom was slurring her words. I should probably have just driven myself after she was passed out on the couch. Even though I don't have a license. It would probably be safer. But as it turned out, she did give me a ride. I was thankful for that.

I ended up showing up at the dance late and all by myself. Totally embarrassing. I had to pretend I was hanging out with different groups of people there all night because Jamie and her friends kept leaving me behind. Again, embarrassing. I really wasn't hanging with anyone, so I spent most of the time in the girls' bathroom pretending to pee until the dance was over and it was time to go home. Beyond embarrassing. It was awful. And when it was time for my stepmom to pick me up she didn't show. The chaperones were watching the last of us kids who were waiting for our rides. I didn't want them to have to stay there all night so when they weren't looking, I ran behind a tree and called my stepmom. She didn't pick up, so I called Max. He's only in middle school but he said he'd come get me if he could find the keys. And he did. Good old Max. By the time he got there, all the lights were off and everyone else had gone home. Pretty awful. But at least I could count on Max.

54.

I'm babysitting for Dana and Dora this coming weekend. All day Saturday and all day Sunday. I can't wait!

When I first asked my stepmom if I could babysit both days, she had a really strange reaction.

"Who's going to do your chores if you're gone all weekend?" she asked. Of course, I expected that.

"I already thought of that," I answered. "I can do all my chores Friday night."

"Who's going to walk Lucky?" she asked next. It was my weekend to walk the dog and I was ready for that, too. Making sure the dog got walked was a high priority in our household.

"I asked Max and he's OK with switching weekends," I answered. Max was so cool about things like that. Like I said, I can count on Max.

I'm supposed to be at Dana and Dora's house by eight in the morning each day and I won't get home until about nine at night. That's two really long days but I don't mind. It keeps me out of my house, and I'll make a ton of money. Dana and Dora are really sweet kids. They're twins and they're only four years old which makes them super cute. I'm going to bring over stuff for making cookies; and we're going to ride scooters to the park; and I'm bringing some paints and a bunch of books to read to them. We're going to have fun!

"Why are the days going to be so long?" my stepmom asked next. "Why does their mom need you all day and until nine at night?"

I wasn't ready for that one.

"I don't know," I answered. "It was actually their dad who called."

My stepmom started to laugh then. And not a nice laugh. It was a really mean laugh, almost more of a cackle. Or a howl. All I could think of was that I was dumb to have asked her about babysitting so late in the day. I should have waited until the next morning when she was sober, before she started drinking.

"Oh, she's completely lost it then!" my stepmom snickered. "She's probably in the looney bin! I heard she's been having bouts of depression. Kids will do that to you, you know, drive you out of your mind! Sure. Go ahead and babysit. We don't need you around here anyway!"

That confirmed it; she was drunk. Usually I saw the signs easily, but I missed them this time. I must not have been watching closely like I usually do. I'll have to be more careful. But at least she said yes.

It was a great weekend at Dana and Dora's house. We did finger painting and we used chalk to draw all sorts of funny pictures on the sidewalks. We played hide and seek and we baked cookies and we watched movies. We rode scooters everywhere and I brought a bunch of picture books to read to them. Of course, I brought Madeline. They love Madeline almost as much as I do.

I brought other books, too, like Amazing Grace by Mary Hoffman. It's one of my new favorite picture books for little kids. It's about this little girl named Grace and she's Black and she wants to be Peter Pan in the class play. One little boy in her class tells Grace she can't be Peter because she's a girl; and a little girl in her class tells Grace she can't be Peter because she's Black. But Grace's mama and her grandma encourage her and tell her she can be whatever she wants to be. Grace tries out for the part of Peter Pan and she gets it! Dana and Dora loved the story, and I told them that just like Grace, they could be anything they wanted to be in life.

And then we read the original story of Peter Pan together and we played Peter Pan for the rest of the afternoon. Sometimes Dana was Peter, and sometimes Dora was Peter, and sometimes I was Peter. We led the bevy of Lost Boys on naughty adventures all around Neverland. And all afternoon I thought about my friend Gracie, and I wondered how she was doing and if someone was encouraging her to be all she could be.

I didn't see Dana and Dora's mom at all that weekend, so I guess maybe my stepmom was right. Maybe she was somewhere getting help for her depression. When I left on Sunday evening, I asked their dad to say hi to their mom for me when he talked to her next. He looked totally embarrassed and uncomfortable when I said that, and he just sort of mumbled an answer that I couldn't hear.

Then I remembered how people don't understand mental health issues. And I thought that maybe I shouldn't have said anything at all.

55.

With tryouts next week, I've been going to Dance Squad practice every morning before school and again in the evenings after track practice. It's a pretty long day cuz then I have to study and do my homework when I get home, but I'm loving it. I've got all the dance routines down that are required. The only thing is, you're supposed to also present an original routine in a small group to some music of your choice, and I don't have anyone to pair up with. Everyone has their own friends and when I've asked a couple of groups if I can join them, they've said no. I don't know what to do. It's really embarrassing to go around begging someone to take me in. I'm feeling pretty bummed.

I was sitting on the bleachers yesterday toward the end of Dance Squad practice while everyone else was practicing their original routines in their groups. I was feeling totally dejected and rejected and kind of sorry for myself. And then Jesse showed up.

"What's the matter, Maddie?" he asked. "You look all bummed."

"Nothing," I said. I sure didn't want to tell Jesse that no one wanted me in their group for Dance Squad tryouts.

"I've been watching you practice the Dance Squad stuff. I think you'll make it – you're really good."

I was embarrassed but secretly pretty pleased that he'd been watching.

"You think so?" I asked.

"Yeah," he said. "But why aren't you out there now? Everyone else looks like they're still practicing."

I decided to level with him.

"Well, I've got all the required stuff down but now we're supposed to be doing an original routine and I don't have anyone to pair up with."

"Just ask someone," Jesse said.

But then he must have read something on my face cuz he said, "Oh, I get it. It's the 'Let's be mean to Maddie' stuff, huh? No one will include you?"

In a weird way, I knew Jesse understood. I'd seen him being excluded by other kids when it came to group presentations in classes. It's like people knew his brother had died in a police chase or something. Or maybe they didn't know the details, but they remembered him from middle school when he was always getting into trouble, and now in their advanced high school classes they didn't want to take a chance on him screwing up and bringing down their grades. I decided to take a chance and admit it.

"Yeah", I replied. "Something like that."

"Well, why don't you just do your own thing? It's not like there's a requirement that it has to be two or more people to do an original routine is there?"

I thought about it for a minute. I wasn't quite sure.

"You know, Maddie, I think sometimes you just need to adapt and create your own rules, and then let someone challenge you on them. As long as it doesn't hurt anyone. I'm thinking about being a lawyer one day, to help kids when they're in trouble with the law. I'm finding that the law isn't always clear on some things. It's open to interpretation. Dance Squad rules might also be open to interpretation."

I liked that. Heck, what was stopping me from creating my own routine anyway? Just myself, and my disappointment at being rejected.

'*Get over it,*' I thought to myself. '*Show them you can do it.*'

"Thanks, Jesse," I said. "I think you're right. I'm just gonna do my own thing and see who decides to try and stop me."

"You go, girl!" he laughed. "I'll bet no one is going to get in your way! And if they do, you'll just run them over!"

I laughed and I headed home to find some music and create my own original routine.

56.

"Let's start with the scar," Max said to me. "If we can figure out how she got that scar then maybe we'll know more about her back story."

Max and I have decided to try to find out more about our stepmom since she's basically the only parent we have left at this point. We want to figure out what happened to make her like she is. Every once in a while, she is incredibly kind and caring, like when she was concerned about my burned foot and she took me to the doctor and she wasn't even mad. She even gives some pretty decent advice occasionally, like about my quitting Scouts and more recently about friends. She told me not to bother with people like Olivia and Taylor who don't appreciate me and accept me, and to find some different friends. But then it all disappears pretty quickly, and she just gets drunk and mean again. We don't want her to know we're investigating, though. We've got to be pretty stealth and surreptitious (strong vocabulary words!) about it.

"Good idea, Max," I said. "It's a pretty severe scar and she's always trying to hide it."

The scar on our stepmom's forehead is a clue. She always wears her hair with bangs hanging over her forehead, so the scar is pretty much hidden. When we do see it though, we can tell it's a significant scar. It's thick and red and ropey, and it goes from just above her nose straight up between her eyebrows to her hairline, and then it cuts across one side of her forehead toward her ear. It must have been a pretty serious accident that caused such a big scar. We've always wondered about it. Max and I are determined to find out what happened.

We have a Grandma Fuches (pronounced like the "u" in "unicorn" - can you believe that name - good thing she doesn't teach middle school!) that isn't our real grandma, just like our stepmom isn't our real stepmom. We know she's part of the puzzle though cuz we know that Grandma Fuches is actually the mother of our stepmom's first husband, Grant. We were told a little bit about him over the years, but we don't know much. We just know that he was this perfect guy that our stepmom married when she was pretty young and that they were really happy and he had a lot of money. He died young of a heart attack and after that she married our loser dad. From that point forward her life just really sucked. At least that's what she always tells us.

Our Grandma Fuches lives in a mansion up on the hill behind some private gates about fifteen miles from where we live. Sort of in the direction that Max and I were riding our bikes that day when we rode along the highway a couple of years ago. It's near the private swim club where we learned to swim and where our dad used to work during the summers. Grandma Fuches' house has what our stepmom calls "manicured grounds", meaning really beautiful landscaping and lots of space around it. It's probably a few acres or something, like the size of three or four football fields. If she lived in England, it would have a name like "Surrey Cottage" or "Avon on the Delles". It doesn't have a name but it's huge and it's beautiful. The house has a red tile roof and white stucco walls, Spanish style architecture it's called. There are actually servants' quarters built into it, too. I guess it should be called "Casa Bella Grande" or something.

Grandma Fuches must be pretty rich. She has a cook and a gardener and a maid, and her towels are super soft, like the maid must know how to use real fabric softener on them and not just the fabric softener sheets that Max and I throw in the dryer at the laundromat. We know because she gave us a bunch of her old towels when she replaced them. We buried our faces in them cuz they felt so soft. I don't know why she replaced them cuz they were still practically brand new! When we've gone to visit, which is just a couple of times cuz our stepmom usually doesn't bring us, we try to be on our best behavior and then Grandma Fuches gives us some treats when we leave. One time she even gave us each a $20 bill. She's actually pretty nice. She has us call her "Grandma Fuches" because of our stepmom, and because she doesn't have any of her own grandkids or anything. It turns out that even though our stepmom was married to her only son, they didn't have any kids of their own. That's all we know so far but it's a start, and we're determined to find out more.

57.

The other day our stepmom was gone visiting Grandma Fuches by herself, so Max and I were home alone.

"Hey, Max," I said. "This is the perfect time! Want to get started on our search?"

"Yeah," Max replied. "We'll have at least a couple of hours."

Max and I began exploring our house, everywhere we could think of for clues to our stepmom's past. We went through all the boxes in the garage to see if there was any information there, but we didn't find anything. We went through her closet – I know – we should respect her privacy. But whatever. There was nothing there either. We looked in all the cupboards and in all the drawers – bedrooms, kitchen, linen closets, bathrooms. Still nothing. We went through the old oak antique desk that has been in our dad's family for years. Nothing. We were careful to put everything back exactly as we found it so she wouldn't know we had snooped. We started getting pretty frustrated and thought maybe our stepmom had a storage shed somewhere or a big safe deposit box where she kept all her secrets.

And then Max said, "What about the attic?"

"What attic?" I asked.

"There's a little bit of an attic above the garage, and there's like a trap door thing in the garage ceiling that leads to it. Maybe there's something up there."

I had never even thought about the attic. It was just a little bit of a crawl space above the ceiling in the garage. I realized that Max could be right. It would be the perfect place for storing old papers: hot, dry, and airless. We headed for the garage.

Max and I found a flashlight, got a ladder, and climbed on up. Max went first since it was his idea. When he got to the top of the ladder, he pushed open the little door to the crawl space and climbed inside. I followed next. It took a few moments for our eyes to adjust even with the flashlight cuz it was really dark up there. But once we got used to the dim light, we were super surprised.

Max was right. There it was. A treasure trove of stuff.

There were about 20 boxes all bundled up and carefully labelled and dated. We realized pretty quickly that it would take a long time to go through them all. There wasn't much space up there, and it was really hot and stuffy.

"We don't have a lot of time right now, Max," I said. "And we're going to have to be really careful so she doesn't find out."

"Yeah," Max answered, looking around at the piles of boxes. "But she'll probably never find out cuz she never even goes downstairs so she's never going to climb a ladder and come up here into the attic."

Since she also doesn't go out all that much though, only to the bank and grocery shopping, and to the liquor stores of course, and once in a while to Grandma Fuches' house, we knew we'd have to be patient and use every opportunity we had.

We smiled and gave each other a "high five" knowing that now we at least had a place to start.

And then all of a sudden, we heard a click and a whirring sound and realized that the garage door was starting to open! We had to scramble out super quickly, dropping the ceiling door back into place behind us. We dashed down the ladder, pushed it up against the wall, and ran into the house through the connecting door, putting the flashlight back in the kitchen drawer right before our stepmom drove into the garage.

58.

I *love* my psychology class! We're doing a unit now on "dys-functional families". I swear, I could teach this stuff! But it's also very enlightening.

I'm learning that in typical (that's the new word for "normal") families, everyone takes a turn at being great or messing up or being the best or failing or whatever. It's just a part of life. Every-one encourages each other and they just try to help each other out and to improve and grow. Of course, they have problems, but they try to solve the problems together. And in typical fam-ilies, there are consistent expectations and rules. The rules might be different in different families or in different cultures or for different ages of family members, but the expectations are pretty clear and pretty consistent and everyone in the family knows what the rules and what the expectations are. The rules and the expectations don't really change much. No big surprises.

But in dysfunctional families, there are "good guys" and "bad guys" and if you're a good guy nothing you do is ever really considered bad; and if you're a bad guy, nothing you do is ever really considered good. It's like you're assigned a role for life, and you can't get out of it! And the expectations are never clear. You never know what to expect. It just changes every day. There is absolutely no clarity about anything, ever, so everyone is always off balance and it's like you're always walking around on egg-shells and never knowing when something is going to break, or when the other shoe is going to drop. Or when the fragile house of cards is going to come tumbling down. (Mrs. Klocki would say that's too many metaphors.) And the funny thing is, all of the atypical (not normal) stuff seems pretty typical (normal) to me.

And then there's this thing about birth order. Like, the first born is usually a good guy, "the hero". They're the high achievers and they usually follow the rules, and they work really hard. The next born is more of "the rebel". In dysfunctional families they are definitely a bad guy. They aren't high achievers, they break all the rules, and they don't appear to work very hard. The youngest no one can ever remember or figure out. They're "the lost child". It's like everyone just forgets about them and no one knows where they are or what they're doing.

I got to thinking about my own family. I think we switched it up a bit. For some reason, Annie is the rebel and I'm the hero, but Max is definitely the lost child. And I don't know why. I thought back to the Probation Officer who showed up at our door way back when. He said that Annie was the smartest of all of us kids. I don't know how he knew that, but he did, and I remember that it surprised me cuz I always got the best grades. I thought I was the smartest kid.

But when you think about it, Annie really is the smartest, and the hero in a rebel sort of way. She always understood everything that was going on and she shielded Max and me from a lot of it. She took the blame for all sorts of stuff that wasn't even her fault. And eventually she had just had enough, and she started fighting back and became the rebel instead. That makes her a hero in my book.

It kind of makes me think about my literature class, too. The archetypes and all. In most stories, there is a hero and there is a villain and there is a victim. I wonder if all of life can be categorized so simply? And I wonder again about our stepmom. What role did she play in her own birth family? Was she likely to have been the hero or the rebel or the lost child? I wanted to find out.

59

I've started to notice that Max is always running to the mail-box to be the first one to check the mail after it's been delivered each day. I wasn't sure why until today when I saw him taking a bunch of big stuffed envelopes out of the mailbox that were addressed to him.

"What are those, Max?" I asked him.

"None of your business," he answered.

"But what are they, Max? I don't want you getting yourself into some sort of trouble."

"Don't worry about it, Maddie," he said. "And don't be such a goodie goodie. My grades are good and I'm doing all kinds of journalism stuff at school. Everyone says I'm doing a great job. So what if I treat myself to a few things? Who cares?"

I just stared at him. I couldn't believe what he was saying.

Max has been hanging out with a kid down the block named Rudy. I don't like Rudy much. He's a little bit older than Max and he's kind of shady. I think he's getting Max to do some risky stuff that they shouldn't be doing. Like putting firecrackers and M80's under cans and blowing the cans up into the air. And spray painting some stupid stuff onto the asphalt on the street. And taking the gas caps off of cars. And lighting little fires. And watching stuff that he's not supposed to watch online. Where does Rudy get all this stuff anyway? Kids can't buy spray paint at the store since it's locked down, and aren't firecrackers and M80's illegal?

"She's never going to find out," Max went on. "She doesn't even read over her credit card bills to see what she's paying for. I know. I've watched her. She just pays the minimum payment and not always on time, but she does pay them eventually. Otherwise, they'd close her accounts. And besides, she actually owes us. She gets all this government money and our grandpa's trust fund and who do you think she spends it on anyway? You should treat yourself to some stuff too, Maddie. I think we deserve it after everything we've had to put up with!"

It finally dawned on me that Max must have been using our stepmom's credit card number to order a bunch of stuff online for himself. I already suspected that he was doing some online gambling, but I couldn't figure out how he could fund it. And now I knew.

Max laughed and headed into the house with all of his packages, sneaking them downstairs so that our stepmom wouldn't see them.

I was worried that he's going to get himself into some big trouble. And I realized that he really is a lost child. The one that we learned about In Psychology class. The one that everyone overlooks. The one that no one ever remembers to check on.

60.

"Look what I found in Max's drawer!" our grandpa yelled. "He's been stealing my coins!"

Annie and Max and I all looked at each other, scared.

Annie challenged him. "What are you doing in Max's room and going through his drawers anyway? And how do we know you found that stuff there? Maybe you just planted it!" Annie was ten years old at the time, I was eight, and Max was only six.

It was several years back when our dad was alive, not too long after we came to live with him. Our grandpa was spending a couple of weeks with us before he moved back to Wisconsin and our dad and stepmom had made a bedroom for him out of the den that was downstairs right next to Max's bedroom. Our grandpa wasn't really big on kids. He wasn't the kind of grandpa that told you stories or took you to the park or taught you how to ride a bike or played frisbee with you or anything like that. He was more the kind of grandpa that was small and skinny and had a mean little dog and just a little bit of long white hair that he combed straight back over the top of his head and his face looked all skeletal and he sort of cackled when he laughed.

He and his dog were only with us for a couple of weeks but none of us kids liked them much – him or his dog. Our grandpa had sent most of his stuff ahead of him to Wisconsin, but I guess he had kept some of his valuable stuff with him that he said he didn't trust to ship back there. And one evening he marched upstairs with a bunch of gold coins in his hand, and he was shouting, throwing a real fit!

Our stepmom started yelling at Max, and Annie started yelling back at our stepmom, and our dad said that everyone should just calm down. But he grabbed his ping pong paddle and he made us all go downstairs to Max's room. Our grandpa pulled open one of Max's drawers and there were more gold coins. Our grandpa looked happy in a sick sort of way, but our dad looked pretty upset.

"Max, you need to tell us how Grandpa's gold coins got into your drawer. You're not in any trouble. Just tell us the truth." Our dad was really calm. I think he was really trying to be a good dad.

"I don't know how they got there!" Max cried. And no matter what our dad and our grandpa said, Max stuck to his story and refused to budge.

Our dad finally lost his temper and started hitting Max on his butt with the ping pong paddle. Max was screaming, our grandpa was laughing, I was crying, and Annie was yelling at them all to stop. No one was paying her any attention until she grabbed our dad's cell phone out of his back pocket and started shouting louder than anyone else.

"Stop right now or I'm calling Child Protective Services!" ten-year-old Annie yelled. "I'm sure CPS knows all about our family anyway!"

Our dad stopped hitting Max, and Annie stared him down until he dropped the paddle. He grabbed the cell phone out of Annie's hand and stormed out of Max's room.

Our grandpa went over to Max's drawers and opened them all and gathered up a bunch more gold coins, laughing to himself as he left the room.

And while our dad and our stepmom and our grandpa went back upstairs for a drink, Annie took Max and me back into our bedroom and hugged Max.

"Don't worry, Max," Annie said. "I'm never going to let anyone hit you again."

Max kept saying over and over that he hadn't stolen those coins.

Now with all the other trouble that Max was getting into with Rudy and using our stepmom's credit cards for online gambling and to order stuff for himself, I wondered what had actually happened that day with our grandpa's coins. Had Max really stolen them or had our grandpa just put them in Max's drawers to be mean? And why would either of them have done that anyway?

61.

We're reading *The Scarlet Letter* in my American Literature class. It's by Nathaniel Hawthorne, and it's about this young woman, Hester Prynne, who gets pregnant in a small town in the 1800's and she's single and she won't tell anyone who the father is. She's really brave, and really independent, but she's also really lonely. No one wants to be her friend. And she puts up with all the embarrassment and the town shunning her, and she has to wear this really bright red letter "A" sewn onto all of her clothing that tells everyone that she is an "adulteress".

It's really pretty awful the way the town treats her, but she puts up with it to protect the father of her baby from being exposed. And eventually, you learn that the baby's father is someone you would never expect to get anyone pregnant and if they did, you would expect him to speak up and help her or marry her or something. But he doesn't, and it makes me think about courage, and honesty, and standing up for what you believe in. It also makes me think about how lonely life can be. I begin to wonder how Nathaniel Hawthorne came up with this story idea in the first place. And I also begin to wonder if our stepmom's big scar on her forehead is somehow her scarlet letter, and maybe that's why she always tries to hide it.

Our teacher says we have to write our own short story around a theme we found in *The Scarlet Letter*. There are a lot of themes we can choose from: Loyalty; Status; Courage; Fear; Hypocrisy. I decide on the theme of "Loneliness". It seems to fit for me.

I write a story about a girl who doesn't have any friends. In my story, the girl tries to make friends, but no one wants her to be around them. The story is pretty lame, but I try to show the girl's emotion by putting her in places where you would want to go with a friend – like to a picnic or the carnival or the beach or the movies or a park or a party. Or a dance. But the girl is just always by herself and even though people notice her being alone all the time and some people feel a little sorry for her, they still don't want to be her friend. After a while, the girl just learns to live with it. And she decides that it's not so bad being alone after all. She has a really vivid imagination, so she just develops some friends in her mind and when she's lonely, she just hangs out there – in her mind with her imaginary friends. Until eventually the girl just stays there all the time, in her mind, and never goes out into the real world again.

62

I really like to run. In fact, I love to run! I run track at school. And I like to run at home in my free time when there's nothing else to do and no one to hang out with. I run a lot. Sometimes when I'm out on a run, ideas come to me for stories or poems or whatever. I think maybe it's inspiration. But then I start to worry. What if it's something else? What if I'm becoming like the girl in my story?

The characters in my mind tell me their stories – it's like they're waiting for me to listen to them and write their stories down. If it's just inspiration and imagination, that seems safe enough. But what if it's not really creativity? What if it's the beginning of insanity and I'm hearing voices that aren't really there? Is that really so different? And how does the brain work anyway? And what about conscience? Is that really just my inner self talking to me and telling me what I should think about and what I should or shouldn't do before I make a decision? Or is it something else? Something more sinister? I have so many questions!

I just watched a video on the internet about something called the hearing voices movement. The speaker was saying that she started hearing imaginary voices in her head when she was in college, and she was afraid of them. She tried to ignore them and pretend they weren't there, but the more she feared them and tried to silence them, the more frightening and intimidating they became. So eventually instead of being afraid of them and trying to silence them, she tried making friends with her voices. And she came to realize that her voices were actually trying to help her, to warn her about something, or to help her make better decisions. And the more she listened to the voices, the fewer of them there were and the kinder they became.

The speaker said that people who hear imaginary voices have often had very traumatic childhood experiences and that the voices start later, in adolescence or early adulthood. That's what happened with her. She said that people who are raised in typical families have their own "inner voice" that they listen to, like a conscience, but it doesn't become a bunch of characters living inside their minds. And she said that hearing voices is not necessarily a disability but just a difference. And that if someone begins to hear voices, they should seek help, but they should also make sure that the helpers are gentle in their assistance.

All of this makes me wonder even more about creativity and genius and madness - how some people say there is a very fine line between them all. And I wonder how much difference there truly is between what is imagined and what is real. And I worry about myself, and about Annie, and about Max. What if one of us starts hearing voices? And for the first time in a long time, I begin to wonder – and worry - about our mum.

63.

Max and I took several months to go through all the boxes in the attic. We had to wait until our stepmom was gone somewhere and we were alone to climb up there. And that didn't happen very often. Our stepmom doesn't go out much.

Max wants to be an investigative reporter one day, so he decided to look for clues to our stepmom's past on the internet, too. He's really smart about stuff like that, and super resourceful. But sometimes he's also a little bit secretive. I'm glad we're in this together.

As we read through all the stuff in the boxes that we found, a pretty sad story began to unfold. We started to see our stepmom in a new light. It didn't make any of her cruelty any better, but it did help us to begin to understand her a bit.

It seemed that our stepmom was a person who wasn't very independent. She wasn't very strong on her own and she depended too much on the wrong people. She made one bad decision after another.

She grew up in a small town in rural New York State. We already knew that. When she was in the fall of her senior year in high school, she went into New York City to go shopping with girlfriends.

"I've met a really great guy," she said in her diary. (I know – privacy - but whatever.)

"He's so handsome! And he seems really interested in me and in what I have to say. He's a lot older than I am but I really like him. He's not at all like the boys at school. He's so mature. His name is Grant and he's from California."

She wrote that they started meeting and going out together, but her parents weren't happy about it. They didn't seem to like him. They thought he was irresponsible and too old for her since he was 27 at the time and she was only 17 and still in high school. And besides all that, he didn't have a job.

"I don't know how to make Mama and Pops like Grant," our stepmom had written in her diary. "They think he just has a lot of family money but not much character. And they think he drinks too much. And they think he's spoiled and way too old for me. But I'm more mature than they realize. I'm old enough to make my own decisions. I think they just want to keep me from growing up since I'm the baby of the family!"

There weren't a lot of entries after that until several months later in the winter. We thought maybe Grant had gone away but apparently he hadn't. Our stepmom had continued to see him. She was probably just too busy sneaking out of the house to write in her diary!

"Something terrible has happened," she said in one of the last few entries in her diary. "I told Mama and Pops that I was going out with my friend, Stella, but I went off with Grant instead. We went into the city, and we went to a couple of clubs – it was great fun! He got me in even though I'm underage. But then on the way home, he crashed his car. I ended up in the hospital with a huge gash on my forehead and it's probably going to leave a big scar. And the hospital called Mama and Pops. I'm in so much trouble. They've absolutely forbidden me to see him again!"

The scar! We finally knew the backstory of how she'd gotten that big scar on her forehead that she was always trying to hide. But we kept reading cuz there was a lot more.

It must have been a truly terrible accident. Max searched on the internet and found an old article about it from our stepmom's hometown newspaper. It didn't list names, but the information matched. It said that there had been a drunk driving accident that involved two people, a 27-year old man who was driving the car and his 17-year old female companion. It stated that the driver was drunk and had lost control of the car, skidding on ice, hitting a light pole and completely destroying the car. The driver was OK but the pregnant young woman sustained serious injuries when she hit the windshield.

Pregnant? Max and I looked at each other in disbelief!

"Grant feels terrible about it," our stepmom said in her diary. "He had been drinking and he says he is old enough to know better. But it wasn't really his fault. We hit ice!"

She didn't say anything about being pregnant though. We weren't sure why. Maybe she didn't want to admit it, even to herself? Or maybe she didn't know? And did she lose the baby?

There were only two more entries in her diary after that.

"We just left. We're running away! We're going to drive to California where Grant's parents live," she wrote in her diary about a month later.

And then the last entry.

"I've just called Mama and Pops from the road, and they've given us permission to marry! They said there is nothing more they can do. I'm so happy! And they said I can finish my high school diploma requirements when I'm ready to do so. I know I'll do it eventually."

We kept searching through the boxes for more information and we found about a million postcards from all over the United States that Grant and our stepmom had written to his parents. It looked like Grandma and Grandpa Fuches had bought them a new car when they arrived in California. After a small wedding, they look a long honeymoon. Grant and our stepmom drove all over the U.S. for at least six months before eventually returning to California. The postcards proved it. Apparently, it was all paid for by the Fuches. And when they got back, they moved into a new house near the beach that his parents had also paid for. We found the thank you card saying so.

Our stepmom eventually did graduate from high school (we found her diploma) and then she went to secretarial school (we found her certificate) and then she got a secretarial job (we found an old paycheck stub) and Grant joined his family's business (we found the newspaper announcement). They didn't seem to have any kids though. Max and I wondered about that. We guessed that after the accident maybe she couldn't have any more.

There were TONS of photographs of the two of them. Grant was very handsome, and our stepmom was actually really beautiful, and they did look pretty happy. They were always very well dressed, with really stylish clothes. A bunch of the photographs were taken in front of new cars, and at the beach where they were goofing around with other friends in the sand. It's really hard to picture our stepmom happy and having fun at the beach and being with friends. But there she was, looking super pretty and super happy and showing off in a bathing suit for the camera. It was hard to believe but old photos don't lie.

64.

Over the next few months, we kept reading through the boxes of stuff in the attic, and Max kept up his internet research. Eventually we learned even more.

"Hey, Maddie," called Max. "Look what I found! Grant's death certificate!"

Somehow seeing the death certificate seemed really sad. They had obviously been in love, and they had a lot of fun together. We already knew Grant had died young. His death certificate confirmed that. It showed that he had died when he was only 36. That meant that he and our stepmom had been married for nine years. Our stepmom must have been just 26 when she became a widow.

On the death certificate, it listed the cause of death. We thought it would say heart failure or cardiac arrest or something like that. But it didn't.

"Maddie," said Max. "He died from cirrhosis of the liver! Look. It says so right here."

"What?!?" I couldn't believe it.

Cirrhosis of the liver? That meant Grant was an alcoholic! And he must have been a **big** alcoholic to die from it when he was so young. But in all the photos we found he and our stepmom had looked like they were super happy together. It just didn't make sense.

Max and I were pretty shocked. Our stepmom had always told us that Grant was this perfect guy and that they had this perfect marriage. And if it hadn't been for him dying young from a heart attack which wasn't his fault, she would have had a really wonderful life and not have gotten stuck with our dad and us kids.

But it wasn't that simple. Or that rosy. In reality, it seems that Grant was just a guy who was spoiled by his rich parents, got a teenager pregnant, drove drunk, lost the baby, and then drank himself to death. He must have really had problems. And he sure wasn't very mature.

But there was more to our stepmom's story. We learned that she was married to a second guy after Grant died and before she married our dad. We found newspaper clippings in the boxes announcing it. But that marriage didn't last, and it looked like they got divorced in less than a year. It was probably a rebound relationship, and we figured the early divorce saved her inheritance from Grant's estate and the Fuches. At least that's what we assumed.

We knew that our stepmom had met and married our dad after that. The dates matched up. Our dad was husband #3, and he turned out to be another alcoholic. And this time with a mentally ill ex-wife and three little kids that needed parenting.

We already knew that our dad wasn't super responsible. He had married our mum who had a lot of mental problems, but she came with some sort of trust fund set up for her in England by her father. And then he married our stepmom who had apparently inherited a big estate from Grant and his family. And then he was dating Mrs. Shambles who was also rich. That made our dad a gold digger. Finding women with money. And not setting them up very well for happy futures.

We wondered what our stepmom's husband #2 had been like. Probably another alcoholic.

I started thinking more about our stepmom and the choices she had made, and I started to feel really confused. On the one hand, I felt kind of sorry for her. She had been married three times and none of her husbands seemed like very mature men. On the other hand, I was really angry with her for making our lives so miserable. She didn't seem to know how to stand on her own two feet without leaning heavily on someone else. And the people she chose for her support people were barely standing up themselves.

I got to thinking about all those old photos of our stepmom and Grant. Sure, they must have had a bunch of happy times. That's when people take photos, right? They take selfies to show everyone what a great time they're having and what a great life they have. They share those pics with everyone – on their phone and on social media and in their holiday cards and everything.

But there must have been plenty of awful times, too. No one dies when they're only 36 from being an alcoholic without causing other people a lot of pain. But no one takes photos of those times. They don't share those. They don't talk about that. Everyone who lives it knows those hidden rules. And no one moves across country and leaves all their family and friends behind without feeling at least a little bit lost and lonely and maybe having a little bit of regret.

All of this made me think about Hester Prynne in *The Scarlet Letter* again. She was from a small town, just like our stepmom.

She got pregnant when she wasn't ready, too. And she ended up alone and having to face life all by herself, kind of like our step-mom did after Grant died. But Hester Prynne seemed to have some sort of inner strength and she faced life head on. She didn't let life crush her. She had courage and confidence. She seemed to hold onto her self-respect and not let other people define her. She made choices that didn't hurt other people. But our stepmom never seemed to be able to do that. I wish she could be more like Hester Prynne.

65.

"When a person becomes an alcoholic or a drug addict, they stop maturing emotionally," Ms. Pensar said. "Turning to alcohol or drugs when problems arise means the person doesn't learn to solve their problems in positive or healthy ways. That can leave them emotionally stunted at the age that their drug or alcohol addiction became severe."

Ms. Pensar is my Psychology teacher. I really like her, and I love the class. She makes complex topics understandable.

"Maturing actually takes practice," she went on. "That's what the teenage years and early 20's are all about. Trying out different decisions and even different personalities. It's almost like changing your clothes. You keep trying different options until you find one that fits. The challenge is to do so without making any seriously impactful decisions that will negatively affect your future or the future of someone else."

Ms. Pensar also told us that some people "self-medicate" by using alcohol or drugs to deal with trauma they've experienced, or to try to correct some misfiring of neurons in their brain – like to calm themselves down if they have ADHD or some sort of mental illness. She said that if they seek help, other medications can be used in a controlled way that won't mess up their lives. But if they don't seek help, the drinking or drugs can get out of control.

I gave what she said about emotional maturity and self-medicating some thought. If what Ms. Pensar says is true, that would make our stepmom emotionally stuck at age 17, when her drinking seemed to have started and perhaps got out of control. And I thought again about birth order. Max and I had discovered that our stepmom was "the baby of the family". She was the youngest. Maybe she was a lost child, the one that everyone forgot to check on. Or maybe she had experienced some sort of trauma that she never dealt with or she grew up in a dysfunctional family. Or in the very least, in a very busy family that overlooked her needs.

I began to see my stepmom in a different light. She was emotionally still a teenager, yet she was trying to raise kids who were nearly as old as she was. She just didn't have the capacity to be a mature adult, much less a parent. It wasn't really surprising that she married a bunch of guys who weren't good for her and that she tried to give away her step kids. She was emotionally a colossal disaster. She had made one bad decision after another beginning when she was 17. She sure had a lot of growing up to do!

Our stepmom's whole life started looking pretty sad to me, and kind of pathetic. And as I thought about the mess she had made of her own life and of ours, the intense anger and resentment I had been building up toward her over the years began to slowly melt away, just dissolving into a puddle of pity. I began to see our stepmom in a new light, one that was filtered through a veil of sadness.

Max and I went up into the garage crawl space one last time that evening after our stepmom had passed out on the couch. We knew she wouldn't wake up and catch us. We looked around for a while with our flashlights to see if there was anything we had missed. Nothing. We made sure that all the boxes were taped shut and stacked neatly, like we'd first found them. We climbed down the ladder for the last time, feeling a little deflated and closed the trap door behind us.

Max headed downstairs to his bedroom, but I walked over to the couch where our stepmom was sound asleep. She was snoring softly. I stood looking down at her for a moment. I could see the scar through her bangs, thick and ropey. I pulled a light blanket over her.

"Goodnight, Mom," I whispered. I lifted her bangs gently and kissed her on her forehead. On her scar.

I went downstairs to my bedroom and sat cross legged on my bed, holding a few of the photos we'd found in the attic of our stepmom and Grant. I studied them. They really did look happy. But I think they were in denial. I think they were living a fairy tale that they desperately wanted to believe. I don't know if we'll really ever know our stepmom's complete story, but we had discovered enough.

I thought about Mlle Cesoir. She was in love with a guy who died young, too. She didn't let herself become an unhappy alcoholic, though. She didn't marry a bunch of guys in a quest for happiness to replace what she had lost. She didn't take on kids and then give them away. She went to college and made a career for herself and ended up helping a lot of kids to learn French and even to inspire a few kids who were having a tough time in life – like Jesse. The more I thought about it, the more I began to have some clarity. I already knew that life wasn't fair. Not at all. In fact, sometimes it just sucked! But now I began to realize that life is also what you make of it – that there are choices and turning points along the way. And that each individual is responsible for the decisions they make. I wanted to make the best of my life, and create a happy future for myself, regardless of what my family life had been like so far. I wanted to make my future a positive one - like Mlle Cesoir's.

66

"Hello, Maddie. How R U?"

It was my cousin, Charlotte. We've been connecting by email and by text. London doesn't seem so far away with the internet. Since I'm almost 14, that would make her almost 24, and I was pretty sure she could fill in some of the gaps for me, so lately I've been asking her about our real mum. Charlotte has just graduated from nursing school and she's really smart. I think it's funny that even with proper English, British people sometimes use shorthand when they text or email.

"I'm good," I emailed back. "Can you tell me more about our mums?"

"2 much 2 text. I'll email U," she replied.

Her email came through a few minutes later.

"I believe I told you your mum was diagnosed with schizophrenia when she was a young adult," she wrote. "I'm not sure if that was before or after she went off to America, but I think it was before. I remember her visiting us before she left and acting rather oddly."

"My mum says that your mum was always a bit off, even in childhood," Charlotte added. "Poor syntax that. LOL. But I'm not sure that my mum's version is completely correct. You see, they never really got on. Not even as children."

So, our mums never did get along, even as kids? That makes me pretty sad. I can't imagine not getting along with my sister,

Annie. Charlotte's mum is nine years older than our mum so I guess they didn't have a lot in common. Not like Annie and me. We're only 17 months apart. We might be pretty different, but we've always been close.

"I think my mum was a bit jealous of having a much younger sister," Charlotte added. And then she shared something I really wasn't expecting. "Auntie Bella who was the eldest of the three sisters, being nine years older than my mum and eighteen years older than your mum, was also diagnosed with schizophrenia."

What? Auntie Bella also suffered from schizophrenia? Annie, Max and I knew that she had been in an asylum, but we didn't know about the diagnosis.

"All three girls were very smart and very good students, and they were all supposed to go to boarding school when they turned 14," Charlotte continued. "That was common practice amongst our grandparents' circle of friends."

Charlotte said that when it was time to go, Auntie Bella refused and after a few years was sent to an asylum instead. We already knew that. Charlotte had told us about the asylum before. But the story was that she was rebelling. And now we learned that she was "having troubles", not rebelling. What the troubles were weren't talked about until much later. That was just about the time that our mum was born.

"When my mum turned 14, Granny and Grandpa sent her off to boarding school. That was expected," she wrote. But then Charlotte said something shocking. "But they also sent your mum at the same time. And she was only 5!" Charlotte went on to say that her mum said that our mum cried for practically the whole first year and it was really hard on both of them.

"It was extremely embarrassing for my mum," Charlotte wrote. "And positively sad for your mum. I believe that your mum was traumatized by the entire experience."

And then another shocker. Charlotte wrote that later our mum had tried to become a nun.

What? It sounded like the title for a poorly written B-grade movie script! *My Mum Was a Nun.* I couldn't believe it. Could our family history get any weirder? If our mum had succeeded in becoming a nun, Annie and Max and I wouldn't even be here.

Charlotte said our family were members of the Church of England. But after our mum left secondary school, she converted to Catholicism, and she went to live in a convent in the South of England where she studied for several years to become a nun. Charlotte said our mum almost took her final vows but in the end she didn't, and she returned home to London.

"I'm not convinced that those pieces of our family history are completely accurate," said Charlotte. "They don't appear to fit. I'm not sure that Auntie Bella suffered from schizophrenia at all. Perhaps she truly was just rebellious and was put away to avoid family embarrassment. And perhaps that was true of your mum as well, though she did act rather oddly at times." Charlotte went on to say that Auntie Bella eventually died as a young woman in a convent. But our mum somehow left and then our grandpa sent her off to the States to attend college at UCLA.

"I've got to dash," emailed Charlotte. "We'll speak again soon."

I was left wondering about our mum's mental health issues and her trauma. Neither of them seemed to have been addressed. And had she originally just been rebellious, too?

The whole thing was very confusing. And shrouded in silence.

Over time as I continued to text and email with Charlotte, I thought more about our mum's diagnosed schizophrenia and her childhood trauma and our Auntie Bella. And I began to worry again. Was I going to be OK? And what about Annie and Max? Were the three of us doomed? Were we going to develop mental illness, too? After all, we hadn't been raised in the best of environments! And now it looked like we might have some pretty suspect genes as well.

I thought again about the hearing voices movement. And about religious people who hear the Holy Spirit. And about artists and authors and other people with super vivid imaginations. And the characters in my stories that seemed to speak to me when my mind was quiet. Could all of these be different aspects of the same thing? Are insanity and genius and creativity just different points on the same spectrum? Is insanity really insanity? How does the mind work anyway? And what about the recent research on the effects of trauma and the neuroplasticity of the brain? And where do a person's strength and spirit and determination and courage and choices fit in? And what about a person's environment? If I wasn't careful, I just might drive myself crazy with all my questions!

I realized I wasn't going to get closer to any answers without a lot more information. I became even more determined to study psychology in college, and perhaps become a researcher or a therapist or someone who helps people with mental health issues. Or maybe even discover a cure for schizophrenia.

I gave it lot more thought. And then I realized what I would need to do to find more answers to my questions. I knew that eventually I would need to find my mum.

67.

Today is Dance Squad final tryouts and I'm really nervous. I'd love to be part of that team. I'd get to wear some cool costumes and uniforms. I'd be part of an official group. I'd get to perform at football games in the fall and in front of the whole school for different events throughout the year. I'd have people to hang out with. I've made it through the first two cuts of the required performances and now it's down to the original routines.

There have been about five or six groups that have already performed and all of them had at least two people in them. Some as many as five. And they all did really well. I'm doing my own individual routine. It's just gonna be me up there – just me, all by myself.

I look up in the stands, and there is Jesse, and he's giving me a double thumbs up, just like Annie did before my speech at my eighth-grade promotion ceremony last year.

I ask the judges to key up my song. And as the music starts and I hear the lyrics come through the large speakers at the sides of the judges' table, I begin to perform my original routine alone. Just me. All by myself. But it's a new me. A more confident me. A defiant me. A "don't get in my way" me.

And I think my song is perfect.

Unwritten
By Natasha Bedingfield

I am unwritten
Can't read my mind
I'm undefined
I'm just beginning
The pen's in my hand
Ending unplanned
Staring at the blank page before you
Open up the dirty window
Let the sun illuminate the words that you could not find....
Today is where your book begins....
(Bedingfield, 2004)

And when I finish, Jesse is standing up in the stands and he's clapping and cheering wildly, and the other girls who are trying out are standing with their mouths hanging open in surprise, and the judges are smiling. And I know I've made it. I know I've made the team! And I know I'm going to keep making it. I think I'm going to be OK.

TENTH / ELEVENTH GRADES

68.

There's a difference between being OK and being satisfied – or happy. I may be OK, but I'm not satisfied. And I'm sure not happy.

Ninth grade ended just fine. I got A's in all my classes. This year I'm taking some Advanced Placement and Honors classes so that's a challenge and it's been keeping me pretty busy. And I made Dance Squad, so that and cross-country practice help to eat away at my empty social hours.

I still don't have any real friends. Not even through Dance Squad. The other girls are nice – but it's all surface stuff. And they don't really include me in anything outside of dance. I never see Annie anymore. Max is hanging out with his own group and besides, he's in middle school and I'm in high school so we have less in common than we used to.

Even Jesse doesn't seem to be paying me as much attention as before. I don't know what's going on with him. Over the summer we went out a few times. We met at the beach and made out behind the lifeguard station. Neither of us has braces anymore so that was pretty cool. And then we went to a couple of parties together. I was pretty much into him, and people were starting to notice that we were a couple. But then he just completely cooled off and stopped calling. I don't know what's going on with him. I've texted him a few times, but he never texts back. He's ghosting me. Jerk.

But I'm liking my AP classes. I can't skate through them like I used to in my other classes. I really have to apply myself to keep my grades up. We always end up in really challenging discussions and we're doing some super interesting projects. Like in AP Biology. We're dissecting frogs.

"Today we're going to follow up on our previous dissection unit with live frogs instead of using frogs that are previously deceased," Mr. Miaguchi said to us last week. The entire class groaned. One of the girls started to cry.

"Because you're in AP Bio, I believe you're mature enough to understand that you will learn much more about bodily systems if you observe them actually functioning," he continued. "You will be able to do that by using a living frog. If it really bothers anyone to dissect a frog while it is still alive, you may opt do an online lab instead. It won't be the same experience and you won't learn as much that way, but it is an option."

No one took that option.

Even though Mr. Miaguchi has us doing weird lab projects, I still really like him. He's got this totally calm approach to life. At all times. Even when we're dissecting frogs. He just never seems to get freaked out about anything. He's got his own style, too. He rolls up his jeans a few inches at the bottom so we can see his colorful argyle socks and his old-fashioned penny loafers, and he always wears a suit jacket and a bow tie. And he never gets upset. He just always seems to be in control and in cruise mode, and he's super smart. He's probably the smartest teacher I've ever had.

But even though Mr. Miaguchi is always calm, I've started picking up on his "tell". That's what Max calls it when someone is playing poker and they have a twitch or a way of pulling at their ear or a blink or something that gives away that they have a really good hand. I've started to notice that Mr. Miaguchi has a tell for when he gets nervous. He still stays calm on the outside but his tell shows that he's uncomfortable on the inside. His outside and his inside don't match.

Mr. Miaguchi chews gum in class even though he knows there's no gum allowed on campus, but I guess it's for his migraines or something. And I've noticed that when he's introducing a difficult topic, like something having to do with human sexuality or reproduction, he just really chomps down on his gum. I mean, really chomps down. It's like he's decided he's trying to macerate it into tiny bits and completely bypass his digestive system by totally liquifying it in his mouth!

And right now, he's really chomping down.

He reached into an enormous burlap bag that was bouncing around on the floor. I don't know why we hadn't noticed it before. And he pulled out a giant frog. He held it by gently pinching it with his thumb and forefinger behind the head and the frog just wriggled around trying to get loose. And then Mr. Miaguchi went into this total humanitarian speech.

"We don't want to hurt the frogs," he said.

Really? I thought. *I kind of think that dissecting them live will hurt them!*

But he continued.

"So, the kind thing to do is to scramble their brains so that they can't feel anything once the dissection begins. We call that pithing."

And he held up this long dissecting needle by its round wooden handle. He started chomping on his gum really hard, and then he inserted the needle into the base of the frog's head. The frog threw all its legs out in a panic. Then Mr. Miaguchi stirred the needle around and the frog went totally limp.

"That's it," he said, withdrawing the needle gently. "That's all it takes. And notice that the frog is still breathing, and the heart is still beating because I was careful not to damage the brainstem that controls the autonomic nervous system at the base of the skull."

He continued.

"Now we can open him up and take a look inside and he won't feel a thing. You have your lab directions in front of you, and you've done dissections on deceased frogs before, so go ahead and work with your partners and let me know if you have any questions."

Mr. Miaguchi pinned the limp frog to a dissecting board and began to slice it open under the oversized mirror at the front of the classroom so that we could observe and follow along if we wanted to. And the frog didn't move at all, so I guess Mr. Miaguchi was right. It wasn't feeling anything.

All I could think of was that I was really glad that they don't perform prefrontal lobotomies on people anymore. Back in the

1940's they used to do a little scrambling of people's brains at the front of the skull instead of the back to try to alleviate depression or to control hallucinations and other mental illnesses. Thank goodness that was before my mum was even born so that never happened to her. That was truly madness in the dark ages of early psychology. At least now we're only doing it to frogs.

69.

I have a job! I'm SO excited! It's only on the weekends but it's going to give me a reason to be out of the house more. It's at a local hamburger spot. It's not a big fast-food restaurant or anything. It's more like a mom-and-pop place that specializes in the best burgers in town. Only there's no "mom", just a "pop". The burgers are really, really good! The place has an old-fashioned counter with red padded chrome barstools that swivel around and then a bunch of red leather booths along the back and side walls. It's really cool! The floor has big squares of black and white linoleum, totally retro. I have to wear a black skirt and a white top and a white apron, old style. But I like it. And since I'm waiting tables, I'm going to make tips! I'm going to put all the money I make into my college savings account. There's not a lot in there yet, just my babysitting money, but it's a start. And this will really help. Oh, and the name of the place is Take-A-Break Café. Kind of cool, huh?

I got the job cuz my stepmom is always taking us there to eat. We never eat dinner at home anymore. I guess it's just too much for her to try to cook anything. Not that she ever really did. But she used to try. Now it's just the three of us anyway – her and Max and me. Whenever we go into Take-A-Break, which is like every other evening, she makes a big deal of ordering something for Max and me but nothing for herself, saying she can't afford it. She's always drunk of course. But Take-A-Break isn't too far from our house so no one ever seems to notice that she can't stay on the right side of the highway without Max or me grabbing the steering wheel and getting us back into our lane.

The owner of Take-A-Break is this really huge man named Dan. He must have a really huge heart, too, cuz I think he sees what a mess our family is, so he offered me a job waiting tables on the weekends. And he offered Max a job washing dishes. And we get free food on our shifts and leftovers that didn't sell to take home. So, it really is a good deal. I start next weekend and I can't wait. I figure if I keep babysitting, too, I should have enough money by the end of my senior year of high school to pay for tuition and books for my first year of college. Then I'll just have to figure out how to find money for rent cuz I'm definitely not living at home after I graduate.

I told Max my plans the other day, the part about moving out once I'm done with high school, and he got really sad.

"What about me, Maddie?" he asked. "You're going to leave me here with her for three more years until I graduate, too? All by myself? What am I supposed to do?"

I hadn't actually considered that. I guess I was just thinking about myself. I thought about it for a minute.

"You're right, Max," I said. "I can't do that to you. You can't be here by yourself for three more years with her. But I don't think I can take another six years of this, either. Don't worry, though – we'll figure something out. We're going to stick together."

I had no idea what the solution was, but I knew I'd have to come up with something cuz neither of us could do six more years here. Now that we know the truth about our stepmom's history, I guess we understand her more. But that doesn't make her any easier to live with. And leaving Max here by himself for three years after I graduate would be cruel. It was simply out of the question.

I'm running for a class office this year. It's a two-year position that would start next year as Junior/Senior Class Treasurer. It's kind of ironic when you think about it. Our stepmom was Parent Teacher Club Treasurer for our elementary school, and she stole all their money. She intended to pay it back but she never did and I guess they eventually figured it out and just took the job away from her. But I'm totally trustworthy; I'll keep the books straight. And besides, there are all sorts of rules and double-checks to make sure that our class money goes toward the right things. We have to pay for our float in the Homecoming Parade, our Winter Ball, our support of the Special Junior Olympics summer games that we host on our campus, and stuff like that. So, I hope I win! I have to make a bunch of posters and put them up everywhere – but I don't think the job of treasurer has much competition actually, because it has a lot of responsibility. That's sort of why I chose it. So anyway, I think I have a chance at winning` – we'll see what happens.

70.

"Hey, Maddie. Can you bring us some coffee, please?"

It was Dan and he was sitting in the very back booth with Freddy the Hat at the Take-A-Break Café. Max and I call the guy Freddy the Hat because he looks like an old-time gangster. He always wears old black slacks, worn brown leather shoes, an old jacket that droops off of his collapsing shoulders, and an old black Fedora. You can see the hat was probably pretty expensive in its time, 40 years or so ago. But it's pretty old and beaten down now – just like Freddy.

Freddy's not very tall but he drives a really big car, an old black Cadillac from the 1960's. It's one of those super long ones that looks like a boat, with the big fins and pointed cone-shaped red taillights. I sometimes wonder how he reaches the pedals. It's kind of a cool car though. He comes into Take-a-Break every couple of weeks and sits in the back booth to talk with Dan and has his coffee.

Freddy's Wife comes in with him, too, but she always sits at the counter and never with Freddy and Dan. And she never says a thing. Not one word. Ever. We don't even know her name so we just call her Freddy's Wife. Freddy orders a coffee for her, and she reaches for it with her way-too-long, dirty, yellow, curling pointy fingernails, and she sits there and sips it, never looking up, until Freddy and Dan are done talking.

"Sure thing," I replied, and I filled two big mugs with coffee and brought them over to Dan and Freddy in the back booth.

And something caught my eye.

"Oh my gosh, Freddy. Those are beautiful!" I exclaimed, looking at the black velvet roll that he had unfurled on the table. There were several pieces of jewelry lying on it, sparkling in the artificial light.

"I love those jade earrings! Are they real?" I continued. "They must be really expensive! Are they for sale?"

Freddy looked alarmed and Dan looked surprised. Freddy started to quickly roll up the velvet display, but Dan stopped him.

"Actually, yes, they are for sale," Dan said, reaching his hand across the table and placing it on Freddy's arm. Dan looked Freddy in the eye. "Freddy just came across some great deals at a garage sale and he was sharing them with me. What did you say, Freddy? Twenty dollars for the earrings since they aren't real jade?"

Freddy seemed to recover. "Yeah, sure. That'll work," he replied.

"That's a great deal!" I exclaimed. I have twenty bucks in tips! Can I buy them from you now?"

"I'll help you out with that since you've been working so hard, Maddie," Dan interjected. "I don't want you to be spending all your college money. I'll put in half so they'll only cost you ten. Right, Freddy?"

"Yeah, sure," Freddy replied again.

"Seriously? Thanks, Dan. That's awesome," I said.

I reached into my apron pocket and pulled out ten one's and gave them to Freddy. Dan gave him a ten-dollar bill, and Freddy handed me the earrings. Then he rolled up his black velvet package and hurried from the Café, dragging his silent wife behind him.

Max was watching the whole thing.

When we got home that night, I showed Max the earrings.

"Aren't these beautiful, Max?" I asked, holding the earrings up to my ears so he could see them. They were a pale green jade laced with white, large teardrop earrings hanging from tiny golden chains. "I only paid $10 for them. And even if they aren't real jade, I still like them!"

"Maddie, you're so naïve!" Max said. And he laughed out loud.

"What do you mean, Max?" I asked. "You don't like them?"

"Oh sure, I like them," he answered. "I like them just fine. And you got yourself a real deal! Over $100 worth of real jade earrings for just ten bucks! It was a real HOT deal!"

"What are you talking about? You think they're real jade? Dan paid the other $10 so they actually cost $20! Freddy got them cheap at a garage sale, so he gave us a good deal. And Dan said they're fake jade."

"Yeah, right," Max said. "You do know what Freddy does for a living, don't you?" I could see the investigative reporter light flickering on in Max's eyes.

"He's retired," I replied. "I don't think he works anymore."

"Oh, he works a lot actually," Max said laughing. "In fact, he works every day! Who do you think is calling Dan constantly on the phone when Dan takes all those calls in the back room? And who do you think Dan is calling when he's holding the race papers in front of him? He's calling in bets! Freddy's a bookie, Maddie! And a fence! Freddy the Fence! He sells stolen goods. Those earrings are hot! I'm surprised they're not burning your hands right now!"

I looked at my beautiful new earrings. Hot? They were stolen? I had just bought stolen earrings that really belonged to someone else? How could I be so stupid? And Dan places bets with a bookie?

"Isn't that illegal to place bets with a bookie?" I asked Max. "Dan is so nice! He's really helped out our family."

"Those things aren't mutually exclusive, Maddie," Max answered. "Yes, Dan is a really nice guy. And he is trying to help us out. And he's also an addicted gambler. He places bets on everything: horses, ballgames, boxing. He's losing a bunch of money on it and if he's not careful, he's going to lose the Café. But enjoy your earrings. You deserve them!" And he walked away laughing over his shoulder.

I stood there bewildered and watched Max walk away.

I wondered to myself, not for the first time – how is it that Max and Annie seem to see through things in a way that I don't? I know I'm smart, but they always seem to know what's really going on. I just seem to see what I want to see. But then again, they don't seem to be very satisfied with all that inside information.

I took my earrings to my room and held them up to my ears one last time as I looked at myself in the mirror, admiring how the gold chains caught the light and the jade seemed to glow from within. And then I opened my jewelry box and tucked them into a back corner, knowing I was never going to bring them out again.

71.

Jesse and I have a bunch of our classes together, so I see him at school a lot. But we never talk anymore. I decided to put an end to that. I finally drummed up the courage to approach him the other day as we left our AP English class and headed out to the campus quad for lunch.

"Hey, Jesse," I said, catching up to him. "Why are you avoiding me? Can we just talk about it?"

Jesse seemed really uncomfortable, and he looked down at his shoes. He was wearing red converse high tops. He's always been his own person when it comes to fashion.

"Maddie, you're great," he said. "I'm sorry if I led you on last summer. It's just that it's not going to work out between us."

"Why?" I asked. "We get along great. We like all the same things. And we really understand each other. We trust each other and we know about each other's families. Each other's secrets. So, what's going on? Did I do something wrong? Or are you interested in someone else?"

"No, not at all," Jesse answered. "You didn't do anything wrong and there's no one else. You're amazing. And you're right – we do have so much in common. I love my conversations with you. You're someone I can really talk to. I wish I could be your boyfriend. But I just can't."

"Why not?" I asked. "At least be honest with me," I said.

He hesitated for a long moment. "OK," he finally said. "I'm going to be really honest with you. Come with me."

And he took my hand and led me down the hall and across the campus and into a classroom in the Science Building. I knew the classroom – it was Mr. Miaguchi's.

We entered and it was filled with a bunch of chatty students sharing lunch together. There were kids of all grade levels, and of all appearances. Some of my AP classmates were there – and other kids that I didn't know. There was a big poster that wasn't usually hanging in Mr. Miaguchi's room during class time. It was super colorful with splashes of pink and green and blue and purple, and it said '**LGBTQ Students and Allies Club – Welcome!**'

Mr. Miaguchi was there, and he smiled warmly as I entered the room. And I noticed he wasn't chewing his usual gum. He wasn't a bit nervous. But still, I hesitated to enter, feeling a bit overwhelmed. Jesse held onto my hand, looked deeply into my eyes, and said something in the most loving tone that I will never forget.

"Maddie, I'm gay."

"What? Why didn't you tell me?" I asked in disbelief. "And how can you be gay? What was our kissing about then? And why would you lead me on?" I could feel the tears pooling in my eyes. I'm such an idiot!

"I didn't know myself," Jesse answered. "At least I wasn't sure. But I am now. And Maddie, I still love you. Just not in the way you had hoped. You're an amazing girl. And I hope we can go back to being the best of friends now that you know."

I could see Mr. Miaguchi and the other kids watching me, kindly, but I just couldn't handle it right at that moment. Jesse is gay? Had there been clues? Was it just my usual naïve way of not seeing what was right in front of me?

"I'm sorry but I have to go," I said. And I dropped his hand and turned around and quickly left the classroom.

I didn't talk to Jesse for a while after that. We still had most of our classes together, but we didn't talk at all. He was letting me have my space, I guess. I felt a little awkward in Mr. Miaguchi's class for the next few days, but he just seemed the same as before. I wondered if he was gay, too, or if he was just an advisor for the LGBTQ & Allies Club. I knew from my preparations to be a class officer that every club had to have an advisor.

One of the kids in my AP Biology class caught me after class a few days after Jesse's "big reveal". Her name is Katie, and she's really popular and a great student.

"Hey, Maddie," Katie called to me as we left class. "Wait up!"

I turned around and wondered what she wanted. She and I had been lab partners a couple of times but it's not like we had anything more than that and some pretty good brains in common.

"I saw you at the LGBTQ & Allies Club the other day. Are you going to come back? We meet every Wednesday at noon right here in Mr. Miaguchi's classroom."

"I don't know," I replied. "I'm not really sure why I went there so I don't know if I'm coming back."

"Well, I hope you do," Katie said. "There are some really cool kids in the club and we all just kind of hang out and talk and support each other. Some of the kids are lesbian or gay or bi or trans or whatever and a lot aren't. It's just a place where you can be yourself."

"Why would you hang out there?" I asked Katie bluntly. "You have plenty of friends. You're super popular. You don't need some club to give you support. Or are you gay, too?"

Katie gave me an awkward smile.

"Yeah, I have a lot of friends," she admitted. "But I can't always be myself with them. I feel like I have expectations to live up to or something. And no, I'm not gay, but one of my friends is lesbian and she invited me to have lunch with her in Mr. Miaguchi's room one day, and I just found that I liked it. I'm straight, and I really like the people there. No one is trying to one-up you. It's not a competition. It's just a place to hang and be yourself. I hope you come back – really, I do. You might find you like the kids there."

I turned around and walked away.

"I'll think about it," I called back to her, but I had no intention of returning. Ever.

When I got home that night, I went to find Max. He was in his bedroom, playing video games.

"Hey, Max. Can I talk to you about something?"

"You're talking right now, aren't you?" he answered. Sometimes younger brothers can be so annoying.

"Well, can you at least put down your game and pretend you're listening?"

Max put his game down and sat up on his bed.

"What's up, Maddie?" he asked.

"Did you know that Jesse is gay?" I asked. I figured I should just put it out there and see what he said.

"Of course, I knew he was gay," Max answered. "At least I was pretty sure he was. Why do you ask?" He paused. "Oh no, don't tell me you had a crush on him? I knew you guys were hanging out a lot. Did you just find out?"

Tears started welling up in my eyes and I looked away as they spilled down my cheeks.

"I'm sorry, Maddie," Max said earnestly. "Truly I am. So, you just found out? Did he tell you? You want me to go beat him up for being mean to you or something?"

I knew Max was just kidding and trying to make me laugh.

"Why didn't I know, Max? What's the matter with me that I just don't seem to see the clues for some stuff, even when they're right in front of me?"

"Oh, Maddie, it's because you have your own way of looking at the world," he said. "You don't want to consider things that might make you upset, so you just sort of ignore them. And it's not a bad thing – just something you should recognize and be aware of. It makes you sweet."

I knew Max was being really kind. I must look a mess if he's being that nice to me. For a younger brother and for only being in middle school, he sometimes could have some pretty good insights.

"Didn't you tell me about your psychology class talking about denial as a defense mechanism or something a while back?" Max asked.

I was surprised that Max remembered that. Sometimes when I share stuff with him, he doesn't seem to be listening. But he's super smart and I guess he takes everything in.

"Yeah," I answered. "We learned that some people use denial as a way to protect themselves from information or situations they don't want to see or hear or acknowledge."

"Well, Maddie, I think you're a denial expert." Max smiled. "There are worse things to be."

I thought about it for a bit. It was true. We did learn that denial was a method of self-protection and that it's not a bad thing unless it's overused. It allows us to deal with difficult or uncomfortable situations, especially things that are beyond our control to change. Denial allows us to not have to face life's harsh realities head on for a while. But if it's overused, it's like a totally rose-colored way of always looking at the world and not seeing facts for what they truly are. Leading to unrealistic expectations and disappointment. I think that's what happened between me and Jesse.

"Thanks, Max," I said. "Sometimes it's like you're the big brother. I'm glad I have you." And I gave him a hug.

"No problem, Mads," he said. "Now get out of my room so I can go back to my game!"

I laughed in spite of my tears and headed down the hall to my own room. I had some more thinking to do.

73.

"What are you guys up to?" I asked. Dan and Max were sitting in the back booth at Take-A-Break Café with cards dealt out on the table between them.

"Dan is teaching me to play poker," Max said, studying his cards carefully.

"Don't worry, Maddie," Dan said. "Poker is a game of skill, not chance. And Max has a real knack for it. He could win some big money if he keeps at it."

I walked away, worried. Max has a really sharp mind – he's great at math. Even if he thinks he's going to keep this new hobby under control, I'm not so sure. He told me later that he's playing Texas Hold 'Em, Five Card Stud, and a bunch of other games, but he doesn't like Blackjack. He claims that one really is a game of chance.

And I found out that he's betting on some online games, too. I'm guessing he's funding those with our stepmom's credit card. That and maybe some of the money he makes under the table at Take-A-Break Café. He was supposed to be saving most of it for college. Dan pays him in cash because Max isn't old enough to get a work permit since he's only 13, but we need the money, so it was all supposed to work out. And Max likes working there. But now he's starting to hang out at Dan's house after his shifts are over and on weekends to play poker with Dan's son who is a lot older than Max is. It just doesn't seem like a good idea to me. I'm not in denial about that.

I was working at the Café the other day when this older guy in his 20's came in. After I got him his hamburger and fries, he told me he was a photographer and that he'd like to take some photos of me. He said he thought I could make it in modeling! I was pretty flattered – I guess I'm looking better than I used to since I've been so busy with cross country and Dance Squad and school and work. I'm pretty toned up these days. But I wasn't sure the guy was legitimate and I'm only 15 so I told him I wasn't interested. He gave me his card, though. It looks like a totally legitimate business so I'm going to hold onto it in case I change my mind.

I've noticed some of the boys at school checking me out, too. They're starting to flirt with me a bit. Maybe I'm like the Ugly Duckling and I'll actually grow into a beautiful swan one day. And maybe I'll have a boyfriend after Jesse after all. We'll see.

I've started hanging out with Katie during lunch. She's actually pretty cool. She gets a lot of attention from the boys, but she says her dad won't let her date yet, so she doesn't go out with anyone. I sometimes wonder what that would be like – having a dad who was looking out for you. It might be nice, although it might also be sort of an inconvenience if he puts limits on you. Like Katie's dad does with her. Katie has a lot of other girlfriends, but she says they're a bit too gossipy for her and she doesn't like how they're always competing with each other for attention and talking behind each other's backs. I guess I'm not much competition so that's why she likes hanging with me. Oh well, she's good company anyway.

We don't hang out at lunch on Wednesdays, though, cuz that's when she goes to the LGBTQ & Allies Club meeting. It's just sort of an understanding that I'm not going. But today is Wednesday, and she asked me to go with her. Again.

"Why don't you come, Maddie?" Katie asked. "The kids there are so cool. I really think you'd enjoy them. And Jesse has been asking about you."

I tried not to look surprised when she said that, but I guess my face gave me away.

"He really likes you, you know. And he misses you. He told me so. Can't you guys go back to being just really good friends, even if you aren't boyfriend and girlfriend?"

"That's not what I want," I said. "I thought he was my boyfriend. Now I just feel really stupid, like he was using me. And I don't know if I want to be his friend."

"Think about it, Maddie," Katie said. "Do you think it's easy for a kid in high school to admit to themselves that they might be gay? Maybe it is for some people, but it wasn't for Jesse. His family has expectations that he'll marry a girl and have kids someday. He's the only kid left in his family. And he didn't want to disappoint them, or you. I really think you should give him a chance at being your friend. You know most boyfriend/girlfriend relationships in high school don't last anyway. But deep friendships do."

"I'll think about it," I said. "But I'm not going to the club meeting today."

"No problem. I get it," Katie answered. "But let me know if you change your mind. See you fifth period." And she left me standing there by myself as she headed to Mr. Miaguchi's classroom.

I did think about it. I thought about it every day. I thought about it constantly. I couldn't get Jesse out of my mind. Maybe our "breaking up" was just as hard on Jesse as it was on me. Maybe he hadn't been leading me on and he'd only been confused. Maybe he was feeling just as miserable about how things ended as I was. And the following Wednesday, I decided to give the club meeting a try.

I walked into Mr. Miaguchi's classroom at lunch, a little awkwardly, and when Katie saw me she came over and gave me a big hug. And right behind her was Jesse. And he hugged me, too.

"Want to talk?" Jesse asked. I smiled.

"Yes," I answered. And we did.

74.

Jesse and I are hanging out a lot these days. And often with Katie, too. And when we talk, it's about all kinds of things – our families and their expectations of us, their good sides and not-so-good sides, where we want to go to college and what we want to study, what we want to do with our lives, the injustices of the world, losing people who are important to us – lots of important topics. And it feels so good. It feels really satisfying to have two kind and sincere friends who I can be pretty honest with and who understand me. They both tell me that I work too hard, that I study too hard, that I need to have more fun. But they also get that for me work and school are my play – they keep me positive and grounded and give me purpose. And they keep me away from my home. And I find success and contentment in them. Like I said, Jesse and Katie get me.

Katie and Jesse are super creative, too. Sometimes we make silly posters and put them up all over school, just things to make people laugh and not take themselves or life too seriously. One time, we made little mini-posters with positive statements on them and glued them to popsicle sticks and stuck them all over the lawns on campus near the lunch areas. It was fun to hear people's comments about them and to hear them laughing at the illustrations that we attempted. A couple of kids actually picked up a few of them and said they were going to take them home as reminders that life is good and to stay positive!

And Jesse and I actually talk about what we want in a partner.

"My boyfriend has to be really smart and understanding and funny and athletic and good looking," I told Jesse.

"Just like me!" Jesse said laughing.

"Well, almost just like you," I smiled back.

"My boyfriend has to have exactly the same qualities," Jesse said. "Then we can all four hang out together."

I laughed at that one.

"That would be pretty cool," I answered.

I'm starting to think that Katie might have been right, that having a high school best friend might be better and more long-lasting than a high school boyfriend.

I've also been thinking a lot about denial lately. How it's pretty unconscious, and how it's a good strategy for getting through tough times that you have no control over. But I've also been thinking that when you're strong enough or mature enough or ready, it's probably a good idea to revisit those things that you've been in denial about – so you can learn from them, and work through them, and not repeat the mistakes you've made or that other people close to you may have made in the past.

And then suddenly a memory started coming back to me. It was pretty fuzzy at first – I wasn't even sure if it was a real memory. I was in a big car with my sister and my brother. We were sitting in the back seat in huge car seats, so we must have been really small. There were two grownups in the front seat, but we didn't know who they were. Max and I were crying, and Annie was telling us it was going to be OK. That's all I remembered......at first.

Then a few weeks after the memory first came to me, it came back – but it was expanded. Annie and Max and I were in this really big place and there were a lot of other children there, too. And the adults were telling Annie and me to go in one direction and Max to go in another. And Max was crying, and Annie was yelling at the adults and saying that we were never separated, we were one for all and all for one, just like The Three Musketeers! And that Max needed to stay with us. And the grownups said, No, that Max was a boy and he had to go to the other side. And they pulled Annie and me in one direction and Max in the other, with Annie still yelling about The Three Musketeers while Max and I were just crying.

I told Jesse about the memory. I tell him pretty much everything these days.

"Maddie, I think it's a real memory," he said. "Can you find Annie and ask her about it? I'll bet she remembers what happened. And have you talked to Max about it yet?"

"I can't tell Max about it," I answered. "He's just barely hanging in there with the chaos at home, and all his schoolwork, and his job, and his gambling. I'm afraid I would tip the balance for him, and he'd just lose it if I asked him about it."

"I get it," Jesse replied. "Then I think maybe it's time to find your sister and talk to her about it. I'm sure she'd love to hear from you anyway."

I actually haven't talked with Annie for way over a year. If I really want to find her, I know I can. I know the name of the family she's living with, and I know she's going to the continuation high school. Gateway. I know she should be graduating next year since she's a year ahead of me, as long as she's catching up on her credits. So, it shouldn't be too hard to find her.

Jesse is pretty insightful, and he's right on this one. It is time to find Annie.

75.

I spot Annie right away. She's grown into her red hair and freckles. Her hair is gorgeous, almost down to her waist in back and it's flowing behind her as she comes out of the front doors. She's holding a bunch of big books and toting a backpack over one shoulder. Always the reader. She's talking to this really good-looking guy whom I've never seen before. I wonder if it's her boyfriend. And I suddenly realize it's been more like two years since I've talked to her.

Gateway Continuation High School has classes every day, plus Wednesday nights for kids who are working, according to their website. I had guessed that Annie might attend Wednesday nights, so I snuck out of the house one Wednesday evening and hung out by the school entrance at 9 pm, hoping I'd timed it right for the end of school. I checked on my stepmom before I left. She was in a drunken slumber, so she'd never know I was gone. And Max was doing homework in his room. I knew he'd be up until at least midnight finishing it since he had had to work at Take-A-Break until 8:00 that evening. He'd be so absorbed that he wouldn't notice I had left.

And then, there I was, hanging out near the entrance of Gateway hoping I'd guessed right, and that Annie would be coming through the doors any minute.

I had guessed right.

"Hey, Annie," I called over to her before I lost my nerve. Annie startled, and then immediately stopped talking and looked around to find me.

"I'd know that voice anywhere!" she said as she dropped her backpack and her books and ran over and gave me the biggest hug ever.

"Sis!" she said. "Oh my God, it's really you! What are you doing here? How are you? Oh my gosh!" And she just sputtered like that for a long while, the whole time hugging me until I started feeling a little embarrassed by all the attention. The other kids had stopped to stare at us.

"Um, I'm good," I answered. "I just miss you and wanted to talk with you."

"Oh my God, it's **her**, isn't it," she said, referring to our stepmom. "Is she driving you totally nuts? I'm so sorry I left you there, but I just couldn't take it anymore! Do you hate me for it?"

"Annie, no," I answered. "I could never hate you and I totally get it. Sometimes I don't think I can take it either, but it is what it is so I'm staying until I graduate. But that's not for a couple of years. And then we need a plan for Max cuz he can't stay much longer either. We've got time to talk about all that later, though. How are you? I've missed you."

The other kids headed out toward their cars or their bikes or their rides and ignored us as we sat down on the steps and started to catch up. It was *so good* to see Annie and to talk to her again. She is so smart and so wise. She totally gets life – and me.

Annie told me that she likes where she's living now. The family is pretty cool, and they have a girl my age and a boy

Max's age. (I worry that we're being replaced in her life!) She said the parents are kind, but unusual. They're both psychologists and they're pretty accepting of Annie and whatever choices she makes. They supported her transfer to Gateway; they don't mind all of her piercings; they like her boyfriend (yes, that was him that she was leaving with); and they don't put a lot of pressure on her. They live in this old house that they are "renovating", which means that they've torn out all of the interior drywall down to the wooden wall frames, but they haven't replaced anything yet. So, Annie says when you walk into the house, you can see through all of the rooms all the way to the back of the house. And I guess the parents like it that way because Annie says it was that way when she got there almost two years ago, and nothing has changed since.

We talked a lot and we laughed a lot. It felt *so* good! And Annie gave me her cell phone number and her address and said I have to come and see her so we can talk some more. I promised to call and I gave her my number, too. I felt like I was floating on my bike as I headed home. It's as if a piece of me was missing and reconnecting with Annie has made me whole once more.

76.

I tell Jesse and Katie all about it the next day at school.

"Good for you, Maddie," Jesse says. "I am so glad you found Annie!"

"Me, too," says Katie. "She's been so important in your life. You have to keep seeing her!"

"Definitely," I answer. "We're going to connect at the beach this weekend so we can keep catching up."

"In the shade, I hope," laughs Jesse. "Both of you sunburn so easily!"

I meet up with Annie at the beach after I get off work at Take-A-Break the next weekend.

"You're still working for that addicted gambler?" Annie asks.

"Was I the only one not to know?" I laugh. "Yeah, I am. But he's really nice – and it's a job."

"Yeah, Dan is nice alright," Annie answers. "But I'm concerned about Max and the gambling."

"How did you know about that?" I ask.

"Oh, you know me. I've got my contacts!" Annie smiles. "I've been keeping an eye on you two. You're both acing school and you're both working too hard. I'm proud of you guys."

Leave it to Annie. She was still checking on us and making sure we were OK.

Eventually, I tell her about my fuzzy memory and ask her what she thinks about it.

"Maddie, you really don't remember more than that?" Annie asks.

"Not really," I answer. "Except I think I remember reaching out to Max through a chain link fence and him crying because we were separated from him, and he had gotten into trouble for not brushing his teeth or something. Does any of that make any sense?"

"Actually, it does," Annie answers. "It makes a lot of sense." And she tells me the story that makes the hazy images fit into my cache of memories.

Annie tells me that the place I'm remembering was called MacLaren Hall, a receiving home for children in Los Angeles County that took care of kids that were between homes and not yet in the foster care system.

"It was pretty much a dumping ground," Annie said. "But social workers didn't have much of a choice when kids were brought into police departments because of abuse or neglect and there was nowhere else to put them. It's been closed down now, though. No one else has to live in that awful place ever again!"

She said that the three of us kids had actually been taken there twice. The first time Annie was only four so I would have been barely three and Max would have been a baby. I don't remember that time, but Annie does. The second time, I was five, Annie was six, and Max was three. That's the time I was remembering.

"The boys lived in one area and the girls lived in another area," Annie said. "So, they separated Max from us. It was awful. But we weren't there for that long – maybe a couple of weeks.

Mummy had been picked up by the police for something and I guess after a couple of weeks they had evaluated her and decided she was well enough to have us back. And I'm sure they couldn't find our deadbeat dad anyway, so there weren't a lot of options. It's hard to know what the issue was that time with Mummy. But I remember she yelled a lot at our neighbors, and was having a bunch of hallucinations, so I'm sure she was acting pretty strangely."

We shared some of our memories of Mummy then. Her grabbing a bag of oranges out of the hands of an old lady in the produce section of the supermarket; her praising Max for making the scale drawing of the sperm whale with a magic marker on the roll of paper towels; her not allowing us to read any children's books with people with disabilities in them – not even Heidi. (We think that was because she didn't want to admit her own limitations.) And of course, her letting me collect the remains of roadkill animals to study and Annie refusing to ride in the car with a bunch of dead bones in the back seat!

We laughed a lot. It was all pretty ridiculous looking back, and good to laugh about. After our visit, I found myself wondering how our mum was doing, and how she'd been able to manage at all, suffering from mental illness, with three little children and essentially no money, in a new country and with no support. It seemed like I was coming into a new practice of leaving my denial behind me and facing life with a bit more clarity. It had been a long time since we'd seen our mum, and I couldn't help wondering if perhaps it was time that we connected with her again, too.

It was so good to talk with Annie. And she had some other news for me as well. About Gracie.

"You know that Gracie goes to Gateway, too, don't you, Maddie?" she asked.

"No, I didn't know that! "

"Gracie's doing really well," Annie went on. "She's super smart and she's in counseling for all her homelife stuff. She doesn't live at home anymore either. She lives in a foster home and it's a really good one. The parents are super caring and they're making sure that she's making good choices and getting the help she needs. And she's in recovery. She's clean and sober."

I was so glad to hear that. I'm going to see if I can connect with Gracie, too.

Annie and I decided to get together at least once a month and to text in between. We both have our own cell phones so it should be easier to stay in touch now. I'm going to tell Max about it so that next time we can include him, too. I think he'd like that.

77.

The other day, Mr. White came down to our house. He's our neighbor from up the street. I guess some of our mail had been delivered to his house by mistake and he was being nice and passing it along to us. The only problem was, he knocked on our door at 11 in the morning. And it was a Saturday.

I happened to have the day off of work so I tried to be the first to the door, but our stepmom was nearby and she beat me to it. She was still in her nightgown and already slurring her words. Uh oh. She opened the door and just stood there in the morning light in her long see-through nightgown with nothing on underneath, leaning against the door jam seductively.

"I'm sure Mr. White has seen this before," she said, smiling at him as she opened the door wider.

I was *so* embarrassed.

Mr. White awkwardly handed her the mail and turned around quickly to get out of there, but he caught my eye before he left. He gave me this totally sympathetic look. I don't know who felt worse – him or me.

We're not the only weird ones in our neighborhood though. We might be the most obviously dysfunctional family, but we have plenty of company in the "strange" department. The area might look totally ordinary and middle class on the outside, but there's a lot going on here beneath the surface.

The neighbors next door are the McLain's. They have three older kids who are all off at college and then a little girl who is younger than Max. I think she's in sixth grade. Our stepmom calls her "The Mistake" – unkind as usual.

The little girl is beautiful. I guess she was walking home a couple of weeks ago from elementary school when some van came by and grabbed her – right off the sidewalk a couple of blocks from home. Just kidnapped her in broad daylight! The police were called and there was this search, but she was missing for hours. And then later that evening, she was found, dumped at a park just outside of town. No one is saying what happened to her. They're keeping it pretty quiet. She was alive and everything, but who knows what they did to her. The police found the van abandoned at the park, but it was stolen so now they're dusting it for prints. Poor kid. Our stepmom said all sorts of mean things about it. I hope she's going to be OK – the little girl, I mean.

Then there are the Fritzes who live up the block. Max swears he's seen an old Nazi convertible coupe inside their garage. He says Mr. Fritz bought it at auction and is restoring it. I asked him how he knows that it's an old Nazi vehicle and Max says you can still see the faded swastika on the side door. I'm not sure I believe Max, but the Fritzes are pretty weird. I don't know why anyone would want an old Nazi car in their garage though.

Two blocks below us, there is a family with two beautiful teenage girls, Fiona and Fatima. They're beyond gorgeous. There are rumors that their dad was sexually abusing them. No one knows for sure if it's true or not, but CPS showed up a little while ago and no one has seen the girls since. We think maybe they were taken out of their home.

And two doors down from them are the Naples. There are three boys, Kiernan, Kyle, and Kaleb. Well, actually just two now, Kiernan and Kyle. And a dad. No mom. We're not sure what happened to the mom. But she's gone. Kiernan is the oldest and he's in Annie's grade. He's super smart. Kyle is the second, and he's in my grade. He's also super smart but really odd. The youngest boy, Kaleb, is in Max's grade and he's on the spectrum. He has a lot of issues, and he just wanders around the neighborhood quoting statistics from basketball games and from wars and other random things. He started getting sort of violent and then he disappeared (sort of like the mom) so we think he's been placed in some sort of a home for emotionally disturbed kids or something. We don't see him anymore. And no one talks about it. It's just really sad.

And I already mentioned Dora and Dana's family. Their mom still hasn't come home.

And then, of course, there is us. A total circus.

The evening of the nightgown incident, I decided I needed some stress relief, so I took our dog for a run. It was a good excuse to get out of the house. Our dog gets treated better than we do. Every night Lucky gets cooked lean ground sirloin steak mixed with cottage cheese while we go out for cheap hamburgers! Before I left, I lifted a couple of my stepmom's half-smoked cigarettes from an overflowing ashtray and a lighter, so I could have a smoke while I walked. I've never smoked before but somehow it just seemed like a good idea.

Our neighborhood is built on the side of a very steep hill, with houses on only one side of the street. The backyards have fences and then there are banks of ice plant that lead down to the street below. I ran down the block with Lucky, and then slowed to a walk when I got to the street below ours. I decided to light up a cigarette. Like I said, I've never smoked before, but I thought smoking might reduce my stress and make me feel better. But it was awful. I took a long drag and thought I was going to be sick right there. But I tried it again – and again – and again. I started feeling pretty light-headed, and I looked up at the back deck of the house above me. There was Mrs. White, our neighbor.

Mrs. White was leaning over the railing of her upper back deck looking down at me. I was scared. *What if she calls my stepmom?* I thought. But she just smiled at me in a gentle sort of way and shook her head. I realized that she probably knew what had happened earlier in the day with my stepmom greeting her husband at the door practically naked, and she was probably just feeling sorry for me. I dropped the cigarette, smashed it under my shoe, and looked back up at the deck. Mrs. White was still there, still watching me. She gave me a thumbs up, smiled, and then disappeared inside her house. I was grateful that she wasn't going to turn me in. And the smoking didn't seem to help, any-way. I rested in my relief over the next few weeks, until I decided to try something else.

Over the next month, I started hitting my stepmom's vodka bottle. I was careful to note the level of the liquid inside with a pencil mark on the label before I poured any out, and then to refill the bottle with water up to that point. She would probably never know anyway since she goes through an entire bottle so fast, but I was determined not to get caught. I only drank a little at a time, usually when I got home from practice or from work and she was already passed out on the couch or in her room.

But one night when I went to get a drink, I noticed a new mark on the label. That scared me a little bit. Was she checking on it? Or was it Max? Was he sneaking drinks, too?

'What are you doing, Maddie?' I thought to myself. *'Are you going to become a secret drinker and continue our crazy family's legacy into the next generation? Are you going to kiss all your goals goodbye?'*

And so, I stopped. I just made the decision and I stopped. I didn't really like the taste of vodka that much, anyway. And I decided I had better keep my eye on Max. He didn't need to get derailed either.

78.

A big box was delivered to our house the other day. At first, I thought it was something Max had ordered with our stepmom's credit card. But it wasn't. The return address said Family Court, Probate Department, Los Angeles County. I guess it was the rest of our dad's stuff that our stepmom said got tied up in probate after he died. It's been four years. Weird. I wondered what was inside.

When our stepmom saw the box, she went ballistic.

"Well, that's about what I would expect from your dead deadbeat father!" she said. "One single box! Nothing more! He sure didn't care about you or me or anyone else - only himself!"

She went on like that for a while and then headed for her vodka cabinet. It looked like Max and I were going to be opening the box by ourselves. Which was just fine with us anyway.

We waited until our stepmom was completely drunk and asleep on the couch and then Max and I started on the box. We weren't sure what we would find inside so we tried to keep our expectations in check. We didn't want to be disappointed.

We got the box open and looked inside. We really weren't very surprised at all. The box seemed to contain a little bit of all of the many lives that we already knew our dad had lived.

There were his old black leather ice skates from his days of performing with Cirque du Soleil. There was a private's cap from his days in the army. There was a collection of seashells from his scuba diving hobby. There were sketches and plans for the lobster traps he had built. There were a few coin sets from the U.S. Mint, a passing hobby or maybe a short-lived investment. There were flash drives labeled with dates and a catalogue to their contents – mostly photographs. There was his college degree. It turns out he had majored in Psychology - go figure! And there were a few books from his early college days.

And then there were some notes that we found at the very bottom of the box that did surprise us. From something called 'Praetorian, Phalanx, and Fusileer - NTS, 1981 – 1984.'

That was new. We were curious about that one. He would have been a young man during those years, before he got married and before he started having us kids. Max and I looked at each other, and I knew that he was going to investigate it. We would know more soon.

And then deeper in the box, we found an essay he had written about his experience at the NTS – Nevada Test Site - for a class when he was at UCLA. It described a count-down, and then lying flat on the Nevada desert so that the ensuing enormous sound boom blast wouldn't knock him and the others involved to the ground. He mentioned one man who tried to stand too soon and was thrown several feet to the ground by the force! He said they all drank heavily that night and wondered what they had gotten themselves into. Max and I looked at one another in shock. What had he gotten himself into?

We put the box back together in case our stepmom wanted to open it herself the next day. But I guess predictably, it turned out she wasn't interested. The box just sat in the entryway of our house for over a month, untouched, until I finally took it out to the garage. She never said anything about it again, so Max and I split up what was inside. And we made a collection for Annie, too. We figured she would like some of our dad's legacy.

Max did his investigative diligence about the Nevada Test Site and about a month after the box had first appeared, he shared with me what he had found.

"Look at these articles, Maddie," Max said. "Praetorian, Phalanx and Fusileer were some of the last of the U.S. Nuclear experiments at the Nevada Test Site (NTS) before they were outlawed in the early 1990's. They were similar to earlier tests on Eniwetok Atoll in the South Pacific."

"Wow," I answered. "Our dad must have been assigned there as a part of his U.S. Army stint – either that or as a civilian shortly after his army days ended. I remember him saying once that the army paid well which was a pretty odd thing to say."

"Yeah, I didn't think serving in the army was a really high-paying job," Max said, still looking over the research he had found. "But he could have been referring to some special operation that he was hired by the Army to do later as a civilian."

Because the nuclear tests were considered classified, Max wasn't able to find out too much about them. But he did learn that a few of the later tests like Divider, Hunters Trophy, Lubbock, and Diamond Fortune resulted in some airborne fallout. We wondered if that would have had any effect on our dad or on the other people involved in the testing? Could it have affected his health? Or his mind? It looks like we'd never find out since the information was classified. We were glad to know as much as we did, though. It was like another little piece of the puzzle of who our dad was had fallen into its place.

79.

I'm finding that I really like the LGBTQ & Allies Club. I go to the lunchtime meetings in Mr. Miaguchi's classroom every Wednesday with Jesse and Katie. Sometimes everyone there just hangs out and talks and has fun and other times we're working on some sort of project – like posters for Pride Month.

A few days ago, I asked Jesse about Mr. Miaguchi.

"Hey, Jesse. Do you think Mr. Miaguchi is gay?" I asked. He and I can talk pretty openly about just about anything, so I felt comfortable asking.

"I don't know, Maddie. And, no offense or anything, but does it really matter?"

"What do you mean?" I asked. "I'm just curious."

"Well, he's a teacher so he's not going to talk about his sexuality with us. That would be so totally inappropriate. But his whole being is based on justice and acceptance. I know his grandparents were held in the Japanese Internment Camps during World War II at Manzanar. Remember he shared that with us when he was a guest speaker in our U.S. History class last year? So, his family has experienced racial prejudice and segregation and the loss of their land and property. He knows on a personal level what it's like to not be accepted and to be discriminated against. I don't know if he's gay or if he's just an advocate for acceptance of all people. He has pretty high standards, though, so it could be that his life work is not only to teach Biology, but to reduce prejudice and to promote acceptance."

I liked that. If we could all model such acceptance, wouldn't the world be a better place?

Our club has decided to take on some issues of equity at our school. I've noticed in my Advanced Placement classes that Jesse is one of the few Hispanic kids enrolled in them. Most of the students are White or Asian; there are almost no Hispanic or Black kids or Pacific Islanders, or other kids of color enrolled in AP, even though those kids make up over 40% of our school's student population. That just seems wrong to me. I pointed this out to Mr. Miaguchi one day, and he listened thoughtfully. Then he responded.

"Well, that is an interesting piece of data, Maddie. What are you going to do about your concerns?" he asked. He smiled at me as I considered my answer.

"I don't know," I said. "It's just an observation."

"Observation can be the beginning of a change," Mr. Miaguchi replied. He smiled at me again and turned to answer another student's question.

I talked with Jesse and Katie about it after school.

"Jesse, does it bother you that you're practically the only Hispanic kid in our Advanced Placement classes?" I asked.

"Well, I did notice there aren't many Hispanic or other kids of color in our classes," he replied.

"That's what I said to Mr. Miaguchi today. I expected him to agree with me or sympathize or something. But do you know what he said? He asked me what I was going to do about it?"

Jesse and Katie laughed.

"That is SO Mr. Miaguchi," Katie replied.

"Yeah, he's totally pragmatic," Jesse agreed.

"So, what are we going to do about it?" I asked them. "We really should do something!"

Katie and Jesse and I continued to discuss our concerns and together we eventually formulated a plan. We decided to develop an outline for a research project and pitch it to our AP Psychology teacher. We thought it might qualify for an additional credit of Independent Study, and that would serve two purposes. It might help us to highlight some of the unjust practices at our high school and it also might look great on a college application. The next week we ran the idea by Mr. Miaguchi.

"I think you have a strong premise here," Mr. Miaguchi said. "Good luck with it. If you need any assistance, let me know." He smiled at us. He's not overly demonstrative, but I think he really liked the idea.

Jesse and Katie and I spent most of our remaining Junior Year outside of school hours on our research project. We collected data from the school registrar on numbers and percentages of students enrolled in AP classes, overall, by racial breakdown, by gender and by socio-economic status. We collected data on grade point averages for those same groups. We collected information from the middle schools on enrollments in Honors and Advanced classes there and on standardized test scores in English Language Arts and Mathematics. We collected data on college enrollments for the same groups. And we gathered samples of all the outreach being done to inform students of the advantages of Honors and AP classes and the supports for success in them. It took a lot of time.

Along the way, we ran ideas past Mr. Miaguchi, and asked him to proofread our work. He offered comments, asked for clarifications, and offered suggestions and insights. Finally, at the end of almost a full semester of work, he smiled at us.

"I think you're ready to present this to our school's administration and to the School Board," he said.

Jesse, Katie and I were dumbfounded.

"We're just turning it in to our AP Psychology teacher for a grade and for Independent Study credits," I said. "We figured then maybe someone else could do something with the information."

Mr. Miaguchi looked at us and smiled.

"And who might that 'someone else' be?" he asked. "If you stop here, whose purposes have you served?"

We looked at one another.

"Our own, I guess," I said.

"Yes," Mr. Miaguchi replied. "And is there a greater purpose which might be served as well?" He smiled again and walked away to allow us to consider our response.

Jesse, Katie and I looked at one another. This project was taking on a life of its own! We knew we might be in a position to advocate for a more equitable education for all the students at our school. But were we really ready to take this on? And did we have the time?

We talked about it for several weeks. Ultimately, we decided that in addition to handing the assignment in for our Independent Study credit, we would see about getting a meeting with our high school principal and then getting on the agenda for an upcoming School Board meeting. This club thing was turning out to be more work than we had expected! And it looked like the work was going to continue into our Senior year.

Oh, by the way, I won the Class Treasurer election! Actually, it was pretty easy – no one else wanted the position.

80

It's the last day of our junior year before summer vacation. Most of our teachers are hosting class parties or letting us just sign each other's yearbooks. They know our minds aren't going to be on learning anything new. In a few classes, students have been frantically finishing off late assignments, hoping to raise their grades. My last period of the day is my AP Psychology class. I like that. Ms. Pensar brought in cookies for all of us and we were just sitting around talking, playing music, and waiting for the final bell to ring.

"There's just one last thing I want to share with you before we say goodbye for summer," Ms. Pensar said about five minutes before we were going to leave.

The class groaned. Ms. Pensar laughed.

"Not to worry," she said. "It's not an assignment or anything you have to do. It's simply something I think you may find useful - a list of resources in case you need anything this summer. As much as you might look forward to the long break, I've found that it can sometimes be a time of challenge," she went on. "Without the typical structure and supports of the school year, you may find yourself lonely or adrift. And if there are issues at home, they may become magnified. These resources might be of some help."

She smiled at me as she passed out the handouts to everyone in the class. I looked down. I don't know why she might think I would need this list. I looked it over anyway.

Alateen jumped out at me. I'd heard about that group. Ms. Pensar had mentioned it before. It was a support group for teenagers who were living with an alcoholic parent. And it met at Angelika's church on Thursday nights. Interesting, I thought. Maybe I should check it out.

The final bell rang and everyone shouted their goodbyes to Ms. Pensar as we headed out the door. She's pretty cool, I thought. I'm going to add her name to my List of People Who Care.

81.

I did check out Alateen that summer. I had my driver's license and my stepmom let me borrow the car occasionally to run errands, so I tagged a few meetings onto shopping and dropping Max off at work. It turned out to be pretty interesting.

It was all teenagers in the group – sometimes as few as seven or eight and other times as many as twenty. I recognized some of the kids from school, but there were a bunch I didn't know. And it's totally confidential so no one repeats anything that is shared there outside of the group. It meets at Angelika's church like I said, and since I'd been there before I felt a bit more comfortable. Everyone was nice and the leaders were real chill. They allowed time for sharing our experiences and frustrations and also time for information.

I learned a lot actually. Like, you can't fix the alcoholic parent – they have to decide to change themselves. And you're not responsible for their choices – there's nothing you can do to make them better or to affect the choices they make. And the situation is not your fault.

And I learned about the Serenity Prayer – asking for help to accept the things I cannot change, and to change the things I can, and to have the wisdom to know the difference. That seems like a simple concept, but it's actually pretty profound. I thought about all the times growing up when I thought that if we didn't make trouble, or if Annie didn't talk back, or if Max were more honest, or if I confessed when I did something wrong things would have turned out differently. But I began to realize there really wasn't anything we could have done as kids to change our homelife situation. There was nothing we could have done at all.

I also learned about the concept of a dry drunk. I thought back to our family trip to Sea World and San Diego when our stepmom got all stressed out and started yelling and screaming and threatening to skip the vacation and drive us right back home. She was completely sober at the time, but she was showing the characteristics of a dry drunk. That's someone who's been influenced by alcohol – either their own drinking or someone else's – and they haven't learned alternative ways to cope with stress. So, they just use the same useless ways of dealing with problems that they used when they were drunk – like yelling, and screaming, and making threats, and blaming others. It all seemed to make sense.

One night when we were all sitting around in a circle at Alateen, someone entered the room that surprised me. It was Angelika. I was pretty shocked. What was she doing at a meeting? We made eye contact a few times, but she didn't share anything. Neither did I.

After the meeting, I went over to her. She'd been pretty quiet and I didn't know if I should say anything, but she obviously recognized me and not saying something would have been even more awkward.

"Hey, Angelika," I said.

"Hey, Maddie," she answered.

There was a pause.

"OK, I'm just going to ask," I said. "What are you doing here?"

Angelika looked right at me.

"My mom's an alcoholic, Maddie," she answered.

"What? But your dad is so nice. And you're so put together. Your life looks so perfect. How could your mom be an alcoholic?"

"Not all alcoholic families are obviously dysfunctional," she answered. "You know that. We learned that in our AP Psych class. My family looks fine on the outside. My mom has a job and everything. My dad is great. We live in a nice house. But my mom drinks too much. She's what you call a functioning alcoholic. And she yells and screams at all of us all the time. And she says really awful things to my dad. And every night she's passed out on the couch and my dad has to put her to bed – like a kid. No one knows though. You won't say anything will you?"

"Of course not," I said. I gave Angelika a hug. "I guess alcoholic families come in all shapes and sizes."

Angelika laughed at that.

"I know your family is pretty crazy, Maddie," she answered. "But in some ways, maybe that's easier. Everyone knows you're in chaos. No one knows about me."

I got to thinking about what she said. I disagreed with her, though. Living in an alcoholic family is never easy, whether the family is an obvious mess like mine, or it looks all put together on the outside like hers. But maybe there are ways to make life a bit more livable. Maybe there are ways we can help each other through.

TWELFTH GRADE

82.

"We got it! We got the approval!"

Katie was holding the official letter from our high school principal, endorsed by the President of the School Board, granting permission for our LGBTQ & Allies Club to have a float in the fall Homecoming Parade. I think after Jesse, Katie and I made our presentations about the inequities of enrollments in Honors and Advanced Placement classes at our school, and our advocacy for changes to be made to benefit ALL students, no one wanted to tell us, "No". It's like we had started a movement that was gaining momentum and now our bid for a float was successful, too.

Mr. Miaguchi encouraged us to utilize the float as a way to share a message of positive regard for ALL marginalized people rather than to try to shock folks.

"Using honey is more attractive to people than vinegar," he said.

"I think he's right," Jesse said.

"I agree," I said. "Let's be careful with our planning. We want our float to be artistic and tasteful, and to carry a message of acceptance." Katie nodded.

We've been working on our float every evening for about three weeks now. We've invited students who represent all kinds of backgrounds and interests to ride on the float with us and almost all of them accepted. They're helping us to build it, too. It's turning into this really cool project. And everybody seems to just be getting along with each other.

There are the traditionally popular kids in their athletic and cheer gear (even Taylor and Olivia - can you believe that?!); and LGBTQ kids and allies, some of them wearing rainbow tie-dyed shirts, hot pink boas and rainbow colored hair and others not standing out in any way; and Muslim girls wearing hijabs; and Sikh boys with turbans; and Jewish boys wearing Yarmulkes; and country kids wearing denim and cowboy hats and boots; and Hispanic kids in white linen shirts and embroidered dresses and red scarves; and kids representing special needs just being themselves; and genius types with button down shirts. It is SO cool! Everyone seems to get what we're trying to accomplish. We have so many students that want to be involved that some of them are going to have to walk alongside our float. There just isn't enough room for everyone up on top.

"I've got a great idea," Jesse said one day last week. "Let's create a super tall sign in the center of our float that says "ACCEPTANCE" on one side and "DIVERSITY" on the other."

"Maybe we can even make it rotate around on a pole so it can be seen from all sides," I added.

"How are we going to do that?" Katie looked dubious.

We thought about it for a bit and tossed a bunch of ideas around. Then at about the same time, Jesse and I had the solution.

"Some of the physics genius students can design the electronics for the rotating mechanism," Jesse said.

"And the metal shop technical kids can create the parts and put it all together so that it actually works!" I added.

"And the art students can create large letters out of colorful tissue paper flowers that say "LGBTQ & ALLIES CLUB – Celebrate Everyone!" to put around the bottom of the float," Katie suggested.

It's going to be amazing. We want people to understand that we really mean accept everyone. And we're modeling acceptance and how important each person is in the way we're creating the float!

We're going to hand out flyers during the parade that explain how to get into Honors and AP classes and why that's important, and about the tutoring supports that are available on campus. There's also going to be information about the Career Center resources that can help students with their goals and the Counseling Center that can help them solve personal issues. We've even convinced Mr. Miaguchi to ride on the float with us. We are SO excited!

I get out of school every day at noon this year since I'm a senior and I have more than enough credits to graduate. But it's not like my day is done at noon. I joined the Future Teachers of America Club on campus and every afternoon I'm a volunteer teacher's assistant in a classroom at my old elementary school. I love it. I don't get paid or anything, but I do get course credit for it. I tutor kids that are super smart but who are having trouble reading and needing some extra help. I work with small groups of kids, and it's really satisfying. Some of the students have learning difficulties, and some have emotional issues, and some are clearly neglected. I can read the signs on that one. And guess who the custodian is at the elementary school? Mr. Dyanchenko! My old custodian from middle school – the one that everyone loved. I guess he took a transfer to the elementary school and no surprise, everyone loves him here, too.

I was finishing my tutoring one day at the elementary school when the new nighttime custodian came over to me and said hello.

"Hey, Gorgeous," he said, walking up to me as I approached my car in the parking lot.

Stupid line, I know, but he's totally hot. It turns out his name is Gabe and he's a little older than I am – he's about 22 but I'm almost 17 – and he's super cute. He says he's just working as a night custodian until he finishes his HVAC certificate program (that's heating, ventilation and air conditioning) at a local technical school. Once he graduates, he's going to leave the custodian job and work for a major HVAC company. He was so interesting. I really like him. I saw Mr. Dyanchenko watching us from the courtyard and he didn't look too happy. I guess he didn't like Gabe taking time away from his work to talk with me. Oh well, we'll see where this goes.

I've already applied for a bunch of scholarships for college. I have a lot of money in my savings account now, too. It's almost enough for my first year of tuition and fees and books at a state college, so I won't have to take out any loans. And I've looked into ways to reduce the cost of room and board.

After my first year of college, I can apply to be an RA, that's a Resident Advisor, which basically means you're a college student who lives in the dorms with the other kids but you're in charge of what happens there. The new freshmen students can ask you for help with stuff, and you make sure there aren't any alcohol or drugs in the dorm rooms, and you plan social events for the kids so that they can get to know one another and adjust to college life. The best part about being an RA is that you get to live in the dorm and eat for free. If I do that for every year after my first year, it would save me a ton of money. So, I'm hopeful.

Max and Annie and I have talked about Max's situation. We can't leave him at home with "the dragon" all by himself. Annie lives with her boyfriend now and Max might be able to live there with them. Or I could maybe spend one more year at home and then we could figure something out for Max's last couple of years of high school. Maybe he and I could get our own place. We'll see. I guess we'll cross that bridge when we come to it.

I've really gotten into reading lately. And not just for class assignments – it's cuz I just like it. I guess it's sort of an escape, at least that's what Annie says the appeal of reading has always been for her. Lately, I've been reading the old James Michener novels. They're each about 1000 pages long and he goes on forever in his descriptions, but the story lines are really compelling. Except for the opening of "Hawaii". I swear, he took over 100 pages to describe the volcanic eruptions that finally formed the island. And nothing else even happened.

The Michener novel I'm reading now is my favorite, and it's fascinating. It's called "The Drifters", and it's about these six young runaway American kids who travel all around Europe with their backpacks seeking meaning after their tough experiences at home. There's a bunch of drug use in it that I don't like, but I can really relate to some of their frustrations and hopes and dreams, and their need to just get away to try to figure life out. That sounds so appealing. Once I graduate from high school and maybe do a year or two of college, I'm thinking I might want to backpack through Europe for a summer, too. What a great way that would be to gain some perspective on life.

There are so many things I want to do and so many options that sometimes I'm not sure where to start. It's all good but at the same time it's pretty overwhelming. Sometimes I wonder what it would be like to have a mom or a dad to talk these things over with. To guide me a bit. Katie and Jesse talk to their parents about all this stuff and their parents actually offer pretty helpful suggestions. They have whole discussions about it. They'd probably help me, too, if I would ask. But I don't. I'm just going to have to figure it out for myself.

83.

The car horn honked outside my house.

"Bye," I called to no one as I headed out the door.

Max was gone working at Take-A-Break Café and I was pretty sure my stepmom was passed out on the couch. No matter – I was heading to my weekly evening college class. It was Jesse's turn to drive this week and I didn't want to keep him and Katie waiting.

We're all starting on our college credits early, even though we're still in high school. All of us qualified for an Early Entry program where high school seniors can take undergraduate college classes at night at their local community colleges. We're enrolled in a Psychology of Learning class together and I love it. Because we took AP Psychology in high school last year, we were able to have it count as college credit. We got to skip the General Psych college class and go directly into higher level courses. There are only three high school kids in the Psych of Learning class: Jesse, Katie, and me. It's so much fun. We share rides together every Wednesday evening, and we talk about what we're learning. We have to act more adult than our usual crazy selves when we're on the college campus cuz we don't want people looking down on us for still being in high school.

In our class, we're learning about how the human brain works, and how typical learners learn and how some atypical learners learn. Professor Nelson uses lots of interesting approaches to make her points.

Last week, she read us some descriptions of famous people and we had to guess who they were. They were either atypical learners or people who had overcome severe childhood trauma that could have affected their brain development. It was sort of like a game of Jeopardy.

"OK," Professor Nelson said. "Famous People With Curious Brains for 100. This person was labeled 'mentally defective' as a child because he couldn't learn to read. But he was exceptionally good at math. He went on to become a famous physicist and his name is now equated with the concept of 'genius'."

"Albert Einstein," someone shouted out.

"Right," Professor Nelson replied. "This next one is tougher. Famous People with Curious Brains for 200. This person had trouble with both reading and mathematics as a child. The letters and numbers seemed to float off the page and rearrange themselves in front of him. He went on to become a famous painter known for cubism."

"Pablo Picasso," shouted Katie.

"Correcto," Professor Nelson said, smiling. "OK, time to make this more challenging. Curious Brains for 500. This famous singer grew up with a violent father who was addicted to drugs. At one point, the father burned down the family home in an attempt to hurt this person and her mother. She was born in Trinidad and moved to New York as a child."

"Nicki Minaj?" I asked timidly. Katie and Jesse looked at me in surprise.

"Max is totally into her music," I whispered. "He told me all about her background."

"Right again! You guys are a smart bunch. Last in the category – Famous People with Curious Brains for 1000. This famous actress is known for her both her beauty and her talent. She has taken on challenging movie roles where her appearance is sometimes grossly altered. She grew up with a violent alcoholic father whom her mother shot and killed in self-defense. This impacted her severely in childhood, making her determined to study people and their choices in life through her acting career."

The class was silent.

"No ideas? Here's a hint. Audiences were shocked when she took on the lead role in the movie Monster where make-up artists changed her good looks into something truly scary."

"Charlize Theron," someone called out.

"Yup." Professor Nelson smiled. "What we've just engaged in is an alternative way to present information, hopefully in a manner that will help you to remember the concepts as well as the details."

Professor Nelson went on to tell us that not surprisingly, most teachers are typical learners themselves. They learned successfully through traditional lecture, note-taking, memorization, and tests so they tend to use those approaches in their teaching. While that usually works pretty well for typical learners and for people who aren't struggling with the effects of trauma, it doesn't always work so well for the others.

She told us that atypical learners and trauma survivors often need things presented somewhat differently. They might need to understand the whole picture before they can deal with the parts, sort of like looking at the whole map first before reading a list of specific directions for a road trip. Or like having a story told about a situation to create a picture in their minds so that they can later attach the facts to it.

I liked that. Figuring out what each student needs to make them successful is what the best teachers do. I've known teachers who teach that way – like Mlle Cesoir and Mrs. French, back in middle school, and Mr. Miaguchi now. They don't just lecture. They tell a story and explain the background and create visual pictures and offer project options. They offer lots of ways to learn and understand and work with the material. And the kids in their classes are always successful. And they end up liking school.

In our Psych of Learning class, we're also learning that early childhood trauma can affect the development of the brain. The patterns for learning and organizing new information that would normally develop in a child's brain can be interrupted by severe emotional trauma. Sort of like the file folders for information don't get organized properly – the snyapses may not connect. But the good news is that it's correctable. A safe and nurturing environment and specific interventions can allow those patterns to develop later so that permanent harm isn't done.

I'm still thinking about becoming a psychologist, but I also might want to become a teacher who specializes in helping struggling students so that they can learn and see themselves as capable. I could help them find strategies to become successful. We'll see. There are lots of options out there. That's what I love about college. It opens up all sorts of new horizons for you.

Next weekend is Homecoming! I can't believe it's almost here. Our club is almost done with our float and it looks just awesome. And everyone who worked on it thinks so too.

84.

Homecoming was a hit! Jesse was crowned Homecoming King (he says he should have been Queen - haha) and Katie was crowned Homecoming Queen. They're both pretty popular. I wasn't even in the running, but I honestly didn't mind. Our LGBTQ & Allies Club float won first place in the competition and our principal had some really nice words to say about our club's efforts to include ALL students on campus. It's been such a great fall. I don't see how it can get any better.

I'm really falling for Gabe, the night custodian I met at my old elementary school. He and I have been dating and my stepmom doesn't even seem to care that he's obviously a lot older than I am. But I'm turning 17 soon, so I think maybe it reminds her of when she fell in love with her first husband, Grant. I guess she has a heart after all.

Gabe is going to take me to our school's Winter Ball. I have to get a guest pass for him since he's not a student at our school, but that shouldn't be a problem since he's enrolled as a student at a technical school nearby. I can't wait. I've started shopping for a dress, but nothing seems right that I've tried on yet. So, that just means I'll have to do more shopping! I'll have to use a little of my college money for the dress, but it will be worth it. Katie's going, too. Even though her dad doesn't let her date yet, she convinced him that it's safe for Jesse to take her. LOL. I wonder again what it would be like to have parents who are looking out for you the way Katie's are for her. That might be pretty cool.

I haven't introduced Gabe to Jesse or Katie yet. I'm not sure exactly why. Maybe it's because I'm afraid they won't like him. Or they won't understand why I do. And maybe it's also because of the red flags I've started noticing with Gabe. They concern me a bit and I guess I should pay more attention to them. But I really just don't want to deal with them. And if I introduce him to Jesse and Katie, I'm afraid they'll notice the red flags, too. And I don't want to lose Gabe.

Like Gabe's HVAC program. I've asked him about his classes but he's always really vague about them. He doesn't give me any specific answers and he doesn't seem to know a lot of details about the program either. I asked what classes he has to take and what he's enrolled in now and when he'll be done. But he just changes the subject and doesn't really answer. But then maybe he just didn't want to talk about it.

And where he went to high school. When I asked, he gave a sort of evasive answer and said I wouldn't recognize the name since it wasn't around here.

And then there's the alcohol. A couple of times when he's come to my house to pick me up, I've smelled alcohol on his breath. That's something I never make a mistake about. That means he must be drinking in the early afternoon. Or even earlier. I haven't talked to him about that yet, but I guess I need to.

I just need to make a decision about whether I'm going to continue to live in the World of Denial like I usually do or whether it's time to face things head-on. I can't really deny this one – especially the alcohol thing. There's just no way to pretend that doesn't exist. I have too much experience with that one. I've decided I'll keep an eye on things for a little longer and then to find the right time to talk to him about my concerns.

"So, when are you going to introduce us to Mr. Mysterious?" Katie laughed at school today.

"Yeah," said Jesse. "Are you afraid I'm going to steal him away from you?"

Katie and I laughed both at that one.

"Not a chance," I answered. "He's not your type."

"Now I'm curious," said Jesse. "In what way is he not my type? That must mean he's not smart, good looking, goal-oriented and accomplished."

I knew he was kidding, but he was actually pretty spot on. Gabe was good looking, but the other things Jesse listed? Um.....not so much. Jesse must have read it on my face.

"Uh oh, Maddie. What IS he like? What are you getting yourself into? We know he's not a student here and you said he's a little bit older. So, he's already graduated? Where did he go to high school?"

I realized I had no idea. I couldn't even answer Jesse's simplest questions.

Katie looked concerned.

"Maddie, what's going on? Who is this guy anyway?" she asked.

"I guess I don't really know," was all I could answer. "But maybe it's time I found out."

The next evening, things unraveled pretty quickly between Gabe and me. We were driving in his car across town to go to a movie when a car pulled up next to us at a stoplight, slamming hard on the brakes. The window rolled down on the driver's side which was right next to my open window and this girl just started yelling past me at Gabe. She was saying all kinds of crazy stuff.

"You got quite the young one now!" she shouted at Gabe, but all the time looking at me. "How could you do this to me and your kid? I'm going to go after you for all the child support I can get! You're not going to have a penny left for yourself when I'm done! You're a first-class A-hole!"

Gabe pulled ahead quickly when the light turned green. I just sat there in shock. When we got to the movie theater, he parked the car.

"Maddie, there's something I haven't told you," he said.

"You think?" I answered. "Who was that?"

"That was my ex-girlfriend," he said.

"Your ex-girlfriend? But what was she saying about a kid?"

"Well, I guess you could technically say my ex-wife. But we weren't married all that long."

"Your WHAT?" I practically yelled it. "You're married? Or you were married? Didn't you think that was sort of important information to share with me?"

"I was waiting for the right time," he said. "And yes. I have a kid. That's why we got married. But it didn't last."

I couldn't believe what I was hearing. I thought back to a conversation I had had with Mr. Dyadchenko earlier in the day when I had finished my afternoon of tutoring at the elementary school.

"Maddie, I'm concerned about you," Mr. D. had said to me. "You're a really smart girl and you're the same age as my daughter and you remind me so much of her. You need to be careful about the decisions you're making at this point in your life. Your decisions can greatly affect your future."

I was a little bit shocked. And a little bit offended. Everyone always tells me what great decisions I make and what a responsible person I am. I'm a good student. I work hard. I'm kind. I'm honest. No one ever tells me they're concerned about my decisions. I have to admit, I didn't like his comments.

"Why would you say that, Mr. D?" I asked. "I'm tutoring here, and I love it. And I'm getting great grades in high school. And I'm acing my night class at college. And I've got a job. And I've applied to a bunch of four-year colleges and for a bunch of scholarships for after I graduate. I'm doing just fine. What is there to be concerned about?"

"Him," Mr. Dyadchenko said, gesturing in Gabe's direction. Gabe was in the parking lot getting out of his car, coming in for his evening shift. "You're too good for him, Maddie. And he's no good for you."

I was even more shocked.

"He's a really nice guy, Mr. D.," I said. "I know he's a little older than I am but I'm really mature for my age. And he's super responsible. He's going to HVAC school and he's working full-time here." And then I played my ace. "And he's a custodian, just like you!"

Mr. Dyadchenko frowned at that.

"He's nothing like me, Maddie," he said. "And is that what he told you? That he's going to HVAC school? You need to take it slowly and find out more about him. I would hate to see him ruin your future. Don't ignore the signs, Maddie. Be observant. You're a smart girl." And he walked away.

I didn't know what he was talking about at the time, but I liked Mr. D. and I trusted him. So, I decided I would tuck away his advice and give it some thought later. Because now it wasn't just Jesse and Katie who had concerns about Gabe. It was also Mr. D.

I came back to the present.

"You're married and you have a kid?" I asked Gabe. I was dumbfounded!

"Correction. I was married and I have a kid," Gabe answered.

"So, you're divorced?" I asked.

"Well, sort of. Almost. I just need to save some money to file the papers."

Oh my gosh! What an idiot I am, was all I could think.

"And are you really in an HVAC program working on your certificate?" I asked.

"I've applied for the program. But it's super expensive and I have to save some money so I can go. And they told me I have to get my GED first."

"Your GED? You said you graduated from high school!"

I stared at him in disbelief.

"You need to take me home," I said.

"What about the movie?" he asked. "We just got here. Everything's going to be fine, Maddie."

"The movie? REALLY?" I shouted. "I just found out that you're married with a kid! And you're not in school like you told me. And you didn't graduate from high school. And you drink too much. Nothing is going to be fine. All you've been telling me until now are lies! I need to go home. And if you won't take me then I'll walk," I said. And I reached for the car door.

"OK, cool off," Gabe replied. "I don't know why you're making such a big deal out of this. She and I haven't been together for over a year. And I'll be starting school soon. And I don't drink all that much. And besides, it's only beer."

"But you're not divorced. And apparently, you're not paying child support either. And you're not in school like you said you were. And you didn't tell me about any of this. And you drink during the day and you show up with alcohol on your breath. So yeah – this is all a big deal. In fact, it's a really BIG DEAL!" And I got out of the car.

"Maddie, come back! I'll take you home if that's what you want," Gabe called after me.

"No, that's not what I want," I yelled back. "What I want is to never see you again!" I walked away shaking and I reached for my phone to call Jesse or Katie or Annie – anyone but him.

85.

On Monday afternoon, after I was through with my tutoring assignment, I went to find Mr. Dyadchenko.

"Mr. D., do you have a minute?" I asked him when I found him cleaning in the kindergarten center.

"I always have a minute for you, Maddie," he replied, looking up and smiling.

"Well, I just want to thank you," I said. I felt pretty awkward and didn't quite know how to begin. I cleared my throat, but no words came out. I fidgeted with my hands, not knowing what to do with them.

"Ah," Mr. D. said. "He showed his true colors, did he?" And he looked at me kindly.

"Did you know he was married and had a kid?" I asked.

"Well, I knew something about that, but I thought it best you find out in your own way," he answered gently. "I was becoming concerned though that maybe it was time for me to say something to you."

"You said just enough," I replied. "You let me know I should watch out for myself and not ignore any red flags."

"You're a smart girl, Maddie," Mr. Dyadchenko said. "Be careful with your choices and you'll do just fine. Maybe wait to date until a bit later?"

I laughed.

"I think you're right, Mr. D. I bet you don't let Angelika date yet, do you?"

"Not on your life!" he replied. And we both laughed.

"Angelika is a lucky girl," I said. And I gave Mr. D. a hug.

Later that week, I talked about all of it with Katie and Jesse. I had already told Jesse some of it when I called him and asked him to come and get me from the movie theater that day, but it was time to fill him in with the details.

"Well, look on the bright side," Jesse said.

"What bright side would that be?" I asked, still feeling the hurt of having fallen for someone who wasn't any good for me. As much as I knew it was the right thing to do, breaking up with Gabe left a huge hole in my life.

"You're not living in denial like you said you used to," Jesse replied. "You're facing issues head on."

"Well, it sure doesn't feel very good," I replied sadly.

"And he really was a poor choice, Maddie. He's nothing like me!"

I had to laugh at that one. And really – Jesse was right. Gabe was nothing like Jesse or Mr. D. I did deserve better. And when it came to the Winter Ball, Jesse and Katie and I all went together as each other's dates. And we had a blast.

86.

"How are the acceptance letters coming?"

It was Jesse. He and Katie and I were eating lunch together in Senior Court. No more nasty embarrassing lunch tables for us. It's spring and there are just a few months of school left before we graduate from high school. I've received acceptance letters from most of the four-year colleges I had applied to. So have Katie and Jesse. Some are in-state and others are way out of state, which is super tempting. I'd love to get far away from this place.

"A couple more emails came yesterday," I replied. "They said I'm in and the official offers would be coming by U.S. Mail soon."

"Me, too," said Katie. "I'm just not sure if I should stay in-state or go out-of-state. So many decisions."

Jesse and I have to worry about scholarships and expenses. But Katie doesn't. She's lucky in that way. Her family is funding all of college for her.

The scholarships I'm receiving won't cover the living costs, but I have my college savings for that. Or I could apply for financial aid and take out a bunch of loans and keep my savings for some of the other expenses like a car and insurance. Or maybe I could work full-time while I'm also going to college. Annie and I still haven't figured out how we're going to help Max out. He's finishing ninth grade, so he still has three more years until he graduates. I'm thinking maybe I should live at home and go to a nearby four-year college so then I could keep an eye on Max and not take out any loans. I'm just not sure yet. I don't seem to be sure about anything these days.

"Have you decided what you're going to do yet, Jesse?" I asked.

"Yup. I'm going to live at home after graduation and go to our local community college," he answered.

"That sounds like a good plan," Katie said.

"Are you sure?" I asked. "How did you decide?"

"Well for one, I'll obviously be able to save money. Living at home and two-year college fees are a lot cheaper than going away to a four-year college. And I can transfer to a university after the two years through the guaranteed transfer program. But it's more than just that. I'm going to run for a seat on our local School Board of Directors. And I have to continue living here to do that."

"What?!?" Katie and I said together? "You're going to run for the School Board?"

"Yeah," Jesse replied proudly. "There's an open seat and a special election coming up this summer. It's a two-year position. I'm 18 and I live within the school district boundaries which are the only qualifications that I need to get on the ballot. And I've already thought about my platform."

I don't know why Katie and I should be surprised at this. Jesse is super smart, and he follows local, national and world news and politics. And he's always saying that he thinks it's time for young people to have more of a say in what is happening within our schools.

"So, what's your platform going to be?" I asked.

"I want to ensure that all students in our district get a high-quality education, not just the kids from educated families or from the more affluent parts of our town. And I want to ensure that all students are supported and encouraged to take advanced classes in middle school and high school so they can achieve their dreams."

"You want to continue the work we started in the LGBTQ & Allies Club," Katie said.

"Yup. We started a good thing and I want to keep it going. There's a real difference in the expectations of kids for achievement depending on which elementary school they attend in our town," Jesse said. "I think that's wrong, and I want to work to change that. It's in elementary school that you start kids off in a positive direction for life and where they start believing in themselves as learners."

I thought back to Gracie and where she lived, and the fact that she was about the only one from her elementary school who ended up in Honors and Advanced classes in middle school with Jesse and me. I wondered why more kids from her neighborhood didn't qualify for or apply to those classes. And I realized that Jesse was right.

"Can I help you with your campaign, Jesse?" I asked. "You know I totally believe in what you're saying."

"I'd love the help," Jesse smiled. "Since the election is this summer, there's a lot of work to do. And if I win, I'll be taking my seat on the School Board in the fall."

"I'll help you, too," Katie said. "But will you have time for the School Board position if you win and for attending college, too?"

"I'll make the time," Jesse replied. "It's a two-year position. So, I can complete my associate degree at the same time and then transfer to a four-year university to complete my bachelor's degree. I want to major in law or criminal justice. I think it'll be perfect timing."

Katie and I agreed.

"I envy you, Jesse," Katie said. "I wish I knew where I was going. I just haven't decided yet."

Katie wasn't going to brag but we knew she had her choice of which college to attend because of her great grades and high test scores. Her family has planned carefully for her college years so she could go anywhere she wanted, in state or out of state, private college or public university.

"I'm not sure either," I lamented. "But I guess we're going to have to decide pretty soon."

Just then, Angelika entered Senior Court.

"Come sit with us, Angelika," I called to her. "We're talking about college and life after high school. We hear there is such a thing." All of us laughed at that.

Angelika looked pleased as she sat down.

"What are your college plans?" we asked her.

"I'm going to go directly to a four-year college – I just haven't decided which one. My dad's been saving money out of every paycheck for years to make that happen. He actually works two jobs. He's got a night job after his custodian work is done. He says he wants me to have a better life than he and my mom were able to make for me."

"Wow. That's pretty cool," I said. "But I don't know about the better life part. From my point of view, your dad has done just fine – both as the best custodian in the world and as a great dad. And he gives pretty good advice, too."

Angelika smiled at that and gave me a hug.

"You know if you need any college advice, all you have to do is ask him," she said.

"I might just do that," I answered.

87.

This final spring of high school, I'm running track. So are Jesse and Katie, which is really fun. And so is Max! Max is on the freshman squad and Jesse and Katie and I are varsity, but it's really cool to have Max there with us. We all practice together, and we go to the same meets. Track meets go on forever since there are so many events and there are so many kids on our team. Our coaches are really cool. They encourage ALL kids to get involved, regardless of how talented they are, and all of us on the team are expected to do our best and to cheer for our very last teammate in races as they cross the finish line. No exceptions.

We were at a track meet in a nearby town last week when Max and I heard an oddly familiar call from the stands.

"You hoo! Madelleine! Maxwell! You hoo! It's Mummy! Hel-llllooooooo!"

Max and I froze and looked at one another dumbfounded. We were down on the track helping to move some hurdles out of the way after one of the events and we looked up into the stands and sure enough, there was our mum. You couldn't miss her. It was a hot day, and she was wearing a brightly colored heavy purple print winter coat, and an orange and yellow knit cap with a huge pompom on top. We were pretty sure she must have made it herself, and her long white hair was sticking out from under it, flying in every direction. Her face was tanned and heavily lined and weathered, and she just kept yelling.

"Helllooooooo! Madelleine! Maxwell! It's Mummy!"

We thought we were going to die of embarrassment. It had never occurred to us that she might be in the area, but then we realized that we were at a school that was pretty close to her last known address. Yet we hadn't seen her for several years. I thought about grabbing Max's arm and running for the buses. But just then, Jesse and Katie came over to Max and me.

"Is that your real mom?" Jesse asked kindly.

"Yup, that's her," I replied looking down at my feet as I scuffed my shoes on the track and looked intently at my fingernails.

"Well then, I think we should all go over and say hello," Katie said firmly. "Would you introduce us, Maddie?"

"I agree," said Jesse. "That's exactly what we should do. Are you OK with that Maddie? Max?"

I was conflicted, but I could have hugged Jesse and Katie right there. They knew all about my mum. I had told them about her over the last year or so as we had become pretty tight friends. I had told them about how smart she was and how much she loved us kids, but that her challenges with mental illness left her unable to parent us and that her behavior was pretty unpredictable. And sometimes downright embarrassing. And I had shared the fact that we hadn't seen her for years.

"I don't know about that," Max said. "Why don't you guys go if you want to."

I thought about it for a minute.

"It's totally up to you, Max," I said. "But you know she'll just keep calling to us. Maybe if we say a quick hello she'll stop."

Max reluctantly agreed.

So, with Jesse and Katie holding my hands and Max close behind, I climbed up the steps on the side of the bleachers and headed in the direction of my mum. To be honest, I had very mixed emotions. On the one hand, I felt like I was facing a missing piece in my life. But on the other hand, it was a tense situation and really embarrassing. I just wasn't sure I was ready to deal with this at this moment. In this very public place. In front of all these people.

"This is just the beginning you know, Maddie," Jesse said. "But maybe you can come up with a plan so that getting to know her again is manageable. It is what you said you wanted after all."

I smiled at Jesse and gave his hand a squeeze. He and Katie truly understood me.

Over the next few months, I met up with my mum every few weeks. Sometimes Annie joined us, but Max usually didn't. Some days, our mum was really lucid, and all of our conversations were easy. Other days, she seemed far away, and the things she said seemed disconnected and really didn't make much sense.

Our mum told us that she was applying for teaching and nursing positions in the area and that she had a business she had started called Pigpen Industries. We weren't sure how much to believe but we were polite. We knew she wanted us to be proud of her and she didn't want to talk about her mental health challenges. She told us how much she had missed Annie, Max, and me and she wanted to catch up on all of our news. I think seeing her was a lot harder on Max than it was on Annie and me. We tried to keep our conversations light and easy. I didn't tell our stepmom that we were seeing our mum though. I thought that might be pretty hard on her, too.

Our mum was excited about my college plans. And Annie's. Annie is attending Community College with plans to transfer to a four-year university. Just like Jesse. And she's studying English Literature, of course. Just like our mum. I'm still planning on studying psychology, but I didn't talk a lot about that either because I was afraid it might upset her. And I'm still not sure where I'll be enrolling.

One day at a time. That's my philosophy about all the changes and challenges these days. I can't control a lot of what's going on in my environment, but I can face it as it comes and do my best to deal with it. The Serenity Prayer at work! I have decided that I'm going to invite Mummy to my high school graduation though. So, I guess I'm going to have to talk with my stepmom about her pretty soon.

My stepmom was actually pretty cool about it later when I told her.

"I've always felt rather badly for her, Maddie" our stepmom said. "She did the best she could and she truly loves you kids."

Wow! Like I said before, my stepmom surprises me. She can be totally supportive at times. I think maybe she's doing the best she can, too.

88.

"You're drunk!" Jesse announced, staring at me.

"What?" I slurred back. "Not even."

"Yup. You're totally plastered," he replied. "What did you drink anyway? And how are we going to get you back into school? You can't miss graduation, but you can hardly walk. They're going to send you home! We've got to think of something."

Graduation day had finally come but I almost didn't make it to the ceremony. There's a tradition at our high school of seniors going to the ocean early in the morning on the last day of school and climbing down the cliffs to the private beach at the bottom for one last time of celebration. It's sort of a time to be together before we have to separate to face the world as young adults. Everyone goes there – all the jocks, and the surfers, and the hippies, and the goths, and the stoners, and the popular kids and the not-so-popular kids. And everyone just gets along. The place is called Mossy Rocks – and it's beautiful. The ocean is a little wild there, the wind whipping around the corners of the jutting cliffs giving the place a surreal feeling. It's the perfect place to hang out and to say goodbye to childhood.

When I got to Mossy that morning, I found the beach already packed with kids, but I couldn't find Katie or Jesse anywhere. There was a lot of drinking going on and some great music play-ing and when someone handed me a big red plastic cup filled with something called Johnny Walker Red Label, I was feeling pretty excited so I just chugged it. I wandered around looking for my two best friends, but I couldn't find them. Things seemed to get pretty fuzzy after that. Everyone was laughing and running into the waves and hugging each other and having a good time until finally someone yelled that we were going to be late for school and we all started scrambling back up the cliffs.

That's where I finally ran into Jesse.

I guess he gave me a ride back to school where we met up with Katie. But I really don't remember. They told me about it later.

"Oh my God," Katie said. "She's a mess!"

"Yeah, I know," Jesse replied. "But what are we going to do? We don't have our first period class together."

"Angelika is in Maddie's first period class," Katie said. "She's really sweet. Maybe we can hand her off to Angie. I think she'd understand."

And that's what they did. Angelika stayed at my side and guided me through first period and then second, praying for me the whole way! By morning break, I had sobered up enough to realize how lucky I was that my teachers hadn't noticed anything. Either that or they decided to ignore my condition and give me a break. Angelika handed me back to Katie and Jesse just before third period.

"You're a good person, Maddie," Angelika said. "My dad is cheering for you. Don't let him down."

That really made me feel guilty. I sure didn't want to disappoint Mr. Dyadchenko. And he had told me to be careful with my choices.

By lunch, I was back to normal. Thank goodness. I had truly dodged a bullet. Never again, I thought to myself as I headed to the gym where we were putting on our graduation caps and gowns before heading out to the field. I was wearing extra gold cords over my shoulder because of my high academic achievement, and a bunch of pins for my AP classes. And I was a line leader, extra responsibility because the adults thought I could be counted on. *I guess I could have let a lot of people down today*, I thought to myself morosely.

Our graduation was outside on the football field since there were so many kids in our class, and the stadium was full of family and friends and onlookers. I looked up into the stands and I spotted Max sitting next to our stepmom, trying to prop her up since she kept falling over to one side. She was obviously drunk. I guess that was predictable. But then I felt a little guilty for criticizing her based on my own recent behavior.

I could see Max on his phone constantly, either playing games or placing bets. I wasn't sure which. I looked around and I didn't see Annie at first, but then I spotted her near the exit area, away from the bleachers. She was standing next to her boyfriend. She caught my eye and then she intentionally turned sideways, and I suddenly noticed her belly. She was pregnant! How had I missed that these past couple of months? *Looks like we have more talking to do*, I thought.

Annie gave me a huge smile and waved at me, and her boyfriend waved, too. I was glad they were there, and I waved back. She patted her belly then and really grinned at me. I grinned back, shaking my head back and forth and she started to laugh. And then I looked around some more, and I realized I was scanning the stands, the exits, the field, everywhere, hoping I might see my mum. I had told her all about graduation and I had given her the date and the time. *I guess she just didn't show*, I thought to myself. *This is my family - it's what I've got.*

The student speeches started, followed by the names of the graduates being called. I continued to scan the bleachers and the far sides of the field, still looking for my mum. I half expected to hear a call of "Yoo hoo! Madelleine!" when my name was read. I crossed the stage to accept my diploma. But there was nothing. Our principal gave a speech about how proud she was of all of us and a couple of the Board Members spoke, and then the band played and there were some student speeches and dedications until finally the ceremony came to an end. I saw Annie waving at me again as she left with her boyfriend, holding her hand up to her ear and mouthing "Call me." I smiled at her and nodded and then I went to find Max and our stepmom, feeling a little bit deflated.

I had just graduated from high school with high honors, but my life wasn't in any better order than it had been for the last few months or years for that matter. I didn't know what I was going to do about college, my sister was pregnant, my stepmom was drunk, my little brother was becoming more and more of a lost child, my dad was dead, and my mum was who knows where. I fell into a funk as we headed home. *Maybe it was OK that my mum hadn't shown up after all*, I thought. I didn't really know which I would have truly preferred - being embarrassed by her if she had come or being disappointed that she didn't.

89.

I soon found out why my mum hadn't attended my graduation. The following Monday morning, the first day of my official summer vacation, there was a knock on the door. An infrequent occurrence at our house. I wondered who it was.

My stepmom answered, sober this time and fully clothed, to find a social worker standing on the doorstep. The social worker asked to speak with Max and me.

Max was gone somewhere with his friends, so it was just me there to talk with her. Our stepmom rolled her eyes and showed her in, telling me to meet with her in the living room. Then she left us alone, as if she didn't want to hear the news, whatever it was. I heard the vodka glass hit the counter in the kitchen as I sat down with the social worker in the living room.

"Your mother was 5150'd by the police for a mental health evaluation last week," the social worker said. "She's being detained. Do you know what that means, Maddie?"

I shook my head.

"5150 is the number of the California Welfare and Institutions Code that allows for a psychiatric hold and evaluation of someone who is behaving erratically and might be a danger to themselves or others," she explained.

"I expect that the 5150 will show that your mother needs support and she will probably be placed in a group home for adults with mental health issues," she went on. "If they can get her to consistently take her medications, she might be able to be released in another six months to a year to live on her own. Your mother is quite intelligent, but she has a documented history of resisting acknowledging that anything is wrong with her or accepting help for her condition."

That sounded about right.

"She didn't come to my graduation last week," I said.

"That must have been really disappointing, Maddie," the social worker replied gently. "But think about how difficult it must be for your mother to deal with all of the challenges of life, not to mention the everyday things, when she's not sure if what she's seeing and hearing is real or imagined. That must be really confusing for her."

I thought about that. It was true that I was sad that she hadn't shown up for my important day. But really in the big picture of life, it was my mum who was experiencing the greater disappointments as she tried to negotiate a world that for her was entirely unpredictable and unmanageable.

I asked the social worker if we could see our mum and she said yes. She also said that the Court was looking to "conserve her".

"What does that mean?" I asked.

"It means that your mother has chronic mental illness, and that she is not expected to recover. She has lived with schizophrenia for many years, and she will in all likelihood continue to do so. She is not able to care for her own finances. The Court will probably decide on a temporary guardianship, which means that for now she won't be able to decide for herself where she is to live. But if all goes well, the Court will reduce that to a conservatorship, which would mean she can make most of her own decisions. But she will need to have someone oversee her finances and check in on her so that she doesn't end up homeless and on the streets."

Apparently, that had happened before.

"It's important that she take her medication. It won't cure her illness, but it will make it more manageable," the social worker continued. "That's also a part of the conservator's responsibilities – to monitor whether she is taking her medication. Fortunately, there are meds that can now be administered through an injection once or twice a month. That makes it much easier on everyone."

I thought a conservatorship sounded like a good idea.

"Could I become her conservator when the time comes?" I asked.

The social worker was surprised by my question.

"It's a tremendous responsibility, and one that I wouldn't recommend. How old are you?" she asked.

"I've just turned 17 last month. I know, I'm young to have graduated already. But I've grown up pretty fast in some ways," I added.

"I bet you have," she replied. "Congratulations on graduating. I hear you're at the top of your class. And being young may be a blessing in disguise for you because I can see that you may be up for the challenge of dealing with your mother's mental illness in the future. But you have to be at least 18 years of age to be appointed as conservator, so that gives you a year to really think about it. And in the meantime, your mother will have a temporary guardianship. Really think it over though, Maddie. It would be a tremendous undertaking and quite frankly, I wouldn't advise it until you've at least finished your college education."

"I will think about it. Truly," I replied. "And thanks for the advice. I guess I'm glad I'll have some time to consider it. Will you keep in touch with us to let us know where she is and how she is doing and when we can visit her?"

"Of course," our mum's social worker answered, handing me her card. "Good luck to you! We'll stay in touch."

I took her card and later that evening, I sat on my bed, turning it over in my hand, and mulling over all the decisions I had to make. I really did have my whole future ahead of me. It had only been a few days since I had graduated. Maybe I needed to slow all of this down a bit.

There was so much to think about. My mum was being taken care of for now. I would be able to continue seeing her and developing our relationship and take my time to decide how much responsibility for her I was ready to take on.

I had college decisions to make.

And it looked like I was going to be an auntie soon! I was anxious to talk with Annie and see how she was going to handle being such a young mom. After all, she was only 19.

I thought about Mr. Dyadchenko's advice to me earlier in the year: to be observant and to be careful with my choices, to take my time and to remember that I was smart and I would be just fine.

I knew there was a lot to think about and that I needed to carefully consider all my options.

I knew I would sometimes mess up, like I had on the last day of school last week and like I almost had with Gabe. But I also knew that I would recover.

I knew that even though everything about my future seemed to be up in the air right now, nothing needed to be decided today, at this very minute. At this very second. I still had time.

I smiled to myself. I was approaching clarity.

I stretched out my legs, took a deep breath, got off my bed, and walked over to my dresser. I tucked the social worker's card into a drawer for safe keeping. Then I grabbed my cell phone and headed up the stairs and out the front door as I called first Jesse and then Katie and then Annie and Gracie and Angelika. There was so much to talk about with each of them.

For right now, though, all of the decisions could wait. For right now, I could hang with the important people in my life. The people who had helped me through. The people who loved me. Together we could celebrate our friendships, our accomplishments, and our futures. And the fact that we were all going to be just fine.

Life might not be fair, I decided. But it was definitely getting better.

EPILOGUE

Maddie continued to live at home for her first semester of college to provide support for Max, while attending a four-year university nearby. Both moved out by Christmas of that year, living in their own small apartment while supporting themselves as Max finished his sophomore and junior years of high school and Maddie attended college. Max moved in with Dan for his senior year and Maddie lived with college friends. Maddie and Max celebrated his graduation by backpacking through Europe for a summer together. Annie had a little girl, finished her Bachelor's Degree in English, and earned her English teaching credential, which she used to teach gifted middle schoolers in neighborhoods plagued by gang violence. Maddie completed her Bachelor's Degree in Psychology, Master's Degree in Special Education, and several teaching credentials, and went on to teach teenagers with emotional and learning challenges. Max joined the armed services, then worked for a recycling company for many years and became involved in community advocacy and local politics. All had some false starts along the way before finding their balance and success. Annie and Maddie made peace with their stepmom as adults. And all became their mum's conservator at different points, sharing the loving responsibility of ensuring she lived to age 94, never being homeless or living in an institution again.

Life may not have been fair, but it did indeed get better.

MENTAL HEALTH RESOURCES

Although Maddie was reluctant to reach out for assistance, there are organizations that can provide help for individuals and families in chaos:

- School/College Counseling Departments
- Local County Mental Health Departments
- Faith Based Organizations – churches, synagogues, mosques
- Alcoholics Anonymous – www.aa.org
- Alateen/Al-Anon – www.al-anon.org
- NAMI – National Alliance on Mental Illness – www.nami.org
- Mental Health Resources – www.mhresources.org
- National Institute of Mental Health - www.nimh.nih.gov
- Mental Health America – www.mhanational.org

You are not alone. People care. Life can get better.

DISCUSSION QUESTIONS

1. Compare young Maddie and her tone in grade four to the more mature Maddie as she graduates from high school. How has she changed? What are her strongest character traits?
2. There are recurring references to clarity, the couch, and choices in the story. Discuss the significance of each.
3. How do you think Maddie's life would have been different if her father had lived? If she and her siblings had stayed with their mum?
4. What is your opinion about Maddie's father? Her step-mother? Her mother?
5. How are Annie, Max and Maddie and the choices they make different? How are they similar? Is there a character you favor or you want to know more about? Why?
6. Do you think that Max stole the gold coins? Why or why not?
7. Who are Maddie's friends in the story and what roles do they play in her life?

8. What significance does Maddie find in literature and how does it help her?

9. Maddie shares toward the end of the novel that she has a "List of People Who Care". Is that a literal reference? Who do you think would be on Maddie's list and why?

10. What do you think of Maddie's statement that there is a caste system relative to dysfunctional families, and that some are more acceptable than others in our society?

11. There are mentions of Maddie's use of denial and her naiveté throughout the story. Do you think the use of denial is healthy? Why or why not?

12. Maddie is worried about her own mental health and wonders about the relationship between creativity, genius, and mental illness. What are your thoughts on this?

13. Maddie is reluctant to tell others about her family's issues. Do you think that was the best decision? Why or why not?

14. Maddie decides that while life is not fair, it can get better. Why do you agree or disagree?

15. Explain what you would choose as the theme of this story.

16. Why do you think the author chose the title that she did?

17. What questions would you like to ask the author?

Mariah Clark Skewes is a relatively new author who has had a lifetime of writing experiences. Known in her real life as Mary Boyle, she chose the pseudonym to honor her late mother, a brilliant woman who lived with chronic schizophrenia and who enrolled Mary in kindergarten under that name. From her own childhood experiences and later professional training, Mariah/Mary developed an intense passion for encouraging the understanding of marginalized individuals and has spent her professional career nurturing tenacious, imaginative, and often misunderstood children and teens toward bright and rewarding futures. Loving a challenge and believing that with enough compassion, understanding, structure and support all children can thrive, including those who have experienced childhood trauma, Mariah/Mary began writing picture books focusing on the antics of children who operate outside the norm. From there, she has expanded to writing for teens and young adults.

Mariah/Mary is a former public school administrator with a Bachelors Degree in Psychology and a Masters Degree in Special Education. She now serves as an advocate for children in foster care and adults seeking their high school diplomas. She lives with her husband on a vineyard in the Sierra Nevada foothills of Northern California where they grow wine grapes and raise honeybees and Southdown Babydoll sheep. When not writing, Mariah/Mary can be found visiting with their four adult children and their families, running on trails, competing in world marathons, and travelling.